Spawn

As he turned to open the door a particularly violent eruption of flame exploded before him. Harold shrieked and felt one side of his face sizzling. The skin rose swiftly into blisters which immediately burst, the welts hardening as the fire stripped his flesh away as surely as if someone had thrust a blow torch at him. Harold clapped a hand to his face and felt the oblivion of unconsciousness creeping over him but the pain kept him awake and he managed to yank open the bedroom door. The hair on his arms was singed and his veins seemed to bulge as his skin contracted. He turned to see his mother, on her hands and knees, crawling towards him, the flesh of her body apparently bubbling, lumps of it falling from calcified bones. She raised an accusing finger at him and screamed:

"You're to blame!"

Also by Shaun Hutson:

SLUGS
EREBUS
SHADOWS
BREEDING GROUND
RELICS
DEATH DAY
VICTIMS
ASSASSIN
CAPTIVES
HEATHEN
NEMESIS
PURITY
RENEGADES
DEADHEAD
WHITE GHOST
LUCY'S CHILD
STOLEN ANGELS
KNIFE EDGE

SHAUN HUTSON

Spawn

Acknowledgements

Some of the research which went into this book was difficult, to put it mildly, and I would like to thank everyone who answered my questions, however bizarre they may have seemed. Particular thanks to Nurse Anne Bozia for her help. I would also like to thank Niki, whose criticism was as hard but as helpful as always. Also thanks to everyone concerned with the production of the book, particularly Mike Bailey, my editor, who put up with my numerous phone calls and lousy spelling. And, as ever, to Bob Tanner. Indirect thanks to John Carpenter, Iron Maiden, Black Sabbath, Tobe Hooper. All worshipped from afar. And lastly and most important, to my family. My parents, who thought I was mad to write a book like this and to Belinda, who *knows* I'm mad. For suffering my obsessions these past few years I am indebted to her One day soon . . .

Shaun Hutson

FOR MIKE BRETT WITH THANKS AND ADMIRATION

A *Time Warner* Paperback

First published in Great Britain in 1983 by
Star Books, a Division of W. H. Allen & Co. Plc
This edition published in 1990 by Sphere Books Ltd
Reprinted 1990
Reprinted by Warner Books 1994
Reprinted 1996, 1997, 1998, 2000
Reprinted by Time Warner Paperbacks in 2002

Printed in England by Clays Ltd, St Ives plc

ISBN 0 7515 1378 4

Time Warner Paperbacks
An imprint of
Time Warner Books UK
Brettenham House
Lancaster Place
London WC2E 7EN

www.TimeWarnerBooks.co.uk

Part One

"... some of us are born posthumously..."
— *Nietzsche*

"... the foetus is conscious or aware. It
can sense and react not only to emotions
such as love and hate, but to more
complex and ambiguous feelings."
— *Dr Thomas Verny*

One

The flickering wings of the crane-flies inside the jar sounded like whispers in the darkness and Harold Pierce held it to his ear, listening. He smiled and looked at the three insects struggling helplessly inside their glass prison. It was the light that attracted them, he had reasoned, as it did the moths. But Harold wasn't interested in moths, they moved too quickly. They were too hard to catch but the daddy-long-legs were easy prey. He smiled as he repeated the name. Daddy-long-legs. He stifled a giggle. His mother called them Tommies and that amused him even more. She was sleeping across the narrow hallway now, alone for once. Harold didn't remember the succession of men who she brought home, he wasn't really interested either. All he knew was that his father would not be coming back.

Jack Pierce had been killed at Dunkirk six years earlier and, since then, Harold's mother had entertained a never-ending series of men. Sometimes Harold had seen them give her money as they left but, it not being in the nature of fourteen-year-olds to question strangers, he had never asked any of them why. One night he had crept across the narrow landing and squinted through the key hole of his mother's room. She'd had two men in there with her. All of them were laughing and Harold had smelt liquor. They had been naked, all three of them, and for long moments he had watched, puzzled by the strange goings-on before him.

It was shortly after that night that his mother announced he was to have a brother or sister. The baby had duly arrived and Harold had been dragged off to church for the Christening, puzzled when there was only him and his mother present to witness the ceremony. In fact, his mother was shunned by most of the women in the neighbourhood. They spoke to her in the street but it was never anything more than a cursory 'hello'.

Harold held the jar of crane-flies up before him once more, wondering if their whispers would tell him the answers he needed to know.

He lowered the jar and looked across at the cot which held his baby brother, Gordon. The child was sleeping, lying on its back with the thick flannelette sheet pulled up around its face. Harold hated having to share a room with his brother. In the beginning, it had been all right. Gordon had slept in his cot in his mother's room but, since his first birthday, he had been put in with Harold. That meant that Harold was forced to come to bed when Gordon was tucked up for the night and that could be as early as seven in the evening. Most of the time, Harold would sit in the bedroom window watching the other kids kicking a big old leather football about in the street below. He had watched them doing that tonight, perched in his customary position until nine o'clock came around and the other kids were called indoors. Then, Harold had switched on his bedside lamp and watched as the crane-flies and moths flittered in through the open window.

Gordon was sound asleep, little gurgling noises came from his cot as he shifted position occasionally. The nylon eiderdown was crumpled at his feet where he'd kicked it off. It was covered with stitched-on rabbits. Beside the heavy wooden cot stood a pile of yellowing newspapers. Harold didn't read very well but he knew that the papers were called *The News Chronicle*. Just why his mother kept them he didn't know. There was another stack downstairs beside the coal fire, those she used to get the fire started in the mornings. Perhaps the pile in his bedroom were destined for the same purpose.

He crouched on the end of the bed for long moments, propping the jar of crane-flies on the window sill. The night was still and windless and, from somewhere nearby the strains of "String of Pearls" came drifting in with the night. Harold listened to the distant music for a moment then he swung himself off the bed and padded across to the door. The lino was cold beneath his feet and he hissed softly as he tip-toed from the bedroom, across the hall to the door of his mother's room. A framed painting of George VI watched him impassively as he gently turned the handle and popped his head round. His mother was asleep, her black hair smeared across her face in untidy patterns. Harold stood there for long seconds, watching the steady rise and fall of her chest, almost coughing as the strong odour of lavender assaulted his nostrils. Finally, satisfied that she wasn't likely to disturb him, he gently pushed the door closed and tip-toed back to his own room.

"String of Pearls" had been replaced by "Moonlight Serenade" when he got back but he ignored the music, more intent on the task at hand. He reached beneath his pillow and took out a box of Swan Vestas matches. Harold held them in his sweaty hand for a moment then he took hold of the glass jar. The crane-flies began flapping about even more frenziedly as Harold began to unscrew the top, as if sensing freedom. When it was fully loosened he held the jar before him, eyeing the insect closest to the neck of the jar. With lightning movements, he reached in and grabbed it by one membranous wing, simultaneously pushing the lid back in place.

The insect tried to escape his grasp and, quickly,

8

Harold pulled both its wings off. He did the same with three of its legs. The unfortunate creature was then dropped onto a sheet of newspaper where it tried, in vain, to scuttle away. Harold watched its helpless writhings for a moment then he picked up the box of Swan Vestas and slid the tray out, taking a match. It flared orange and the smell of sulphur filled his nostrils momentarily. He bent lower, bringing the burning match to within an inch of the crane-fly which immediately began to wriggle more frantically. Harold pressed the tiny flame to one of its legs, watching as the spindly limb seemed to retract, much like hair does when it is burned. The insect rolled onto its back, its two remaining legs thrashing wildly, its tiny head moving frenziedly. Harold burnt off another of its limbs then pressed the spent match-head against its slender abdomen. There was a slight hiss and the creature's head and remaining leg began moving even more rapidly.

Harold hurriedly lit another match.

This one he held right over the crane-fly, giggling when the stumps of its legs moved spasmodically as the flame drew closer. He dropped the match onto the insect, smiling as it was incinerated, its body rapidly consumed by the flame, charred black by the tiny plume of yellow. A whisp of grey smoke rose into the air. When the match had finished burning, Harold took another and prodded the blackened remains of the insect. It merely disintegrated.

Totally enthralled, Harold stuck his hand inside the jar and took out another of the crane-flies. This one he held by its wings, waving the match beneath it until all its legs had been burnt off. He twisted the wings so it couldn't fly away then he dropped it onto the newspaper and finished the cremation job with another match.

For the last insect, Harold had reserved something

9

special. His *pièce de résistance*. He took a handful of matches from the box and, with infinite care and patience, built them up until they were stacked cross-ways, on top of one another in a kind of well. Into the centre of this well, after removing its wings, he dropped the last insect. Then, quickly, he covered the top with three more matches. There must have been about twenty-five in all comprising that miniature funeral pyre and Harold sat back for a second admiring his handy-work. He could see the crane-fly inside the little stack of matches, its long legs protruding through the slits here and there as it tried to escape.

There were half a dozen matches left in the box and Harold struck one, gazing into the flame for a second before carefully applying it to the head of the match at the bottom of the pile.

It ignited with a hiss, burning for a second then setting off a chain reaction. The little structure went up in a flash of yellow and white flame and Harold grinned broadly.

He grinned until he saw that his blazing creation had set light to the paper it rested on.

The newspaper was dry and the flames devoured it hungrily. Harold felt a sudden surge of panic and he snatched up the blazing paper, scattering the burning remains of the tiny pyre as he did so. Matches which still hissed, alive with wisps of yellow, were scattered all over the room. One fell beside the pile of *News Chronicle*s and licked at the edge of the dry papers. Flames began to rise. The room was filled with the smell of charred paper and smoke wafted in the still air.

Another of the blazing matches fell into Gordon's cot. It hit the nylon eiderdown and seemed to explode, the quilt suddenly flaring as bright tongues of fire sprang from it.

Gordon woke up and began to scream as the fire touched his skin.

10

For long seconds, Harold was frozen, not knowing what to do. He took a step towards the cot, then backed off, his eyes bulging wide. Gordon's night-shirt was on fire. The baby was screaming, trying to drag itself away from the all-consuming inferno. Already, the skin on its arms and legs was a vivid scarlet.

Harold opened his mouth to scream but no sound would come out. The pile of newspapers beside the cot had ignited with a frightening vehemence and the tongues of flame rose a full three feet into the air. The whole room was ablaze. His own bed was seething, a mass of writhing fire. Smoke, thick and noxious, filled his nostrils and finally, as a piece of burning wallpaper fell and stuck to his arm, Harold found the breath for a scream. For interminable seconds, the paper clung to his arm, searing the flesh. He tore it away to see that the skin was red and blistered. His head swam and for a second he thought he was going to faint but, as he saw the cot disappear beneath a flickering haze of fire, he spun round and dashed for the door.

His mother had heard the screams and they crashed into one another on the landing. She saw the smoke billowing from the children's room, saw the leaping flames and she shook her head in disbelief. Pushing Harold aside, she ran into the room – into the furnace and flames which seared her flesh and set her clothes ablaze. Harold followed her back in, watching as she fought her way to the cot, reaching in to lift something which had once been her baby son. The body of Gordon was little more than a blackened shell. One arm had been completely burned off from the elbow down, the stump was still flaming. His mouth was open to reveal a blackened, tumefied tongue. The flesh looked as if it had been peeled away with red hot pincers. Through the charred flesh, white bone showed in places.

Harold's mother screamed and clutched the baby to her. Her own hair was now ablaze, the stench filling the room. She turned, a look of agony etched on her face and she screamed something at him but he couldn't hear through the roaring flames. As he turned to open the door a particularly violent eruption of flame exploded before him. Harold shrieked and felt one side of his face sizzling. The skin rose swiftly into blisters which immediately burst, the welts hardening as the fire stripped his flesh away as surely as if someone had thrust a blow torch at him. He felt something wet dripping from his burning cheek. Things went black as his right eye swelled under the intense heat then, in a moment of mind blowing agony, the sensitive orb seemed to bulge and burst. Blood gushed freely from the ruptured eye, turning immediately to charcoal under the ferocity of the flames. Harold clapped a hand to his face and felt the oblivion of unconciousness creeping over him but the pain kept him awake and he managed to yank open the bedroom door. The hair on his arms was singed and his veins seemed to bulge as his skin contracted. He turned to see his mother, on her hands and knees, crawling towards him, the flesh of her body apparently bubbling, lumps of it falling from calcified bones. She raised an accusing finger at him and screamed:

"You're to blame!"

The empty box of matches lay close beside her. Her hair was burnt off and the stench of charred skin was overpowering. Smoke poured from the open window and those living nearby hurried out into the street to see what was happening. The fire-engine was called.

Harold reeled amongst the flames, screaming in agony as what remained of his face was stripped clean by the flames. But, shielding himself as best he could, he stumbled out onto the landing, throwing himself against the wall in an effort to put out the fire which still devoured his clothes. He stumbled and fell, crashing heavily to the floor.

Downstairs, someone was trying to batter down the front door.

Harold looked round.

Through the haze of pain he saw his mother, a blackened vision which seemed to have risen from the fires of hell, standing in the bedroom doorway. She had her arms outstretched, the skin like crumbling parchment. When she opened her mouth, smoke billowed forth. Her eyes were gone, they were now just black pits in a bleeding, ruined face. Bone shone through the charred skin as blisters formed then burst with rapidity. She no longer had hair just the dancing snakes of flame which topped her skull, like some kind of fiery Gorgon.

She swayed for long seconds then, as the front door was broken down, she toppled backwards into the flames.

Harold began to scream.

"Mr Pierce."

Everything was darkness, he could feel his body shaking.

"Mr Pierce." The tone was more forceful this time.

He could hear screams, close by, drumming in his ears.

"Harold. Wake up."

He realized that the screams were his and, suddenly, he opened his eye and sat up, panting for breath, his body bathed in sweat. He looked round, fixing the woman in a glassy stare.

"Harold, are you all right?" she asked him.

He exhaled deeply and rubbed his eye. His hands were shaking madly, like a junkie who needs a fix. But, finally, his breathing slowed and he felt his heart returning to its usual rhythm. He looked at the woman, at her blue and white uniform, the small triangular hat which perched precariously on her head. Gradually the realization spread over him and he smiled thinly.

"I was dreaming," he said apologetically.

The woman smiled and nodded.

"I know," she said. "But you frightened the life out of all of us."

He apologized once more and wiped his forehead with the back of his hand. He looked up to see two maroon-coated interns standing on the other side of his bed. He recognized one as Pat Leary, a big Irishman who bore a bottle scar just above his right eye.

"You all right, Harold?" he asked.

The older man nodded and swung himself onto the edge of the bed. His pyjama jacket was soaked with sweat, a dark stain running from the nape of his neck to the small of his back. He pulled it off and began searching in his locker for his clothes.

His audience left, the interns moving off towards the exit at the far end of the ward, Nurse Beaton ambling across to the bed next to Harold to wake its occupant. He was a man older than Harold, completely bald and with skin like the folds of a badly fitting jacket. In fact that was what his face reminded Harold of. Harold watched as Nurse Beaton woke the man and then took two red pills from a plastic container she held. She supported the bald man while he took the pills, wiping away the water from his chin when it spilled over his rubbery lips. He heard her ask the man if he'd swallowed them and he nodded slowly. The nurse gently lowered him back into bed and moved on.

Harold was dressed by this time. He picked up a small imitation leather shaving-bag from his locker and headed towards the toilets at the far end of the corridor. The place smelt of disinfectant, as usual, but it was a smell with which he was well acquainted after so long.

Harold Pierce had been a patient in Exham Mental Hospital since 1946. Apart from the first fourteen years of his life, the institution had been his only home. It had been his world. And, in all that time things hadn't changed much. He'd seen scores of people, both staff and patients, come and go and now he was as much a part of the hospital as the yellow-painted walls.

He reached the toilets and selected his usual wash basin. He filled it with water and splashed his face, reaching beneath to find a towel. Slowly he straightened up, regarding the image which stared back at him from the mirror.

Harold sucked in a shaking breath. Even after all these years the sight of his own hideously scarred face repulsed him. It was a patchwork of welts and indentations, the whole thing a vivid red. The hair over his left eye was gone, as was the eye itself. A glass one now sparkled blindly in its place. His left ear was bent, minus the lobe it was in fact little more than a hole in the side of his head. One corner of his mouth was swollen, the lip turned up in a kind of obscene grin. A dark growth of flesh, what had once been a large mole, protruded from just below his left cheek bone, jutting out like the gnarled end of an incinerated tree branch. His left nostril was flared wide. What little hair remained on the left side of his head was thin and grey, a marked contrast to the thick black strands on the other side.

In fact, the right side of his face was relatively unmarked except for a slight scar on his forehead, most of the damage had been done to the left side of his body.

Harold took out his electric razor and ran it swiftly over the right cheek and beneath his chin. No stubble would grow on the left side.

He turned to see two interns carrying another patient from a wheel chair into one of the toilet cubicles. The old man was paralysed from the neck downwards, leaving one intern with the unsavoury task of cleaning him up when he'd finished. The old man was well into his eighties and suffered from Senile Dementia too. A common complaint amongst most of the patients at the institution.

One of the other patients, a man in his thirties who Harold knew as John, was cleaning the floor of the toilet with a mop, slopping the water everywhere in his haste.

"Careful, John," said Phil Coot, trying to slow him down. "You'll drown us all."

John laughed throatily and plunged the mop back into the bucket making a monumental splash. Coot, who was senior male nurse on the ward shook his head and smiled, watching the patient merrily slopping his way across the tiled floor.

"How are you this morning, Harold?" he said as he passed.

"Very well, Mr Coot, thank you."

Coot paused.

"You had some trouble last night?" he said.

Harold looked puzzled.

"The dream," Coot reminded him.

"Oh yes, that." Harold smiled thinly and raised one hand to cover the scarred side of his face but Coot reached up and gently pulled the hand away.

"The usual thing?" he asked.

Harold nodded.

"You're not on medication any more are you?" asked the male nurse.

"No, Mr Coot."

"This is the first time you've had this dream for a long time isn't it?"

"Yes, I don't know why. I'm sorry."

Coot smiled.

"No need to be sorry, Harold," he said. "Some of it is probably just tension at the thought of leaving here after so long." He patted Harold on the shoulder. "Once you get out of here you'll be OK. You'll settle into your new job and forget you've ever seen this place." He gestured around him, his tone turning reflective. "To tell you the truth, I shan't be sorry when we all leave here. The place is falling down around our ears it's so old."

"Where are you going then?" Harold wanted to know.

"The staff and patients are being moved to a new hospital on the other side of Exham in a couple of weeks time."

Harold nodded absently, lowering his gaze. He felt Coot touch him once more on the shoulder and then the male nurse was gone.

Harold took one last look in the mirror then pulled the plug in the sink, watching as the water swirled around the hole before disappearing. It was something which never failed to fascinate him.

Back by his bed, Harold put away his razor and smoothed out the creases in his trousers with the palms of his hands. He glanced out of the nearest window and scanned the grounds. The wind of the previous night had dropped and the leaves which had fallen from the trees now lay still on the lawns below. There were already a number of patients at work with large rakes, gathering the leaves up. Two interns stood close by, smoking.

Three nurses were walking past and they paused to speak with a doctor. Harold could see that they were laughing together and he saw the doctor kiss one of them on the cheek. They all laughed again. Laughter was something which Harold didn't hear too much of these days. He watched the little group almost enviously for long moments then turned away from the window and set about making his bed.

Finally satisfied that all was in order, he wandered off towards the staircase which would take him down a floor to the Therapy rooms.

There were already two other patients at work in the

large room when Harold walked in. He inhaled deeply, enjoying the odour of the oil paint. His own easel was set up close to one of the meshed windows and he crossed to it, inspecting the canvas which he had lovingly decorated these past three weeks. The picture was a series of bright colour flashes, mainly reds and yellows. What it was no one was quite sure, not even Harold, but he swiftly hunted out a brush and some paint from the wooden cupboard nearby and set to work.

Harold looked carefully at his canvas before applying the first vivid brush stroke. It was as if he saw something in those reds and yellows, something which stirred a memory inside him. His brush hovered over the place on his palette where he squeezed a blob of orange.

Flames.

He swallowed hard. Yes, they looked like flames. The memories of his nightmare came flooding back to him and he took a step back from the canvas as if he had discovered something vile and obscene about it. Perhaps, unconsciously, he was painting that nightmare scene as it had appeared to him all those years ago. Was this his punishment? To commit his crime to canvas for eternity? He bowed his head and, with his free hand, touched the scarred side of his face. A single tear blossomed in his eye corner and rolled down his unmarked cheek. Harold wiped it away angrily. He looked up and gazed at the painting once again. The bright colours *did* look like flames.

He dabbed the brush into the puddle of orange paint and tentatively applied a few strokes. For some reason, he found that his hand was shaking but he persevered. Why, in the last few weeks, had the canvas never appeared to be a canopy of dancing flames, he wondered? Was it because of the nightmare? The re-kindling of memories which he thought he had at last succeeded in pushing to the back of his tortured mind? Harold could not, would not, forget that horrific night in 1946 and he had more than his scar to remind him of it.

Along the length of his arms, from elbow to wrist, long white marks showed. They were all that now remained of the near-fatal attempt he'd made to kill himself. The scars were barely visible now but he would sit and look at them sometimes remembering the day when he'd inflicted the cuts which he had hoped would bring him the welcome oblivion of death – the ultimate darkness which would rid him of the guilt that gnawed away at his mind like a hungry rat. He had locked himself in the toilet and slashed his forearms open with a piece of broken glass. He'd smashed the window in the toilet with one powerful fist and then drawn his arms back and forth across the jagged shards on the frame until his thin forearms were crimson tatters. The blood had pooled at his feet and Harold could still remember the strange feeling of serenity which had fallen over him as he'd watched his arteries and veins spewing forth their vivid red fluid. The pain had been excruciating but not as bad as the fire. The fire. That was all he could think of as he stood there that day, his arms reduced to dripping rags as he tugged them back and forth across the glass.

But two interns had battered the door down and found him. They dragged him away, one of them applying make-shift tourniquets to his arms while Harold burbled:

"I'm sorry, I'm sorry."

They tried to comfort him as he slid into unconsciousness, not understanding that his words were for his dead brother and mother.

Now Harold stood in the Therapy room, brush in hand, his eyes lowered. The thoughts tumbling over in his mind.

He had learned to live with the guilt. He knew it

was something he would always have to bear and he accepted that. He *had* been responsible for the death of his brother. He knew that and it was something that would haunt him forever. There was no atonement for him, no way of releasing that guilt. It grew and festered in his mind like some kind of poisonous growth, the dreams which it brought like the discharge from a rank boil.

"Good morning, Harold."

The voice startled him and he turned quickly, almost dropping his palette. The Occupational Therapist, Jenny Clark, stood beside him looking at his canvas. "What are you going to call your painting, Harold?" she asked.

"It looks like a fire to me," he told her. "Can't you see the flames?" He looked directly at her and she tried to fix her gaze on his one good eye, deliberately avoiding his burned skin. She held the questioning stare for long moments then looked back at the canvas.

Jenny smiled thinly,

"Yes, they do look like flames don't they?" she said, softly.

They stood in silence for long moments, both inhaling the cloying odour of the oil paint, then Harold spoke again.

"Have you ever done anything you're ashamed of, Miss Clark?"

The question came completely out of the blue and took her by surprise. She swallowed hard, her brow furrowing slightly.

"I suppose so, Harold. Why do you ask?"

"This painting," he told her. "I think it's like a punishment. A reminder to me never to forget what I did to my brother. I was ashamed of that. I still am. I killed my brother, Miss Clark. I think that's what I'm painting."

Jenny exhaled deeply.

She was about to say something when he spoke again.

"I think it's my way of saying sorry. Sorry for what I did."

She was silent for a moment, her eyes searching his, straying from that wretched glass orb to the real one and then back again.

His tone suddenly lightened.

"I'll call it 'Fire'," he announced. "Just 'Fire'."

More patients were arriving now and Jenny left Harold alone with his masterpiece in order to help the others. Soon the room was alive with activity and noise. Someone knocked over an easel but Harold ignored the clatter and continued with his painting. Finally, satisfied that it was complete, he picked up a tube of red paint and squeezed some of the sticky liquid onto his palette. He dipped his brush into it and, in thick letters at the top of the canvas, painted one word:

FIRE

Two

The road which led from Exham itself, to the larger town of Cornford twelve miles away, was flanked on both sides by wide expanses of fields. Some belonged to the handful of small farms which dotted the countryside round about, but others just sprouted weeds, they stood unwanted and untended.

The road was usually busy but, as the early morning mist cleared slowly, it was strangely devoid of the customary bustle of commuters who clogged it. The

Panda car passed just three other vehicles, one of which was a large lorry carrying vegetables.

Constable Bill Higgins stepped on the brake, simultaneously easing the Panda to one side of the road, its nearside wheels actually mounting the footpath at the side of the tarmac. The lorry swept past, its tail flap rattling loudly and Higgins watched it in the rear view mirror, half expecting to see it spill its load behind it. He swung the car back in lane and drove on.

Beside him, in the passenger seat, his superior gazed out of the side window, watching as the trees sped past. The window was open to allow some cool air into the stifling confines of the car. Despite the slight chill, the refreshing breeze was welcomed by both men. The Panda's heater was on the blink, jammed at maximum output it transformed the vehicle into some kind of mobile sauna.

Inspector Lou Randall fumbled in the pocket of his jacket for a packet of Rothmans and lit one, the wind blowing smoke back into his face. He coughed and waved a hand in front of him. A stronger smell reached his nostrils through the bluish haze of fumes and he winced as he realized that it was manure.

"Why does the countryside always smell like a shithouse?" he said, blowing out a disapproving breath.

"What is it about fresh air that you hate so much, guv?" asked the driver, grinning.

"I wouldn't call *that* fresh air."

Randall had been born and brought up in London, always used to its cramped confines. To the steady crush of buildings and people around him. He felt strangely exposed in the countryside, as if light and space were somehow alien to him. Apart from holidays when he was a kid, he'd never been out of London longer than two weeks at a time. He remembered how his parents always took him to the Lake District when he was a nipper, and how much he hated water too. Large

22

expanses of it always put the fear of Christ into him even though he was a good swimmer. The strange brooding silence which seemed to hang over the lakes always disturbed him just as now the perpetual solitude of endless fields brought back that youthful unease. Randall was thirty-six, stocky and heavily muscled. He usually put himself through a routine of exercises three or four times a week to keep in shape. Not that much happened in Exham to compel sudden strenuous physical activity though. In his sixteen months as head of the small force, he'd dealt with nothing more serious than a couple of rape cases.

He slumped in the seat, the plastic hot against his back, puffing on his fag, his blue eyes scanning the endless tracts of arable land. He ran a hand through his brown hair and exhaled deeply. The clock on the dashboard showed 8.09 a.m. and Randall yawned. He hadn't slept too well the previous night and his eyes felt as if someone had sewed the lids together. He took a last drag on his cigarette and tossed the butt out of the window. Grunting, he straightened up in the passenger seat. He reached over onto the back seat and picked up a manila file, which he flipped open. Inside was a report and, clipped to that, another sheet of paper which bore the signature of the county coroner. Randall yawned again and ran his eyes over the typewritten report which he'd already looked at half a dozen times that morning.

"Paul Harvey," he read aloud. "Age twenty-nine. Detained Cornford Maximum Security Prison, June 1979. No previous prison record." He closed the file, drumming on it agitatedly. "Convicted of two murders, sentenced to life."

"I can still remember when he was arrested," said Higgins, some of the colour draining from his normally ruddy complexion. "It took four of us to hold the

23

bastard down long enough to cuff him. He was a bloody maniac."

Randall raised an eyebrow.

"The reports seem to agree with you," he said. "It must have been quite a shaker for a little place like Exham."

"It was," Higgins confirmed.

"The killings were random. There was never any motive established," said the Inspector, reflectively.

"What exactly *did* he do to them?" Higgins wanted to know. "We never did find out for sure."

Randall opened the file again.

"Both victims were dismembered," he read. "Apparently there was so little of them left that identification was almost impossible. Fond of the old carving knife our Harvey," he added, sardonically.

"Most of the bits were never even found."

"Oh Jesus," murmured Higgins.

"And now he's out again," said Randall, flatly. "He escaped at five o'clock this morning."

The two men continued their journey in silence. Higgins swung the Panda off the main road and down a narrower off-shoot flanked on both sides by trees. Through the windscreen both men could make out the gaunt edifice of Cornford prison. It was built of red brick, discoloured with the ravages of time and the elements. The high wall which surrounded it was similarly scarred, a row of iron spikes and barbed wire running along the top. Two huge black-painted doors barred their way as the constable brought the Panda to a halt.

Randall straightened his tie, cursing when one of the buttons popped off. Higgins grinned.

"Get your wife to sew it. . ."

The smile and the sentence trailed off and the constable coloured as he felt Randall's eyes on him.

"Sorry, guv," he said, softly.

Randall found the button and dropped it into his pocket. Then, clambering out of the car he said:

"I don't know how long I'll be."

Higgins nodded and watched as his superior walked across the tarmac towards the towering black gates. On his way he passed a blue sign which proclaimed in large white letters:

HER MAJESTY'S PRISON: CORNFORD

There was an old mini parked outside the gates, its side panels rotting, the white paint peeling away to reveal the rust beneath. The decaying metal was the colour of dried blood and the peeling paint reminded the Inspector of a picked scab.

He reached the huge gates and banged on a small door set into the right hand one. After a few seconds a panel slid open and a face appeared.

Randall showed his ID and the panel closed. A moment later the door opened and the policeman stepped through to find himself in the courtyard of the prison. A uniformed warder showed him the main entrance of the building and Randall set off across the vast expanse of wet tarmac.

To his left a group of prisoners, dressed in their familiar dark blue overalls, were standing or shuffling idly about while two warders stood chatting. One or two heads turned as he made his way towards the huge main building which was still wreathed in the early morning mist, the grey fog drifting round it like some kind of ethereal shroud.

The Governor's office was enormous, fully thirty feet long and perhaps twenty wide. A huge oak table stood in the centre, an oval shaped antique which sparkled brightly. The legacy of many years polishing. It had nine chairs around it and, suppressing a smile, Randall wondered where King Arthur and his knights had got to. The thought quickly vanished however.

The walls were a sky blue colour dull with the dust

of the years, as with most of the paintwork in the prison it seemed. The ceiling rose high above him, three large banks of fluorescents set into it – the only concession to progress. The rest of the room seemed forty years out of date. Large windows looked out onto the West Wing of the prison, the office itself separated from the prisoners' quarters by a high stone wall and a large expanse of well-kept lawn. The carpet on the floor was so threadbare that Randall's footsteps echoed as he walked towards the desk at the far end of the office. As he approached, Governor George Stokes rose to greet him.

The two men introduced themselves, a sign on Stokes's desk adding a silently corroborative affirmation that he was indeed Governor. He was well into his sixties, his hair almost white, even the wisps that curled from his wide nostrils. But his handshake was strong, belying his years. He was tall, ungainly. Dressed in a two piece brown suit, the trousers of which were an inch too short, he looked like some kind of be-spectacled stick insect.

Stokes introduced the other man in the room as Doctor Kevin Hayes. He was, or had been up until his escape, Harvey's psychiatrist. A short, nervous looking man in his fifties, he was prodding one ear with the blunt end of a pin.

"You're probably wondering why I called you, Randall?" said Stokes, clasping his hands before him and leaning on his blotter.

"It had crossed my mind," said the Inspector.

"We have reason to believe that Harvey will return to Exham," Stokes told him. "We thought you should be forewarned." The older man plucked at the end of his nose. "If there's anything we can do to help you, ask."

"Well, for one thing, I'd like to know why he was having psychiatric treatment," the Inspector said.

26

"From what I've read about the case there was never any hint of mental disturbance."

"During the last six months," said Hayes, "Harvey had become very introverted. He brooded. He'd always been a loner but he seemed to become more hostile towards the other prisoners. He got into fights frequently."

"We had him in solitary most of the time," Stokes interjected. "As much for the safety of the other men as anything else."

"How dangerous is he?" Randall wanted to know.

Hayes stroked his chin thoughtfully.

"It's difficult to say," he said, evasively.

"Could he kill again?" Randall demanded. "*Would* he kill again?"

The psychiatrist exchanged a brief glance with Stokes then looked at Randall.

"It's possible," he said, almost reluctantly.

"How the hell did he manage to get out of here in the first place?" Randall snapped, just a little too forcefully.

"That, Randall, is not your concern," rasped Stokes. "Catching him again is all that matters. *That's* your job I suggest you set about doing it." The two men locked stares for long seconds and the Inspector could see the anger in the older man's eyes. The escape had hurt his pride, it might, Randall reasoned, cost him his job. He probably had every right to be angry. But there was fear there too.

Randall got to his feet.

Randall didn't speak much on the way back to Exham, his mind was too full of thoughts and questions, one in particular nagging at him.

Where and when would Paul Harvey turn up?

Three

Paul Harvey stumbled and fell, crashing heavily against a nearby tree. He lay still on the damp moss for long seconds, sucking in painful breaths, each of which seemed to sear his lungs. His calves and thighs were stiff, as if someone had clamped a vice on each leg and was slowly turning the screw. He dragged himself upright, using a low branch for support. Panting like a bloodhound, he leant against the tree and massaged the top of his legs. He licked a furred, tumefied tongue over his cracked lips. It felt as if someone had stuffed his mouth with cotton wool. He stood still for a moment longer then blundered on through the small wood.

He walked awkwardly, like a drunkard and was forced to use the trees and bushes to hold him up. He couldn't remember how long he'd been running. Four, five hours. Perhaps more. He wasn't sure of anything except the gnawing pain in his legs and the burning in his belly. He must have food, that much he *did* know. The prison was a good six miles behind him now and he afforded himself a smile as he continued his haphazard course through the woods.

A bird twittered overhead and he spun round, taken aback by this sudden sound. He raised a hand as if trying to pluck it from its perch. When that failed he attempted to shout at it but no sound would come. His throat was like parchment. He slumped against another tree, head bowed, ears alert for the slightest movement. *They* would be after him by now but they would not catch him. Not this time.

He cocked an ear expectantly but heard nothing, just the ever-present sound of the birds and. . .

A twig snapped close by and he froze, pressing himself closer to the trunk of the elm, trying to become a part of it.

As he watched, a small boy, no more than twelve years old, pushed his way through the bushes and picked up a football. With the object safely retrieved, he scrambled back towards the clearing beyond where two of his companions waited. Harvey could see the other children now. He relaxed slightly and moved forward with surprising agility for a man of his size. He was well over six feet two, weighing around fourteen stone. His hair was black, closely cropped and shining. Pupils like chips of emerald glittered amidst whites criss-crossed by bulging red veins.

He moved closer to the edge of the woods, keeping low, well away from the children playing beyond. There were three of them he could see, all engrossed in their game. Harvey parted a bush to peer out at them. His large fingers twitched spasmodically but a look of bewilderment crossed his face when he saw them stop kicking the orange ball around and cross to a large plastic bag which lay behind one of the make-shift goal posts.

They took out some sandwiches and began eating.

Harvey put a hand to his stomach as it rumbled loudly.

He watched the three of them eating.

The time would come.

He watched and waited.

Graham Phelps stuffed the remains of the ham sandwich into his mouth and chewed noisily.

"Let's have a drink," he said, motioning towards one of the two thermos flasks.

Colin Fulton dutifully poured him a cup of steaming hot chocolate which he swigged, burning his tongue.

"Fucking hell," he gasped. "That's hot."

Colin and his younger brother, Miles, both chuckled.

Graham, on the other hand, didn't see the joke.

"What's so fucking funny?" he demanded, angrily.

He swore a lot. His father and his elder brothers did it too. His eldest brother had been in Borstal for six months and Graham hero-worshipped him, as he did his father. Both of them would think nothing of smacking a woman in the teeth too, if the need arose. They were really hard. Graham's mind contained a simple equation because he was somewhat simple minded:

Swearing and hitting women = manliness.

As easy as that.

Now he rounded on Miles again. The twelve-year-old, three years younger than Graham and Colin, was an ideal target.

"I said, what's so fucking funny?" he persisted.

"You, burning your mouth," Miles told him. "You shouldn't be such a pig."

"Fuck off," rasped Graham and got to his feet, kicking the ball about, dribbling it close to the brothers, bouncing it off Miles's legs every so often. They finally took the hint and got wearily to their feet, dropping the remnants of half-eaten sandwiches back into the plastic Tesco bag.

Paul Harvey kept perfectly still amongst the trees and bushes, his breath now slowed to a rasping hiss. He watched the three boys kicking the ball about and a twisted grin spread across his face.

Graham decided to show off his shooting ability and lashed a shot in the direction of the makeshift goal but a gust of wind caught the ball and it went flying wide, hurtling into the trees beyond. Graham planted his hands on his hips and looked at his companion.

"Well, go and get the fucking thing," he shouted, watching as Miles sloped off in the direction of the trees.

Paul Harvey saw him coming.

Miles pushed his way into the bushes and onward until he was surrounded by trees. For the first time that morning he noticed just how quiet it was inside the copse. His feet hardly made a sound as he walked over the carpet of moss, glancing around in his search for the ball. It obviously must have gone further than usual. Even its bright orange colour seemed invisible in the maze of greens and browns which made up the small wood. He stepped up onto a fallen, rotting tree stump, hoping to get a better view. At his feet a large spider had succeeded in trapping a fly in its web and, for a moment, Miles watched the hairy horror devouring its prey. He shuddered and moved away, his eyes still scanning the copse for the lost ball. He stepped into some stinging nettles and yelped in pain as one of them found its way to the exposed area between his sock top and the turn-up of his jeans. He rubbed the painful spot and wandered further into the wood. Where the hell was that ball?

He stood still, hands on his hips, squinting in the dull light. Mist still hung low on the floor of the copse, like a blanket of dry ice, it covered his feet as he walked. Droplets of moisture hung like shimmering crystal from the few leaves which remained on the trees. They reminded Miles of cold tears.

Something caught his eye.

He smiled. It was the ball, about ten yards away, stuck in the top of a stunted bush. He hurried towards it, suddenly aware of the unearthly silence which seemed to have closed around him like some kind of invisible velvet glove. He shivered and scurried forward to retrieve the ball, tugging it loose from the grasping branches of the bush.

Something moved close behind him, a soft footfall on the carpet of moss. He spun round, his heart thumping hard against his ribs.

A sudden light breeze sprang up, whipping the mist into thin spirals.

Miles started back towards the openness of the rec, away from the stifling confines of the copse. He clutched the ball to his chest, ignoring the mud which was staining his jumper. The odour of damp wood and moss was almost asphyxiating, as palpable as the gossamer wisps of fog which swirled around him.

Something cold touched his arm and he gasped, dropping the ball, spinning round, ready to run.

It was a low branch.

As he bent to pick up the ball, Miles could see that his hands were shaking. He straightened up, a thin film of perspiration on his forehead. And it was at that moment he felt the hand grip his shoulder.

This time he screamed, trying to pull away but the hand held him back and he heard raucous laughter ringing in his ears.

"All right, don't shit yourself," said a familiar voice and Miles finally found the courage to turn. He saw Graham Phelps standing there, his hand gripping Miles's shoulder. "Just thought I'd give you a bit of a fright." He laughed again, pushing Miles towards the clearing ahead of them.

"How would you like it if someone had done that to you?" Miles bleated.

"Oh shut up and give me the ball," said Graham, snatching it from him.

The huge frame of Paul Harvey loomed ahead of them, rising from behind a fallen tree stump as if he had sprung from the very ground itself. He towered over them, huge hands bunched into fists which looked like ham hocks. Wreathed in mist, he looked like something from a nightmare and, when he took a step towards them, both boys screamed and ran. They darted in opposite directions, the football falling to the ground where it bounced three or four times. Forgotten. They ran and Harvey ran after them.

They crashed through bushes, ignoring the low branches of trees which clawed at their faces, oblivious to the thorns which scraped their flesh. They both burst into the open, running like frightened rabbits. Colin saw them, saw the terror in their eyes and he too, without knowing why, joined them in their crazed flight.

Harvey watched the children as they dashed across the clearing. He waited until they were out of sight, then, scanning the open ground ahead, anxiously emerged from the trees. He crossed to the Tesco bag and rummaged inside, finding several sandwiches, some of which he stuffed into his mouth immediately. The others he jammed into his pockets. He picked up the first thermos flask, flinging it to one side when he discovered it was empty. The second one, however, was full and he could hear the contents slopping about as he shook it. Pieces of half-eaten sandwich fell from his mouth as he tried to swallow as much as he could.

Beyond the clearing lay the rolling fields which marked the outskirts of Exham. Careful not to drop any of his food, he loped off.

In twenty minutes he had disappeared.

It was 10.05 a.m.

Four

The Exham police station was a two storey red brick building set on the perimeter of the town centre. A small construction, barely large enough to house the force of nine men and three women, Randall himself excluded.

At 2.56 p.m., the entire force was crowded into what normally passed as the rest room. There wasn't enough seats for everyone to sit down so one or two of the constables leant against the white-washed walls, their attention focused on the Inspector who stood beside a board at the far end of the room. There were several monochrome photos stuck to it and, resting precariously on the chair in front of him, Randall had a dozen or so more of them.

"Paul Harvey," he said, motioning towards the photos. "Get to know that face because we've got to find him and quick."

The Inspector lit up a cigarette and sucked hard on it.

"Exham's quite a big town," he said. "So there's plenty of places for the bastard to hide. That's if he's even got here yet." He paused. "Or even coming that is."

A murmur of sardonic laughter rippled around the room.

"I want a thorough search of the whole town. Any disused houses, places like that and ask people too. Take one of these with you." He held up the photo and waved it before him. "But just be careful with your questioning. If word gets around that Harvey is on his way back to Exham then we could have a panic on our hands. It's going to be difficult enough finding him without having people ringing up every five minutes wanting to know if we've caught him." He blew out a stream of smoke. "And if the local press ask any questions, tell them to sod off. This lot around here can't write about jumble sales without getting the facts wrong so we don't want stories about Harvey splashed all over the front page of the local rags." A lump of ash dropped

34

from the end of his fag and Randall ground it into the carpet.

"Any questions?" he asked.

"Did Harvey have any family, guv?" The question came from P C Charlton,

"Yes he did. If you can call it a family. The information's a bit vague but it seems he lived with his father up until three years ago when the old boy died. Nobody could find any trace of his mother though. The murders were committed after his father's death."

"How do you know he's coming back here?" It was Constable Reed this time.

Randall repeated his conversation with Stokes and the psychiatrist, expressing his own doubts about the killer returning to Exham. Reed seemed satisfied with the explanation.

There was an uneasy silence and Randall scanned the collection of faces before him

"Any more questions?" he asked.

There were none.

"Right," he glanced at his watch. "There's a couple of hours of daylight left. We may as well make a start."

The uniformed men and women got to their feet, filing past Randall and the board, each one picking up a couple of the black and white photos. The inspector himself waited until they had all departed and then made his way up to his office on the first floor. He lit up another cigarette and sat down at his desk, flicking on the desk lamp. Already the sky outside was overcast, heavy with rain, it hastened the onset of dusk and the watery sun which had tried to shine for most of the day had finally been swallowed up by the banks of thick cloud.

Randall held one of the photos before him, studying Harvey's chiselled features. There was a piercing intensity in those eyes which seemed to bore into the policeman even from the dull monochrome of the picture. Harvey carried two distinctive scars on his right cheek which Randall guessed were bottle scars. They were deep and the Inspector wondered how and when the escaped prisoner had sustained them. He sat back in his seat, tossing the photo onto his desk. The smoke from the cigarette drifted lazily in the air, curling into spirals around him. He closed his eyes.

The wind moaned despairingly at his window.

Five

He couldn't remember how long he'd been running, only that it had been daylight when he'd begun but now the countryside was wrapped in an almost impenetrable cloak of darkness. He wondered if he had been running in circles, chasing his own tracks round and round as he sought some vague escape route. The hills and fields all looked alike in the blackness. His legs felt like ton weights, burdened as they were by clods of mud. His heart thumped hard against his ribs and the breath rasped in his lungs as if it were being pumped by defective bellows.

He paused for a moment, atop a hill, and looked around. Below and behind him lights were shining. In some places the sodium glare of street lamps, in others the brighter glow which spilled from the windows of houses. If he had been able to calculate distance, Paul Harvey might well have guessed that he was about two miles from the centre of Exham. The town was little more than a collection of dim lights in the distance. Like a scattering of fire-flies. He panted loudly, his mouth filled with a bitter taste. He was cold, the first particles of frost now sparkling on the grass around him as the moon fumbled its way from behind a bank of thick cloud. Harvey looked up at the wreathed white orb and blinked. He put up a hand, as if trying to sweep it from the sky and, when this ploy didn't work he decided to keep on running.

The hill dipped away sharply before him and he slipped on the slick grass as he descended the slope. He lay still for what seemed like an eternity, ignoring the dampness which he felt seeping through his clothes. He merely lay on his back, gazing up at the moon, sucking in huge lungfuls of air. Every muscle in his body ached but he knew he couldn't stop. Not yet. Grunting painfully, he hauled himself upright and stumbled on. As he ran he could feel the sandwiches bumping in his coat pockets. He'd eaten one or two since taking them from the children earlier in the day and the flask was now half empty, its contents only luke-warm. He realized that he would have to eat as soon as he found shelter. Eat and drink. But what would he do when that source of food was exhausted? The question tumbled over in his mind as he ran. Yes, the food was important but so was shelter. The night was already digging icy fingers into him, he needed somewhere to hide. And not just from the elements. From *them*. *They* would be looking for him. He knew they would come soon but perhaps not for a few days. Even *they* would have difficulty finding him out here.

The moon escaped a bank of cloud once more and, in its cold white light, Harvey saw a group of buildings ahead of him.

He stopped dead in his tracks, even his breathing slowed for a moment.

Shelter.

He was sure it was a farm. There were. . .

He clenched his fists. Why was it so difficult to think? One, two, three. There were perhaps more buildings, arranged in a quadrangle, with a large open area at their centre – a farm house, a barn, a pig pen, another barn. He moved closer, his wide eyes ever watchful. There were no lights on in the house, perhaps whoever lived there was out, gone to bed maybe. Or perhaps *they* were in there, watching him. Just waiting for him to walk into their trap. He stood still, panting. No, there was no possible way they would find him here, they couldn't know he would find this place. Harvey smiled crookedly and licked his lips, advancing a few more yards. It was certainly quiet, there didn't appear to be anyone around.

He reached the broken fence which surrounded the entrance to the farmyard. It was rotten with damp, the wood black where at one time it had been regularly creosoted. The gate hung from one hinge, an invitation to enter which Harvey took. The yard itself was covered with weeds, some as high as his knees. He walked across to the overgrown hedge which surrounded the garden. There was no gate here, just a weather-beaten arch covered with the spidery remains of a rose plant. Harvey moved tentatively up the path towards the front door of the house, his eyes moving back and forth, waiting for the slightest sign of movement.

When nothing had happened by the time he'd reached the front door, he began to relax slightly. He went from window to window, trying to peer through the grime-encrusted panes in an effort to see what lay inside the house but he could make out no shapes in the gloom. He thought about breaking in. He could smash a window. With his tremendous strength he could even break down one of the doors.

But, what if someone came by? They would see that the farmhouse had been damaged. They would know something was wrong. He would be found. *They* would come for him again. He smiled crookedly again, pleased with his own cunning. He turned and scuttled back down the path, crossing the yard in the direction of the barn. This time, two huge wooden doors stood open and Harvey walked cautiously into the black maw which lay beyond.

The barn smelt of dampness and rotting straw. Bales of it were stacked in one corner and also up in the loft. A rickety looking ladder offered a route up to the loft and the big man put one huge foot on the first rung, testing it. It groaned under his weight but held and he began to climb.

There were about a dozen bales of damp straw in the loft, the wooden floor itself covered with a thin carpet of the fibrous stuff. The stench was almost overpowering but Harvey seemed not to notice it. The darkness inside the barn was broken only by the weak light provided by the moon, the beams creeping in through the numerous cracks in the roof. Here and there, large chunks of the slate roof were gone and Harvey shied away from these as if anxious to remain in the enveloping darkness. He settled down against a straw bale and rummaged through his coat pockets for the remaining sandwiches he'd taken from the three boys that morning. He ate ravenously, stuffing the food into his cavernous mouth until it was gone then he reached for the thermos flask. He took a large mouthful but the contents were cold and Harvey spat the liquid out angrily, hurling the empty receptacle away.

He felt tired, needed to sleep and something told him that this was the safest place to spend the night. Even *they* would not find him in this place, he was certain of that. He stretched out his arms and yawned.

Something cold touched his right hand and he almost shouted in surprise.

He spun round, crawling away but simultaneously trying to see what his hand had brushed against. He listened for sounds of movement but there was nothing, just the hammering of his heart against his ribs and, gradually, he regained his composure. The moon, spilling through one of the many cracks in the roof, fell onto the cold object and, eyes fixed on it, Harvey got slowly to his feet.

It was a sickle.

Stuck into a straw bale, it protruded from the rotted bundle, its rusty blade still wickedly sharp. Harvey reached out and grasped the handle, pulling the sickle clear. He hefted it before him, tracing the curve of the blade with his forefinger. He grinned and swung it through the air, the swish disturbing the solitude of the silent barn. Harvey chuckled throatily, excited by his discovery as a child would be with a new toy. He wiped the wooden handle on his trousers in an effort to remove the dampness which seemed to have penetrated the wood. His stomach rumbled noisily and, once more, he was reminded of the craving gnawing deep inside him. He gritted his teeth and swung the blade at a nearby bale of straw, watching as his powerful blow hacked off a large chunk of it. He rubbed his belly with his other hand and grunted irritably.

The big man turned the sickle over in his hand, his eyes drawn to the cutting edge. He rubbed it with his thumb, pressing just a little too hard and a small globule of blood welled from the cut. He cursed and sucked the wounded digit. He grunted. So sharp. His father used to have an open razor and occasionally, as a child, Harvey had watched the man shaving with it. It always remained in its wooden case at other times, on a small ledge in the bathroom. The strop hung next to it. Harvey remembered the strop well, its smell. That cloying odour of oiled leather which he had come to hate.

And he remembered how it felt.

A vision swam into his mind and it brought almost physical pain with it. The vision of a small child being

40

beaten by a raging drunken man who laughed as he brought the strop down across the boy's pale body.

Across Harvey's pale body.

He swung the sickle through the air, slicing off more of the straw bale. The memories of his childhood were burned indelibly in his mind like a brand. A festering sore which would always be there to torment him.

He was an only child. There had never been brothers or sisters for him to share his miserable world with. His mother, Elizabeth, had seen to that. Harvey had been a breech birth. The labour had been long and agonising and, after it, his mother had vowed never to go through that hell again. Eventually she came to deny Harvey's father intercourse so great was her fear of another pregnancy. But Richard Harvey was not a man to be refused. In the beginning he had sought solace in drink, turning in three years from a large muscular man to a dark, haunted, shadow. When he drank, it seemed a part of himself was sucked into the bottle.

Harvey could still remember the night he had come home, drunk as usual, but this time raving, demanding that Elizabeth allow him what he said was rightfully his. Young Harvey, then just four years old, had heard them rowing in the room next door. He had heard the words turn to shouts and finally to screams and at that point he had climbed out of bed and padded along the landing towards the sounds of the screams and curses. He had pushed the door open and stood watching as his father tried to hold Elizabeth down, forcing her legs apart with one rough hand. Attempting to guide his own puny erection towards her with the other and, when she screamed, he would butt her with his wrinkled forehead until finally, he broke her nose and they were writhing on the bed like bloodstained puppets. Their movements jerky and uncoordinated.

Young Harvey had turned to leave but his father had roared at him to stay. And he had obeyed. Quivering

41

helplessly, watching in bewilderment as his mother moved painfully beneath his father who finally achieved his climax and rolled off the bed, leaving Elizabeth almost unconscious. Richard Harvey had grabbed his son by the shoulders and rasped some whisky soaked words into his face, then he had dragged him to the bathroom and beaten him with the strop until the skin had risen in welts all the time screaming at him that *he* was to blame for what had gone wrong between his parents. If *he* had not been so difficult to bring into the world then things might have been different.

His mother had left the next day.

But for Paul Harvey, the nightmare had just begun. His father's drinking had grown worse. He would drag Paul out of bed at nights and shout and curse at him. Telling him that it was *his* fault Elizabeth had left.

And there was always the strop.

But, even as he grew older, Harvey was forced to put up with it because it became his accepted way of life. Abuse, both physical and verbal became commonplace for him and he stayed with his father in that tiny house in Exham where he had lived his life because he knew nothing else. He had no friends, no relatives he could go to and, somewhere, beneath that hatred which he felt, there was something akin to pity for this shrivelled-up piece of humanity which was his father. For perhaps Harvey had come to believe that he *was* responsible for the break-up of his parents' marriage. Maybe the punishment *was* deserved.

His father had died three years earlier and Harvey's world had collapsed around him. What remained of his self-control and esteem had died too.

Freed from the living hell in which he'd grown up, alone in a harsh world where there was no one he could turn to for solace, he had snapped.

He didn't know how to make friends. He was spurned by the people of Exham, and treated with ill-disguised scorn, for everyone had known what Richard Harvey had been like. Why should his son be any different?

Paul Harvey had taken a fearful revenge. He had killed two of them those three years ago. They had not spoken to him but he had sensed, behind their eyes, the disgust which they felt for him. And he had killed them. For that he had been locked away but now things were different. He was free once more and the people of Exham would be made to pay. *They* would not find him. Not until it was too late.

He smiled crookedly and hefted the sickle before him.

There was movement below him.

He froze, listening to the sound. A steady but cautious sound which wafted up from below on the reeking air. Harvey dropped to his knees and peered through the gaps in the beams, trying to see what was making the sound. Could *they* have found him already? He gripped the sickle tighter.

There was more movement.

He spun round, his heart pounding.

This time it was in the loft.

Harvey struggled to his feet, squinting in the gloom. He gripped the sickle tightly, ready to defend himself.

The moon was suddenly enveloped by clouds and the barn plunged into deep, impenetrable darkness. Harvey felt a strange mixture of fear and anger. He sucked in an anxious breath.

Something brushed against his leg and he shrieked.

He heard a rustling sound from behind him and turned, blind in the darkness, striking out helplessly with the sickle. Something else touched his leg and he jumped back, twisting his ankle in the gap between two beams. He fell forward and a foul smell filled his nostrils. Something rubbed against his face. Something wet.

At that precise moment, the moon broke free of the

enveloping cloud and cold light flooded the barn once more.

Harvey found himself staring into the cold black eyes of a rat. There was another one behind him. It had been their scratchings and scurryings which he'd heard. He got to his knees, grinning, watching the rat as it sat on its haunches nibbling at something it held between its forepaws. Harvey kept his eyes fixed on it, then, with a devastatingly quick movement, he brought the sickle down. Before the rat had a chance to move, the lethal point of the blade had pierced its back, the steel itself ripping through its tiny body until it thudded into the beam beneath. The rat squealed and Harvey grabbed it by the head, ignoring its feeble attempts to bite him. He pulled it free of the sickle, ignoring the blood which dripped onto his trousers. The big man held it in one huge hand, thick streamers of saliva dripping from his mouth. The rat felt so warm. So warm. The gnawing in his belly seemed to become a raging fire.

So warm. . .

He bit the creature's small head off with one powerful bite, chewed twice, feeling bones splinter and then swallowed. With his bare hands he tore the rat open, chewing on the raw flesh, tugging the matted fur away with his teeth, swallowing the jellied pulp of intestines. He even chewed on the tail before tossing the remains away. His stomach glowed, despite the fact that he thought, for a second, he was going to be sick. But, nevertheless, he wiped the rat's blood from his chin and, sickle in hand, went looking for another of the furry creatures. As he grabbed a second one he decided not to eat the head and lopped it off with the sickle. Blood spurted from the tiny arteries and Harvey giggled childishly for a second, watching the headless animal bucking spasmodically in his huge hand.

He ate that one too.

By the time the gnawing in his belly had been quelled,

he felt drowsy, ready for sleep. He was even more satisfied now that this place was safe. *They* would not find him here. Not yet anyway and even if they did, it didn't matter. He touched the blade of the sickle and smiled.

Besides, he had other things on his mind.

He went to sleep with the vicious blade held in one hand.

Six

Harold Pierce brushed away an imaginary speck of dust from the sleeve of his white overall and swallowed hard. He was staring at the floor of the lift as it descended, listening to the steady drone as it headed for the next floor. On the other side of the cramped enclosure stood Winston Greaves. He glanced across at Harold, his eyes straying to the disfiguring scar which covered half of his companion's face. He looked at the burn with the same hypnotic fascination as a child stares at something unusual and he felt all the more self-conscious because of this. He tried to look away but couldn't. Only when Harold raised his head to smile sheepishly did Greaves suddenly find the ability to avert his eyes.

Harold knew that the other porter was looking at him. Just as he had felt the stares and sometimes heard the jibes of others, so many times before. He could understand their fascination, even revulsion, with his own disfigurement but their prolonged stares neverthe-less still made him feel awkward.

For his own part, Greaves had only succeeded by a

monumental effort of will from openly expressing his horror at the sight of Harold's face. He told himself that, in time, he would come to accept it but, at the moment, he still found his attention drawn to the red and black mess. His eyes fastened like magnets to the vision of tissue destruction. And yet, he had been a hospital porter for over fifteen years, he had seen many appalling sights during his working life. The road crash victims (one of whom, he remembered, had been brought in DOA after taking a dive through his wind-screen – when Greaves and another man had lifted the body from the gurney on which it lay, the head had dropped off, so bad were the lacerations to the man's neck), the injured children, other burn victims, casual-ties of modern day living such as the victims of muggings. The youth who had staggered into casualty trying to push his intestines back through a knife wound which he'd sustained in a gang fight. The woman who had been so badly beaten by her husband that, not only had her skull been fractured, part of her brain had been exposed. The child with the severed hand, a legacy of playing near farm machinery. The old lady with a cut on her hip which had been left unattended for so long there were actually maggots writhing in the wound.

The list was endless.

Small wonder then that Greaves's black, wiry hair was shot through with streaks of grey. They looked all the more incongruous against his black skin. He was a small man with large forearms and huge hands which seemed quite disproportionate to the size of his body. He was a hard worker and good at his job which was probably the reason, he thought, why he'd been saddled with the task of showing Harold the ropes.

For the first week, until he became accustomed to hospital procedure and proficient in his duties, Harold was to be under almost constant supervision by

Greaves. Now he looked across at his black companion and smiled again, conscious of his scar but trying not to hide it. Greaves smiled back at him and it reminded Harold of a piano keyboard. The black man's teeth were dazzling. It looked as if someone had stuck several lumps of porcelain into his mouth. His eyes however, were rheumy and bloodshot but nevertheless there was a warmth in that smile and in those sad eyes which Harold responded to.

He had arrived at Fairvale Hospital just the day before. Phil Coot had driven him there from the asylum and helped him unpack his meagre belongings, moving them into the small hut-like dwelling which was to be his new home. The small building stood close by the perimeter fence which surrounded the hospital grounds, about 400 yards from the central block, sheltered by clumps of beech and elder.

Fairvale itself consisted of three main buildings. The central block contained most of the twelve wards and rose more than eighty feet into the air, each storey bore an A and B ward, both able to maintain over sixty patients. The children's wing was attached to the ground floor part of the hospital and connected to it by a long corridor, thus it was effectively classified as a thirteenth ward. Also separate from the main building was an occupational therapy unit where a small but dedicated staff helped the older patients, and those recovering from debilitating illnesses, to regain some of the basic skills which they had possessed before being admitted. It was here that the previously simple task of making a cup of tea now seemed like the twelfth labour of Hercules. Also attached to this wing was a small gymnasium where patients with heart complaints were encouraged to undergo mild exercise and those with broken legs or arms underwent rigorous tests to regain the proper use of their damaged limbs. Also separate from the main building, accessible only by a brief walk across the car park, were the red brick buildings of the nurses' quarters.

Fairvale, standing as it did about a mile from the centre of Exham, served an area of about thirty square miles. It was the only hospital within that radius to offer emergency care and its turnover of patients was large. It also boasted a dazzling array of medical para-phernalia, including a cancer scanner and many other modern devices. Its X-Ray, EEG, ECG, and Pathology departments ensured that the turnover of out-patients matched, if not exceeded, the number of those confined. But the Pathology department which the out-patients saw was the one which took blood samples and urine samples. The real work of Fairvale's team of pathologists took place in the basement of the main building. Here, in four separate labs, each containing three stainless steel slabs and a work-top, bodies were examined and dissected. Pieces of tissue were pored over. Moles, growths, even skin-tags were examined and put through the same rigorous tests. There were no secrets to be kept in the pathology labs, detailed notes were made on each specimen be it a full scale post-mortem or the examination of a lump of benign cells. The filing cabinets which held this information stretched the full length of two of the large rooms. Each one was more than twenty feet wide, double that in length. Inside the labs, cold white light poured down from the banks of fluorescents set into the ceilings but, outside, in the wide corridor which led from the lift to the labs, it seemed to be forbiddingly dark. A perpetual twilight of dim lights which reflected a dull yellow glow off the polished floor and walls.

Harold looked up as the lift came to a halt and saw that the line of numbers and letters above the lift entrance were now dark. Just the "B" flared in the gloom. Winston Greaves ushered him out into the corridor which led towards the pathology labs and

Harold felt a curious chill run through him. He shivered.

"It's always cold down here," Greaves told him. "The labs are kept at fifty-five degrees. Otherwise, things start to smell." He smiled, his teeth looking yellow in the dim light.

Harold nodded and walked along beside him, his skin rising into goose-pimples as they neared the door of the nearest lab. A sign greeted them defiantly:

NO ENTRY BY UNAUTHORISED STAFF

"That includes you at the moment," said Greaves, smiling at Harold. He told him to wait then he himself knocked and, after a moment or two, heard a voice telling him to enter which he duly did, closing the door behind him. Harold was left alone. He stood still for long moments, wrinkling his nose at the odour which came from inside the lab. It wasn't the familiar antiseptic smell to which he'd become accustomed, it was something more pungent, more unpleasant. It was in fact, formaldehyde. He dug his hands into the pockets of his overall and began pacing up and down before the door, looking around him. The labs seemed to be silent, if anyone was working inside there, they certainly weren't making any noise. Harold walked past the door of first one then two. He came to a bend in the corridor.

Straight ahead of him, another twenty feet further down a shorter corridor, was a plain wooden door. Harold advanced towards it and stood silently before the entry way. There were no signs on this door telling him to keep out and, as he stood there, he could hear no sound coming from inside. Except. . .

He took a step closer.

There was a low rumbling sound coming from inside the room, punctuated every now and then by what sounded like extremely loud asthmatic breathing.

He put his hand on the knob and turned it.

49

The door was unlocked and Harold walked inside.

The heat hit him in a palpable wave and he recoiled. For long seconds he struggled to adjust to his new surroundings; then, as he looked around he saw just how large the room really was. It must have been a good forty feet square, the ceiling rising high above him. The paintwork which had once been white, was dirty and blackened in places and, directly ahead of him, over a bare floor, lay a huge metal boiler. A chimney thrust up from it, disappearing through the ceiling. It was the boiler that was rumbling but now Harold noticed another sound. A loud humming and, turning to his left he saw what he took to be a generator. It was covered by a profusion of dials, switches and gauges but Harold's attention was quickly diverted away from the generator back to the boiler and its adjacent furnace. The heavy iron door was firmly closed and the metal looked rusty. The wall above it was blackened and scorched and there was a faint odour of burning material in the air. Harold shuddered, felt his hands beginning to shake, his body trembling slightly. He sucked in a slow breath which rattled in his throat and when he tried to swallow he found it difficult.

There were half a dozen trolleys in one corner of the room, each piled high with linen and as Harold took a step closer towards the strange bundles he coughed at the vile stench which emanated from them. He recognized them as sheets; some soiled with excrement, some stained dark with dried blood or vomit.

A bead of perspiration formed on his forehead and he wiped it away with a shaking hand as he moved closer towards the door of the furnace, the heat growing more powerful as he did so. He saw a pair of thick gloves lying on a ledge close to the tightly sealed door, beside them a set of long tongs and a wrench. Coal was piled in countless buckets nearby, some of it having spilled over onto the floor, its black dust swirling in the hot air.

Harold was trembling uncontrollably now and, as he strained his ears, he could actually hear the sound of the roaring flames from within.

A nightmare vision of his mother flashed into his mind. She was on fire, the skin peeling from her face and arms as the flames devoured her and she was holding something in those blazing arms. It was Harold's baby brother. The child was little more than a ball of flame, one stubby, blackened arm reaching out from the searing fire-ball which consumed it.

Harold closed his eyes tight, trying to force the image from his mind. He took a step back, away from the furnace.

"Harold."

He almost shouted aloud when he heard the voice behind him. He spun round, his face flushed, his breath coming in short gasps.

Winston Greaves stood in the doorway looking at him.

"Are you all right?" he asked, seeing his companion's obvious distress.

Harold nodded.

"I'm sorry," he said. "I wandered off. I found this room."

Greaves nodded.

"The furnace," he said. "The boiler heats some parts of the hospital and that," he motioned to the generator, "that's for auxiliary power, in case we get any power failures or anything, the system is wired so that the emergency generator switches on straight away."

"What about those?" said Harold, motioning to the piles of reeking laundry.

"Some of it is kept here until the laundry department can take it away," Greaves told him. "Some of it is so bad, we just have to burn it." The black man turned

51

and motioned Harold out of the room, closing the door behind him. They made their way back down the corridor, back to the lift. "I would have showed you that room anyway," said Greaves. "That was what I came down here for in the first place. You and I have got some work to do in there this afternoon."

Harold swallowed hard but didn't speak. He gently, almost unconciously, touched the scarred side of his face and remembered the awful cloying heat inside the furnace room, the terrifying vision of his mother and brother flashing briefly into his mind once more. Greaves had told him they had work to do in there. What sort of work? His mind was spinning.

As they waited for the lift to descend, Harold felt the perspiration clinging to his back.

For some unfathomable reason he felt terribly afraid.

For the remainder of that first morning, Greaves took Harold on a conducted tour of the hospital, telling him what his duties would be, showing him where things were kept, introducing him to other members of staff all but a couple of whom managed to disguise their revulsion at the sight of Harold's scarred face. Greaves chattered good-naturedly about all sorts of things, the weather, hospital work, football, politics, and Harold listened to him. Or at least he gave the impression that he was listening. His mind was elsewhere, more specifically on just what he and Greaves had to do in the furnace room that coming afternoon.

The two of them went along to the hospital canteen at about one fifteen and ate lunch. Harold managed a couple of sausages but merely prodded the rest of his dinner with his knife and fork. Greaves, on the other hand, between mouthfuls of fish and chips continued to babble happily to his new companion. But, gradually, the extent of Harold's worry filtered through to the other porter.

"What's wrong, Harold?" he asked, sipping at a large mug of tea.

Harold shrugged and looked around him. The canteen was full of people, nurses, porters, doctors, all sitting around tables eating and chatting. The steady drone of conversation reminded him of the hum of the generator.

"Is it about the furnace?" Greaves asked, cautiously.

"I'm frightened of fire," said Harold, flatly.

Greaves studied his companion over the lip of his mug.

"I'm sorry to ask but. . ." He struggled to find the words. "Your face. Was that . . . is it a burn?"

Harold nodded.

"I've had it since I was fourteen," he said but didn't continue. The rest was knowledge for him alone. He tried to smile and, indeed, his tone lightened somewhat. "I suppose I'll get over my fear sooner or later."

Greaves nodded, benignly and took another hefty swallow of tea. The two men sat and talked and, this time Harold found himself contributing to the conversation instead of merely acting as listener. The images of the morning began to recede somewhat. He relaxed, telling himself that he was tense. After all, it was his first day at work. His first *ever* day at work. Greaves asked him, coyly, about the asylum but Harold answered his questions candidly not wishing to hide anything. He felt no shame about having spent over thirty-five years in a mental home. No, his shame was reserved for that particular subject which Greaves had touched on briefly just moments before. Fortunately the coloured porter didn't ask how Harold had come to be in a mental home since he was fourteen and he himself certainly didn't volunteer the information.

Greaves finally finished his meal and pushed the plate away from him, downing what was left in his mug as well. He patted his stomach appreciatively and smiled at Harold who returned the gesture with more assurance. He looked around him and saw a group of nurses sitting nearby. They were all in their early twenties, pretty girls tending towards plumpness as is the habit of their profession. Harold found himself captivated. One of them, the youngest of the group, her brown hair tucked up beneath her white cap, noticed his obvious interest and smiled at him. Harold smiled, lowering his gaze, one hand reaching up to cover the scarred side of his face in a gesture which had become all too familiar for him. He coloured and turn back to face Greaves who was smiling.

"Are you married?" Harold asked him.

"Yes," his colleague told him.

"What's your wife's name?"

"Linda. We've been married for twenty years."

Harold nodded. He wondered what it was like to be married. What was it like to have someone who cared for you, who needed you? To be wanted, loved – it must be a wonderful feeling. He had loved his mother but it had been so long ago he'd forgotten what the emotion felt like. All that was left inside him now was a hole. A kind of emotional dustbin filled only with guilt and want. He needed someone but was equally resigned to the fact that he would end his life alone, dying with only his memories and his shame for company. He swallowed hard.

Greaves got to his feet and tapped the table top.

"Well, we'd better get on," he said. "I think it's about time you and I did some work."

Harold nodded and followed his companion out of the canteen, leaving the sounds of joyful chatter behind, moving out once more into the hushed corridors of the hospital.

He worked hard that afternoon. On the third floor landing between Wards 3A and 3B, Harold swept and polished the lino until it shone. He muttered to himself when visitors walked over his handiwork in their muddy shoes, for it was raining outside, but no sooner had they passed than he was scrubbing away again.

It was approaching 3.15 p.m. when Winston Greaves arrived. Harold stopped what he was doing, put the cleaning materials away neatly in the cupboard indicated by Greaves then followed his coloured companion into the lift. The senior porter punched a button and the car began its descent towards the basement.

Harold felt a chill filling him, an unexplainable foreboding which seemed to intensify as they drew nearer the basement.

The lift bumped to a halt and the doors slid open. Both men walked out, immediately assailed by the cold. They walked to the end of the corridor to one of the labs, outside which stood a gurney. Whatever was on the trolley was hidden beneath a white plastic sheet. Hanging from one corner were two aprons. Greaves handed one to Harold and told him to put it on which he did, repeating the procedure with a pair of thin rubber gloves that the porter handed him. Suitably decked out for their task, the two men headed left, pushing the gurney towards the room which housed the furnace.

As he opened the door, Harold once again felt the heat, smelled the cloying stench of the coal dust. He saw the black particles swirling in the warm air. The piles of filthy linen had been disturbed, one or two of them removed.

"We'll have to burn what's left as well," said Greaves, indicating the reeking material. He pushed the trolley close to the furnace and, as Harold watched, he slipped on the pair of thick gloves which lay on the ledge before the rumbling boiler, pulling them over his rubber ones. That done, he reached for the wrench and used it to knock the latch on the furnace door up. Immediately the rusty iron door swung open. A blast of searing air swept out, causing the men to gasp for breath. Harold stood transfixed, gazing into the blazing maw. White and yellow flames danced frenziedly inside the furnace which yawned open like the mouth of a dragon. Like the entrance to hell, thought Harold.

"Fetch those sheets," said Greaves. "We'll do those first."

Harold paused before the roaring flames, seemingly hypnotized by the patterns they weaved as they fluttered before him. A low roar issued forth from the blazing hole. Even standing six feet away, the heat stung him and he took a step back.

"Harold," said Greaves, more forcefully. "The sheets."

He seemed to come out of his trance, nodded and crossed to the corner of the room, gathering up as many of the soiled sheets as he could carry. The stench was appalling and his head swam. A piece of rotted excrement squashed against his apron and he winced, trying to hold his breath as he struggled back to the waiting furnace. Greaves took them from him and began pushing them into the flames on the end of a large poker. The ferocity of the fire hardly diminished and even sheets damp with urine and blood were quickly engulfed by the furious fire. Dark smoke billowed momentarily from the gaping mouth of the furnace, bringing with it acrid fumes which made both men cough.

"I hate this job," gasped Greaves, pushing more of the filthy material into the fire.

Harold returned with the last of the faecal linen and together they shoved it into the furnace, watching as it was consumed.

"We'll clean those trolleys up later," said Greaves, motioning to the reeking gurneys in the corner of the room.

Harold nodded blankly, his eyes now turning to the trolley before them and its blanketed offerings. He watched as Greaves took hold of the blanket and pulled it free, exposing what lay beneath.

Harold moaned aloud and stepped back, eyes rivetted to the trolley. His one good eye bulged in its socket, the glass one regarded all proceedings impassively. He clenched his teeth together, felt the hot bile gushing up from his stomach, fought to control the spasms which racked his insides. The veins at either temple throbbed wildly and his body shook.

The foetus was in a receiver, dark liquid puddled around it. It was a little over six inches long, its head bulbous, its eyes black and sightless. It had been cleaned up a little after coming from pathology but not enough to disguise the damage done to it. The umbilicus was little more than a purple knot, gouts of thick yellowish fluid mingling with the blood that oozed from it. Its tiny mouth was open. There was more blood around the head which looked soft, the fontanelles not having sealed yet. The entire organism looked jellied, shrunken, threatening to dissolve when touched.

Harold backed off another step watched by Greaves.

"Not a pretty sight is it?" he said, apparently unperturbed. But then why should he be? He'd done this sort of thing often enough before. Harold gagged, put both hands on the trolley to steady himself and stared down at the foetus, his heart thudding madly against his ribs. He watched as Greaves picked up a pair of forceps, large stainless steel ones, from the trolley beside the receiver. Then, he picked the occupant of the tray up by the head, having to readjust his grip when the body nearly fell out. A foul-smelling mixture of blood, pus and chemicals dripped from the tiny body and Greaves wrinkled his nose slightly. Then, almost with disgust, he cast the foetus into the furnace. Immediately the body was consumed and there were a series of loud pops and hisses as the tiny shape was devoured by the flames.

Harold watched, mesmerized.

"Gordon," he whispered, watching the tiny foetus disappear, reduced in seconds to ashes.

He thought of his brother.

"Gordon," he whimpered again.

But, this time there was no screaming. His mother didn't dash in and try to drag the small creature from the roaring inferno. There was nothing this time. Just the terrible feeling inside himself. A cold shiver, as if someone had gently run a carving knife into his genitals and torn it upward to his breastbone. He felt as if he'd been gutted.

Greaves pushed the furnace door shut and hammered the latch back into place with the wrench then he turned to look at Harold who was still swaying uncertainly. For a moment, the senior porter thought his companion was going to faint.

"Are you all right?" he said.

Harold gripped the edge of the gurney and nodded almost imperceptibly.

"You'll get used to it," Greaves told him, trying to inject some compassion into his voice.

Harold was confused. He looked imploringly at Greaves as if wanting him to elaborate on the statement.

"That's how all the abortions are disposed of," the coloured porter told him. "We get through above five a month."

"Will I have to do this?" said Harold.

"Eventually."

The two of them stood there for long moments, neither one speaking, only the roaring of the flames from inside the furnace and the persistent hum of the generator interrupting the silence.

Harold drew a shaking hand through his hair. His face was bathed in perspiration and he was finding it difficult to swallow, as if the furnace had sucked in all the air from the room. He was suddenly anxious to be out of this place, back into the chill of the corridors. Away from the furnace. Away from the dragon's mouth that devoured children. Away from the memories. But he knew that they were one thing that would always pursue him. No matter where he ran or hid they would always find him because they were always inside him and now, as he thought about that tiny body being incinerated, his mind flashed back to another body burning, to another time. To 1946. To Gordon.

He turned and blundered out of the room, leaning against the wall, panting as he waited for Greaves to join him. The black man closed the door behind them, sealing off the sounds of the generator and the furnace.

He touched Harold gently on the shoulder, urging him to follow.

"Come on," he said, softly and Harold walked beside him, brushing one solitary tear from the corner of his eye.

And Greaves's words echoed in his mind:

"You'll get used to it."

Seven

One of the barn doors creaked loudly in the wind and the high pitched whine made Paul Harvey sit up. He gripped the sickle tightly in his hand, trying to control his breathing. The creak came once more and he realized that it was the door. Exhaling wearily, he lay down on the bed of straw again, gazing up through the hole in the roof immediately above him. Clouds skudded past, buffeted by the wind, passing swiftly before the moon until it resembled some kind of celestial stroboscope. The unrelenting glare reminded Harvey of an unshaded light bulb.

There are many things which stick in the memory, some of them inconsequential, and one of the things which now came to the big man's mind was the fact that, in the house where he grew up, not one single light possessed a shade. The rooms downstairs were bright but those upstairs were lit by dim sixty watt bulbs. His own bedroom included. He could still see it in his mind's eye. The unshaded bulb, the large bed with its rusty legs, the dusty floorboards. After his mother had left, the house had become steadily filthy. His father was never there to clean it and, even when he was, the dirt and grime didn't seem to bother him. During summer, the kitchen became a playground for all kinds of insects. Flies would feast on the congealed grease and rotting food which coated plates and saucepans. They were tossed, unwashed, into the chipped sink. Perhaps once a week, Harvey's father would force him to wash them and Harvey would obey because he feared his father. Fear was a stronger emotion even than hatred, over the years Harvey had come to learn that much. He had, even as a teenager, been a big lad, powerfully built. It would have been relatively easy to snap his father's frail neck with one strong hand. But, the spectre of fear, ingrained within him for so long, always seemed to be there, preventing him from harming his father who was, after all, the only person he had to share his worthless existence with. He cooked for him, he cleaned as best he could. Sometimes forced to launder sheets which his drunken father had fouled the night before. Harvey had done it all because, along with the fear was a perverted sense of duty. He owed this shrunken, sadistic little bastard his existence and that was what hurt most of all.

He wondered what it would have been like if he had left home with his mother. Would it have been different? Perhaps there wouldn't have been the beatings and the abuse but words sometimes hurt more than actions and his mother did not easily let him forget the pain she had gone through to give him life.

Harvey pressed both his hands to his temples as if the thoughts hurt him. He screwed his eyes up until white stars danced behind the lids. The knot of muscles at the side of his jaw throbbed angrily and he kept his teeth clenched until his head began to ache. Only then did the images begin to recede somewhat. He sat up rubbing his face with both huge hands, head bowed. And he remained in that position for some time.

The wind howled around the barn.

Eight

Harold watched the milk bubbling in the battered pan and listened to the powerful wind outside. At times, the gusts grew to such awesome proportions it seemed they would demolish the little hut. Built only of wood, it shook with each fresh onslaught of the gale.

The solitary dwelling was about 300 yards from the main building, which was itself visible through the window in the other room. There were no windows in the kitchen and Harold now stood in the yellowish light provided by an unshaded fifty watt bulb which dangled from the ceiling by a worn flex. The kitchen contained a hotplate, an old enamel sink and some cupboards which had been hastily nailed to the wooden wall at some time. The rusted heads of the nails were still visible in places. The tiny room was less than twelve feet square and it smelt of damp. There was mould on the west wall but at least, thought Harold, the place didn't leak. It had been cleaned up somewhat before his arrival but still showed the signs that it had been uninhabited for more than six years. There was a deep layer of dust and grime on nearly everything and Harold decided that he must clean the place up on his day off. It was, after all, to be his home from this point onwards.

He switched off the gas and removed the saucepan of milk, carefully pouring the contents into a mug which stood nearby. He then dropped the pan into the sink where it landed with a clang. Harold shuffled into the other room. It was slightly larger than the kitchen, boasting a single bed, a table and two battered chairs and more cupboards which looked as if they'd been assembled by a group of unenthusiastic woodwork students. The room was heated by a parafin stove which stood close to the bed and Harold warmed himself beside it before crossing to the window and peering out. He scraped away some of the accumulated muck from the window pane and squinted through the darkness. The lights of the hospital blazed in the night.

Harold lowered his head, the memory of what he'd seen that afternoon suddenly filling his mind. He turned his back on the hospital as if, by doing so, he would be able to blot out the visions of what he'd witnessed there earlier. He crossed to the bed and sat on the edge of it, sipping at the milk. It was hot. It burned.

He exhaled deeply, the thought of that tiny foetus consumed by the hungry furnace causing him to shudder. My God, that sight brought so many unwanted memories with it. He had thought that when he took this job it might help him to forget or at least come to terms with what had happened all those years

62

ago. But now he had learned that it was to be his duty to burn things. Things. Were they human? he asked himself. The one in the tray had looked like something from Outer Space but it was still human. It was still a child. They were asking him to burn children. Asking him to relive his nightmare day in, day out.

Asking him to burn Gordon, to burn his brother, over and over again.

Harold walked slowly towards the door of the furnace room. Even ten feet away he could hear the steady hum of the generator. His footsteps echoed in the dimly lit corridor and his breath formed small vapour clouds in the heavy air. For some reason it seemed colder in the basement than usual. Behind him, the pathology lab doors were closed, retaining their secrets. Harold put his hand on the furnace room door and pushed it open. He stepped inside, immediately recoiling from the all too familiar smell of soiled linen. He walked across to the furnace itself, the generator humming noisily nearby. He could hear the muffled roar of the flames as he picked up the thick gloves which lay on the ledge before the furnace door. He pulled them on then reached for the wrench, giving the lock a hefty whack.

It sprang open.

Flames, white and orange, danced madly before him and Harold felt their searing heat on his face. The air seemed to be sucked into the blazing hole and he struggled to get his breath. He took a step back, wincing at the intensity of the heat.

The door behind him swung shut with a loud bang and Harold spun round, heart thumping hard against his ribs. For long seconds he watched the door, expecting someone to walk in – Winston Greaves or maybe one of the other porters. The door remained firmly closed. Harold turned slowly back to look into the roaring furnace. As he stared into the raging inferno his one good eye began to pick out shapes in the blazing hell which was the furnace. Much as children watch the dancing flames of a coal fire. A vision slowly formed before Harold.

He wanted to move away but it was as if his feet were nailed to the ground and, all he could do was stare into the fire.

A single tear blossomed in the corner of his eye and rolled down his cheek. They were in there, the charred remnants of countless children like the one he had seen Greaves burn.

He had felt so powerless as he had watched the tiny body consumed. Just as he had felt powerless that night in 1946 when he had seen his mother and Gordon burned to death in the fire.

The fire which *he* had started.

The leaping flames seemed to alter shape, reform until Harold found himself looking into the face of his dead brother and, all at once, he realized that he must pluck Gordon from the flames.

He plunged both hands into the firebox.

Mind shattering pain enveloped his arms, the gloves which he wore disintegrating in seconds as the flames devoured them. Harold found that he could not move and, as the agonizing pain began to spread through his entire body he actually saw the flesh of his arms turning black, huge blisters growing and bursting like flowering plants which spilled their fluid in thick gouts. Bone showed white through the charred stumps and finally Harold found the breath to scream.

He was still screaming when he woke up, propelled from the dream with a force he could almost feel. For long seconds he continued to scream but then, as he realized where he was, he quietened down and his screams turned first to whimpers and then to tears.

Curling up beneath the covers he sobbed uncontrollably.

Nine

Judith Myers stood before the bedroom mirror and studied her reflection in the glass. She ran a hand over the small, almost imperceptible bulge below her sternum then turned sideways for a better view. She touched the shape gently, allowing her eyes to stray momentarily from it, studying the rest of her naked body. Her hair was still wet from the shower she'd just taken and it hung in dark dripping strands, the droplets of water making brief circlets on the beige carpet. Her make-up had been washed off but her face was all the more striking for that. It seemed to glow in the half-light cast by the bedside lamp, her cheeks seeming sunken and hollow in the twilight. She ran an appraising eye over the rest of her body – the taut breasts, the unwanted bulge of her belly, the dark nest of pubic hair at its base. She'd put on some weight around her bottom and that fact made her even more irritable. Finally, after taking one last look at her slightly distended stomach, she turned away from the mirror and reached for the large fluffy towel which lay on the bottom of the large double bed. She began to dry her hair.

"You still intend to go through with it then?" said Andy Parker. He was stretched out beneath the sheets, watching her. He took a last drag on his cigarette and ground it out in the ash-tray on the bedside table.

"I thought I asked you not to smoke up here," said Judith, still rubbing frenziedly at her hair.

"Don't evade the question," he said.

She paused for a second and looked at him.

"Yes, I am still going through with it."

Parker held her gaze for a moment then he shook his head resignedly.

"Look, Andy," she said, irritably. "We've been over

65

this time and time again. Now I don't want to keep talking about it."

"I wonder sometimes if you've given it enough thought," he said.

"Christ," she threw the towel down. "I've done nothing *but* think about it ever since I found out I was pregnant." There was a long silence then Judith retrieved the towel and set about drying her hair once more. Her tone was more subdued when she spoke again. "Look, I can understand the way *you* feel, but try and understand how *I* feel. A baby at this time just wouldn't be. . ." She struggled to find the word.

"Convenient?" said Parker.

She nodded.

"I don't know why you're so worried, Judith. I mean, if it's the money that's bothering you, my wage is plenty for the two of us. We don't *need* the money you bring in."

"The money's got nothing to do with it and you know that," she told him, folding the towel. She shook her head, her shoulder-length hair flowing tantalizingly as she got up and crossed to the linen basket in the corner of the bedroom. He watched her, still naked, as she tossed the towel in amongst the other dirty washing. She stooped to pick up one of his handkerchiefs which was lying nearby. She glanced at it, saw that it was clean so proceeded to fold it neatly and push it into the drawer with the others. She was a stickler for neatness, everything must be in its place. It was one of the many little things which Parker had noticed about her during their six years together. She was twenty-five, eight years younger than him and they had shared each other's lives for the past six years, four of which they had spent living together in a house on the edge of Exham town centre. There had never been any mention of marriage, in truth it was an unspoken fact that they would probably live out their days together without the intrusion of matrimony. It was something which suited them both. But the subject of children was another matter. At thirty-three, Parker was keen, almost anxious, to be a father. He had everything else he wanted. He owned a highly successful restaurant in Exham, he had gone through his hell-raising days and enjoyed every minute of it but now he was ready to set the seal on his success, their relationship and his own newly-found passivity by drawing the cosy cocoon of a family around himself.

Judith, apparently, had other ideas. She worked for one of Exham's biggest firms as a graphic designer and she took her job very seriously. She was in with the chance of promotion, the opportunity to take charge of her own department and she certainly didn't want to jeopardize the impending promotion by the unwelcome intrusion of a child.

She crossed to the dressing table and picked up a brush, sitting before the mirror to sweep the bristles through her hair. She glanced at Parker's reflection as she removed the knots and tangles from her hair, brushing away enthusiastically until it sprang up to its usual lustrous fullness. She dug fingers into it then crossed to the bed and slid in beside him.

"Is this bloody promotion *so* important?" Parker demanded, scarcely concealing his annoyance.

"To me it is," she told him. "I want that department."

"You could go back after you'd had the baby," he suggested.

She snorted.

"And start at the bottom again? No thanks."

She put one hand on his chest, curling the thick hair with her index finger, tracing the outline of his muscles with her long nail, allowing it to glide down towards his navel. The muscles of his stomach tightened slightly as she drew patterns across his belly, working lower until she was at the forest of his pubic hair. The head

67

of his erection nudged against the probing digit and she enveloped it with her whole hand, feeling its hardness. With her free hand, she reached up and touched his face, curious at his apparent lack of response.

"You realize the moral implications of what you intend to do?" he asked, unexpectedly.

She looked puzzled.

"You're over four months pregnant."

She released his penis immediately, rolling onto her back. Judith let out a long, angry breath then propped herself up on one elbow, glaring at him. "You never give up do you?" she said. Her voice took on a hard edge. "Just drop it, Andy. Once and for all. Drop it."

"Judith, it's a human life," he insisted.

"For God's sake, shut up about the bloody child." She sat up, looking down at him. "For the last time, I'm having the abortion. Don't start this philosophical crap about taking a human life because, apart from being about the lowest trick you've pulled so far to try and stop me, it doesn't make the slightest bit of difference to the way I feel. Nothing you can say or do will make me change my mind." Her face was flushed with anger and it was reflected in her voice. "I don't *need* this baby. I don't *want* this baby."

She suddenly sucked in a tortured breath as a violent stab of pain lanced through her.

"Oh God," she gasped and rolled onto her back again.

Parker threw back the sheets, seeing that her hands had gone to her belly, were pressing the slight distension. She winced again. It felt as if someone were jabbing her stomach wall with a red hot knife, just below the navel. She inhaled deeply and the movement brought a renewed wave of pain. As a child she had been bitten by the family cat once, and the pain which she now felt inside her abdomen reminded her of that pain.

She allowed her hands to slide away from her belly and both she and Parker watched as the flesh rose slightly, first above the navel and then to one side of it. Her stomach undulated slowly for long seconds then was still. The pain ceased as abruptly as it had come.

She lay still for what seemed like an eternity, afraid to move in case the agonizing torment returned. Her forehead was greasy with perspiration and her breath came in shallow gasps. Eventually she touched her stomach. There was no discomfort.

"What the hell happened?" Parker asked, anxiously.

Judith smiled thinly, her face pale.

"I don't know. I think it must have been a muscle spasm," she said. But, even as she spoke, she looked down at her stomach, remembering the undulations.

She turned, trembling, to face Parker, who took her in his arms.

It was a long time before either of them slept.

Ten

Randall got out of the car and walked across the pavement towards the front of the cinema. A few red letters still hung from the track which ran around its canopy, others had been displaced long ago by the wind. He looked up and read:

TH P LA E

"I can remember when the Palace used to be the best cinema in Exham," P C Higgins told him, scanning the front of the building.

"Well, it's been empty for two years," said Randall. "It's as good a place as any to hide."

"You don't really think he'd pick somewhere in the middle of town do you, guv?" asked the constable.

"I doubt it," Randall confessed, "but we'd better check it anyway." He pulled a large key from his jacket pocket, one which they'd picked up from the owner of the building earlier that morning. He owned both The Palace and The Gaumont further up the road and had asked why the police should be showing so much interest in the deserted cinema. Randall had told him there'd been a spate of arson recently and they wanted to check the building out in case the fire-raiser should strike there next. The owner had not asked any more questions.

"You stop in the car," Randall told his driver. "Just in case anything comes over on the two-way."

Higgins hesitated for a moment.

"I'll be OK," the Inspector reassured him. He waited until the constable had retreated to the car then inserted the key in one of the padlocks which hung from the four sets of double doors. The Inspector threw his weight against the doors and they swung open reluctantly. He coughed at the smell of damp and decay inside.

A door to his left led into the stalls, to his right, a staircase which would take him up to the circle. He checked the stalls, the beam of his torch scarcely able to penetrate the gloom. Dust, at least a couple of inches thick, swirled up and around him, the particles drifting lazily in the glow of the torch.

The circle was worse.

Seats had been torn up and piled at both sides of the balcony and Randall had to put a handkerchief across his face so foul was the odour of decay. He checked everywhere, including the projection box, but all he found up there were a couple of yellowed copies of *Men*

Only. He glanced through one, smiling thinly to himself then dropped it back into the dustbin. Rusted spool cans lay discarded on the stone floor.

Satisfied that the cinema was, indeed, deserted, Randall made his way back outside and across to the waiting Panda car.

"Not a bloody trace," he said, dropping the torch on the parcel shelf.

It had been the same story all day, not just in the places where Randall had searched but from the other members of the force. The Inspector had ordered hourly reports from each car but, as yet, with the time now approaching noon, no sign had been found of Harvey. There was no hint that he was anywhere near, let alone in, Exham. As Higgins moved the Panda gently out into traffic, Randall looked at the people who thronged the streets of the town. Some were shopping, some stood talking. There were children with their mothers, young-sters standing in groups smoking. The Inspector exhaled deeply wondering what any of them would think or say if they knew that there was a psychopath heading for their quiet little town. If that fact was correct of course. Randall hated trusting other people and he felt especially reluctant to trust the opinions of a prison psychiatrist and a jumped-up bastard like George Stokes.

As yet another report came in, again drawing a blank, Randall began to think that he and all of his force were on one big wild goose chase.

Paul Harvey slept until almost one o'clock in the after-noon, a fitful, dreamless sleep which he awoke from abruptly. He tasted something bitter in his mouth and he spat as he clambered to his feet. He stretched, the joints in his arms cracking loudly. He bent and picked up the sickle, gripping it tight in one huge hand. From his perch inside the barn, he could see the farmhouse.

71

His stomach rumbled noisily and he belched loudly. Perhaps there was food in the house.

Either way, he decided to find out.

Eleven

Harold Pierce worked unsupervised now and, freed from the watchful but helpful eyes of Greaves, he became more confident. Now, as he mopped the floor, he hummed a tune merrily to himself.

Harold was still humming his tuneless ditty when the lift nearby opened and Brian Cayton stepped out. He too was dressed in a porter's overall, a small blue name badge attached to his lapel. Cayton was a young man, yet to reach his thirties, with a shock of red hair and a smattering of freckles, Harold had seen him about the hospital many times.

"Harold, do me a favour will you?" he said.

Harold put down his mop.

"What is it?" he asked, smiling, noticing that Cayton made a point of not looking at him. He was one of the few members of staff who had not yet become accustomed to the sight of the vile scar.

"There's some work to be done down in bloody pathology," said Cayton. "I would help you only there's an emergency op. about to go ahead on nine and I'm supposed to be there. So, if you wouldn't mind helping them out down in pathology."

Harold's smile faded quickly and he swallowed hard.

"What do they want?" he asked, warily.

"I'm not sure," said Cayton, stepping back into the lift and punching the button marked nine.

The doors slid shut and there was a loud burring as the lift rose.

Harold stood still for long moments, gazing at the floor, staring at his own distorted image on the wet surface. Then, leaving the mop and bucket in the middle of the floor, he headed for the steps which would take him down to the basement.

Harold found that, by the time he reached the door of Pathology One, his body was sheathed in a fine film of perspiration. He knocked tentatively and stood waiting, listening to the sound of footsteps approaching from inside. The door opened and a middle-aged man in a white plastic apron peered out. He looked at Harold over the rims of his thick spectacles, brushing a loose strand of hair from his forehead. He glanced briefly at the scar then ran an appraising eye over the nervous porter.

"Wait there," said the man, attempting a smile but not quite managing it.

Harold peered through the half-open door, at the stainless steel slab nearest the door which, he noted, bore an occupant. The other men in white overalls were poring over it. There was a type of scale suspended over the slab and, as Harold watched, one of the men lifted a crimson lump from the slab and laid it in the bowl which registered a weight on the metric scale it bore. The man ran a blood-soaked finger along the scale, recording the weight to the last gramme. He then said something about the liver and Harold saw his companion jot the weight down on a clipboard which he held. The crimson lump was removed and placed on a trolley nearby, some congealed blood spilling in blackened gouts from the organ. Harold blenched and turned away, his stomach somersaulting.

"Here you are."

The voice startled him and he turned to see the

73

bespectacled man standing in the doorway, leaning on a trolley covered with a white sheet.

"Just some specimens to dispose of," he said and pushed the trolley out.

Harold took a firm grip on the gurney and began to push it in the direction of the furnace room, hearing the door close behind him as the pathologist retreated back inside the lab. One of the wheels squeaked and it offered a discordant accompaniment to the rhythmic tattoo beaten out by Harold's shoes which echoed through the chill, silent corridor. He looked down at the trolley as he walked, running a suspicious eye over the sheeted exhibits hidden from view. He could detect that familiar smell, the cloying, pungent odour of chemicals which made his eyes water. Harold tried to swallow but found that his throat was parchment dry, his tongue felt like a piece of sun-baked meat. He paused at the door of the furnace room and opened it, feeling the familiar blast of warm air as it greeted him. The generator hummed unceasingly as he dragged the gurney in beside him and closed the door. Unable to contain his curiosity any longer he pulled back the sheet, uncovering the objects which lay on the trolley.

He moaned as if in pain. His one good eye riveted to the foetus which lay in the tray. For long seconds, Harold stared at it, tears brimming in his eye. He didn't know at what stage the thing had been aborted but it was slightly larger than the one he'd seen Greaves incinerate on the first day. Its eyes were sealed shut by membranous skin. The head once more looked swollen and liquescent but this time it had a thin, almost invisible covering of fine hair. The whole body was covered by the langou and Harold reached out a shaking hand to touch the silken fibres. But the body was cold and dripping with chemicals and it felt so obscenely soft that he hastily withdrew his hand. The forceps lay beside the

74

receiver and they glinted in the cold white light cast by the overhead banks of fluorescents.

Harold pushed the trolley closer to the furnace, using the wrench and gloves to open it as he had seen Greaves do. The door swung open and a blistering wave of heat gushed forth, sweeping over Harold like a burning tide. He took a step back, recoiling from the sudden intense temperature. He pulled on a pair of thin rubber gloves and looked down at the foetus, then at the forceps. The furnace yawned invitingly. Harold picked up the metallic clamp and prepared to pick up the tiny body. His breath was coming in gasps, a single tear now rolling down his unscarred cheek.

He reached for the foetus.

"No."

He threw the forceps down and gripped the side of the trolley to steady himself.

"No," he said again, his voice cracking. "No."

He looked at the body, lying in its pool of rancid fluid, the arms and legs drawn up stiffly in a pose which reminded him of some kind of vile, hairless cat waiting to have its belly stroked. He sucked in huge lungfuls of stagnant air, his head bowed. When he finally managed to straighten up he looked into the furnace until the roaring flames burned yellow and white patterns on his retina. He could not, *would* not, put the foetus into that hungry mouth. His anxious gaze strayed back to the liquid-covered body and he shook convulsively.

"Gordon," he whispered, softly.

His head was beginning to throb, his nostrils and eye stinging from the odorous substances which lay in the tray with the abortion. He looked around him, at the generator, at the filthy trolleys which stood in one corner of the room, at the piles of fouled linen. There was something else too, something which he hadn't noticed the first time. It was like a large plastic dustbin

75

standing near to the piles of filthy laundry. Harold crossed hastily to it and lifted the lid, immediately gagging at the disgusting stench which rose from it. He looked down and saw that it was full of old dressings. Some were stiff with dried blood, others still crimson and fresh. There were gauze pads soaked with yellowish fluid, bandages that had pieces of skin sticking to them. Harold backed away, his mind churning with ideas. He crossed to the gurney and, with infinite care, as if he were lifting a sleeping child, picked up the foetus with both gloved hands. A drop of fluid burst from the umbilicus and splashed Harold's overall but he ignored it, carrying the tiny creature towards the bandage filled dustbin. There, he gently layed it on the ground and dug deep into the mass of bloodied dressings, making room at the bottom. This done, he once more lifted the foetus and placed it in the dustbin, covering it with the used bandages and pads, hiding it from view. He wiped some pus from his glove and then hastily put back the lid of the dustbin.

The furnace room door opened and Winston Greaves walked in.

Harold spun round, heart hammering against his ribs. Greaves looked at him for a moment, at the dustbin, at Harold's bloodstained hands. Then he smiled thinly.

"I thought I'd see how you were getting on," said the senior porter.

Harold walked back to the furnace, satisfied that Greaves suspected nothing. After all, he reasoned, what *could* he suspect? Together they disposed of the remaining things on the gurney, consigning them to the blazing fire then returning the trolley to pathology.

As they left the furnace room, Greaves leading the way, Harold took one last look across at the dustbin. The foetus would remain hidden in there, free from prying eyes. As far as anyone else was concerned, it

76

had been incinerated along with everything else. He had told Greaves that he'd burned the contents of the dustbin along with the pathology specimens and the coloured porter nodded his approval. Harold smiled to himself and pulled the furnace room door closed.

The foetus would be safe in its hiding place until he could return.

Night came without bringing the rain which had threatened earlier. Instead, the air was filled with a numbing frost which glittered on the grass and trees, reflecting the light from the hospital like millions of tiny diamonds. Harold stood at his window, watching as more and more lights were extinguished in the huge building as the hour grew late. He watched with almost inhuman patience, his mind a blank; the only thing scratching the surface of his consciousness being the persistent ticking of his alarm clock. He stood in the hut in darkness, not having bothered to turn on the light and, when he glanced behind him, the phosphorescent arms of the clock radiated their greenish glow revealing that it was almost 12.36 a.m.

Harold didn't feel tired, despite the fact that he'd been up since six that morning. His mind was too full of ideas for him to notice any fatigue. In another twenty-five minutes or so he would slip out of the hut, cross the few hundred yards of open ground which separated his own dwelling from the main building and go through the entrance which faced him.

It led past the mortuary to a flight of steps and a lift which would take him down to the basement and, eventually, to the furnace room.

The hands of the clock crawled slowly to one o'clock and Harold decided that it was time to leave. He slipped silently out of the door and locked it behind him, hurriedly making his way across the large expanse of grass between his hut and the nearest entrance. The frost crunched beneath his feet but, despite its severity, it had done little to harden up the ground and Harold twice nearly slipped in the mud. His breath came in short gasps, each of which was signalled by a small cloud of misty condensation. As he drew closer he realized just how dark the hospital was. There seemed to be only a couple of lights burning on each floor and that was not enough to illuminate his dark shape in the blackness.

He paused, ducking behind a nearby bush when he heard a clicking sound. Looking up he saw that it was two of the nurses returning to their quarters. They were laughing happily, the sounds of merriment drifting through the chill, silent night. Harold watched them until they disappeared out of sight then he continued forward, almost running the last few yards to the entrance.

A blue sign to his right proclaimed:

MORTUARY

He pushed open one of the swing doors and moved as quietly as he could into a short corridor which led to a staircase. He blinked hard in the darkness, for no light had been left on. Indeed, as he reached the top of the stairs, he grabbed the handrail to guide himself, so impenetrable was the darkness.

It seemed even colder inside the building than out and Harold shuddered as he made his way tentatively down the stairs. How he wished he had a torch. He was completely and utterly blind, unable to see a hand in front of him and this sensation made him feel all the more uneasy. He could feel his body trembling and, as he put his foot down to find the next step, he stumbled. Harold gasped in shocked surprise and fell hard on the base of his spine. The impact sent a pain right through his body and, for long seconds, he sat where he was, moaning softly, one hand still gripping the handrail, the other massaging his back. He slowed his breathing, afraid that someone might hear him, worried that his little venture would be halted because some conscientious pathology assistant had decided to stay late and finish some work in the labs. His trepidation grew stronger when he noticed that there was a light burning at the bottom of the staircase. He had to round a corner to reach the base and that was still a dozen or more steps down. As yet the light was indistinct but, hauling himself up, Harold moved on, drawn towards the light like a moth to a flame.

He reached the bottom of the stairs, emerging in the area before the lift. The doors to all the labs were closed. Perhaps, he reasoned, someone had left and forgotten to turn out the light. But another part of his mind told him that the men who worked down here were too thorough to let such a minor thing as a light escape their notice. Heart pounding against his ribs, he walked to the door of the first lab and pressed his ear to it.

There was no sound coming from inside.

He twisted the handle and found that the door was locked. The same procedure was repeated with the other three labs and Harold was finally satisfied that the light had simply been overlooked. For that, to some degree, he was grateful. Although it lit only the area near the lift, it did provide at least some light for him as he made his way up the corridor.

In the furnace room the heat was as powerful as ever, but this time he welcomed it for it drove some of the chill from his bones. The generator kept up its ceaseless humming. Harold crossed quickly to the plastic dustbin and lifted the lid, pulling the used dressings aside, ignoring the blood and other discharge which sometimes stuck to his flesh. He finally felt something soft and jellied beneath his hands.

Very carefully, he lifted the foetus out, holding the tiny body before him for long seconds. Even in the half-light, he could see that the skin was already turning blue. He turned and laid it on one of the soiled sheets which were stacked on the gurneys behind him, then, as if he were wrapping a fragile Christmas present, he carefully pulled the dirty linen around the foetus. A rank odour filled his nostrils but he tried to ignore it and, with his "prize" secured, he made his way back towards the door, holding the small thing as a mother would hold her baby.

Harold ran across the open ground towards his hut finally slowing down when he reached the flimsy dwelling. He leant against the wall, trying to catch his breath, his one good eye squinting through the gloom to the doors he'd come through. No one had heard or seen him. There was no one following. Harold smiled thinly and closed his eyes. He took great gulps of cold air, trying to ignore the rancid stench which rose from the sheet and its dead occupant but that didn't seem to matter any longer. He had completed the first and most hazardous part of his venture, the second step was merely a formality.

The hut in which Harold lived stood about ten yards from a low barbed wire fence which marked the perimeter of the hospital beyond it lay large expanses of open fields, some of the ground was owned by the hospital but it was fenced off nevertheless. In the far distance, Harold could see the lights of Exham and, occasionally, the headlamps of a vehicle travelling along the dual-carriageway which led into the town. He headed towards the fence and cautiously stepped over it, catching his trousers on one of the vicious barbs. The material ripped slightly and Harold pulled himself free.

The ground sloped away before him slightly, leading down towards a deep cleft in the field which looked like an open black mouth in the darkness of the night. Harold steadied himself and made his way towards the depression. Above him tall electricity pylons rose high into the sky, their metal legs straddling the field, the high voltage cables they carried invisible in the gloom. There was a smell of ozone in the air, rather like the aftermath of a thunderstorm and Harold could hear a distant crackling sound from overhead.

He reached the foot of the small hill and stood close by the foot of a pylon. He was exhausted, both mentally and physically drained. His eye felt gritty and his throat was dry but he walked on, finally finding what he thought looked like a suitable spot. There was enough natural light for him to see what he was doing. He paused and laid the bundle of dirty sheet on the frosty grass, then he knelt and began scraping at the earth with his bare hands. He found that it was soft enough for him to achieve the necessary depth. Like a dog who's found a good spot to hide a bone, Harold pawed the earth away until it began to form a sizeable mound behind him. By the time he'd finished he estimated that the hole must be about two feet deep and twice that in length. He was panting loudly, his hands caked in mud, his clothes already reeking from the foul smell of the soiled linen. With the hole prepared, he unrolled the sheet, exposing the foetus inside. He lifted it gently from the cover and laid it in the hole.

For long seconds he stared down at it, tears brimming in his eye. He lowered his head, his body shaking.

"Gordon," he whispered. "Forgive me."

He felt a strange contradiction inside himself, a great sadness but also something akin to relief. Had he at last found a means of atonement? He began pushing the wet earth back into place, covering the tiny body.

"Mother," he said, as he continued to pile earth back into the grave. "It's different this time. This time I won't let it happen again. There'll be no more burnings."

He looked up, as if expecting to see someone standing

81

over him. Expecting to hear voices. There was only the far-off whistle of the wind in the pylons.

Harold finished piling in the earth and stood up, flattening it down with his shoe. He wiped his hands on the piece of soiled sheet then balled it up and hid it beneath a nearby bush. That done, he returned to the small grave. At first, when he tried to speak, no sound would come and his lips fluttered noiselessly but he swallowed hard and clasped his dirty hands before him.

He didn't know anything religious. No prayers. No hymns. He lowered his head, his eyes closed.

"Now I lay me down to sleep," he began, falteringly. "I pray the Lord. . ." He struggled to remember. "I pray the Lord my soul to keep." A long silence. "If . . . If I would . . . should," he corrected himself. "If I should die before I wake. I pray the Lord my soul to take." Tears were coursing freely down his cheek by now.

"Amen."

He turned and headed back to his hut.

It was not to be the last time he performed the cathartic ritual.

Twelve

Lynn Tyler prodded the bacon with a fork, turning it over in the hot fat. She hated fried food and the small kitchen already smelt strongly of it, the odour making her feel queasy. How the hell anyone could ever eat a cooked breakfast she didn't know but, in about five minutes, Chris would come downstairs and devour his usual four rashes of bacon, two eggs and a couple of slices of fried bread. He was sleeping upstairs at the moment, undisturbed by the sounds coming from the room below him. The radio competed with the frying bacon for supremacy in the cramped area.

Lynn jumped back as the fat spat at her, some of it catching the arm of the sweatshirt which she wore. At least three sizes too big for her and with "Judas Priest" printed across it, the garment came to just below her bottom. She wore nothing else and the lino in the kitchen felt cold beneath her bare feet. She ran a hand through her uncombed black hair and exhaled deeply, looking down at the pan but also at herself. She was almost shapeless beneath the thick folds of the sweatshirt but even that wasn't enough to disguise some painfully obvious facts about her body. Her breasts, for so long unfettered by a bra, were beginning to droop – legacy of all those years she had spent enticing men. Ever since she'd reached her fourteenth birthday, just over five years ago, she had flaunted herself in every flimsy blouse and T-shirt she could find. There had been dozens of men in the intervening years, too many for her to count, attracted not just by her sizeable bust but by her easy manner – and easy was the operative word. She knew that some called her a tart, a slag, someone had even called her a whore once, but to Lynn Tyler the moral double-standard which governed the sex lives of men and women was ludicrous. And unfair. If a man slept around he was patted on the back and admired, earning the name of stud with each new conquest. If a woman chose to take different men to bed for her own private pleasure, she was sneered at, insulted and, in Lynn's case, thrown out of the house. Her parents had kicked her out when she was seventeen after coming home to find her locked in a torrid embrace on the floor of their sitting room with her boyfriend of the time. Since then she had shared a three-bedroomed house near the centre of Exham with her best friend, Jill Wallace. Jill worked in nearby Camford and her job often took her away from the house for days at a time. It was during these respites that Lynn invited Chris to stay. She herself was unemployed and had been for over a year. Chris worked in Exham's largest engineering firm. They had been together for over nine months. It was something of a record for Lynn and, during that span of time, something had happened to her which she had always consciously avoided before. She had fallen in love. All the countless other men, they had been for *her* private gratification although more often than not it had not turned out that way. But it was different with Chris. She had never had any intention of falling in love, in fact the emotion had proved so alien to her that at first she hadn't been sure what she was feeling, but she knew it was ten times stronger than anything she'd felt in her life before. And she knew she wanted Chris on a more permanent basis than meetings three times a week and the odd weekend together. She wanted to marry him.

That was why she had stopped taking her pill. For the last three months she had left it untouched in its green packet. And, finally, she was sure. She was pregnant. She'd missed two periods, and a trip to the doctor last week had confirmed her suspicions. Surely with a baby on the way Chris would marry her? But she had yet to tell him her news.

She finished cooking his breakfast and while the kettle boiled for coffee she lit a cigarette, went to the bottom of the stairs and called him. She waited until she heard the creak of the bedsprings, signalling that he was up then she padded back into the kitchen and sat down to her own breakfast – a cup of Nescafé and a Marlboro.

He was down in a matter of moments, chest bare to expose his hard lean body with its tangled growth of light hair on the chest and stomach. He wore a faded pair of jeans, held up by a studded leather belt. Around one wrist was a leather band, similarly dotted with studs. He rubbed his stomach and sat down in front of the plateful of food.

"Don't you ever wash in the mornings?" she asked him, smiling. She watched as he started hacking away at the bacon.

"Well, I didn't have time this morning," he told her, chewing furiously. "I felt hungry."

She shuddered.

"I don't know how the hell you can eat *that* first thing in the morning." She took a drag on her cigarette, blowing out a long stream of smoke. She crossed her legs beneath the table, tapping her feet together agitatedly. Should she tell him now? Excuse me Chris but you're going to be a father? She took a sip of her coffee instead.

The DJ on the radio was babbling some hip bullshit which neither of them seemed to hear. Chris because he was too engrossed in his breakfast and Lynn because she was too wrapped up in her own thoughts. She watched him as he set about the first egg, slicing it in two, dipping his fried bread in the runny yolk. He looked up at her and smiled that warm, welcoming smile she had come to know so well these past nine months. She wondered if there was room for love in that smile.

"What's on your mind?" he said.

She looked surprised.

"Not a lot," she lied. "Why do you ask?"

"You're not usually this quiet," he told her.

Lynn smiled weakly, taking mock offence.

"Thanks a lot."

He smiled again, pushing half the egg into his mouth. She sucked hard on her cigarette, held the smoke in her mouth for long seconds then blew it out in a long blue stream.

"Chris, I'm pregnant."

The words came out as easily as that but, once she'd said them, it felt as if a hole had opened up inside her. Well, there it was. She'd told him, flat out. She sipped at her coffee and eyed him warily over the rim of the mug.

He slowed the pace of his chewing, looking down at his plate, not, as she'd expected, at her. He didn't speak.

"I said. . ."

He cut her short.

"Yeah, I heard you." There was an edge to his voice, almost imperceptible but nevertheless present. Like a knife blade in the darkness, invisible but razor sharp.

She ground out the fag in a nearby saucer, the plume of smoke rising mournfully, disappearing above her like a forgotten dream.

"Haven't you got anything to say?" she wanted to know.

"Are you sure?" he asked, still looking at his plate.

She told him about the visit to the doctors, the missed periods. He nodded.

They sat in silence for an eternity then he dropped his knife and fork onto the plate where they clattered noisily. Finally, he looked her in the eye.

"I thought you were on the bloody pill," he said, exasperatedly.

"I was," she told him. "I just didn't take it for a few weeks."

With the deception now revealed, it was she who dropped her gaze, unable to meet the unrelenting stare from his green eyes.

"Jesus Christ," he murmured, then his voice gradually grew in volume. "You bloody tricked me didn't you?"

86

"I didn't," she countered although the accusation bore weight and she was crumbling beneath that weight.

"You had me thinking it was safe and all the time you weren't taking your pill. You made a fucking mug out of me for all that time?" He was struggling to keep his anger in check and he wasn't making much of a job of it.

"It was just two months, Chris," she said.

"Two months. Two *years*. What's the difference? It's still me who ends up looking the twat, isn't it?"

She could feel the tears building but she fought them back, angry with herself now. They sat in silence for a long time. A silence finally broken by Chris.

"So what are you going to do?" he demanded.

"What do you mean?"

"About the kid."

"I'm going to have it."

He shook his head.

"Well, it's your business I suppose but I think you're stupid," he told her.

Her brow furrowed.

"It's not just *my* business," she said, defiantly. "It's yours too. You are the father after all."

"Are you sure?"

The remark was barbed and it cut deeply.

"You bastard," she growled. "Yes, I'm sure it's yours. If anyone else had been fucking me in the last nine months I think you might have found out about it."

"So, what are you going to do about it?" he asked again.

"I've told you once. I'm going to have it. I wanted the child. It's *our* child."

The realization gradually swept over him and a bitter smile creased his face.

"You know, Lynn, you've got more brains than I gave you credit for," he said.

"What's that supposed to mean?" she said.

"The baby. Not taking the pill. You planned it all didn't you?"

She reached for his hand, almost surprised when he didn't pull away. When she spoke again her tone was low, almost pleading.

"Chris, it was the only way I knew of keeping you," she said. "I love you. I've never loved anyone else in my life before. I didn't want to lose you."

"So you thought you'd trick me into becoming a daddy?" His voice was heavy with sarcasm.

She pulled her hand away.

"I hoped you'd marry me when you heard about the kid," she confessed. "You are its father after all."

"Only because you didn't take your fucking pill," he rasped. She watched as he got to his feet. "I'm sorry, Lynn but I'm not ready for this." He swallowed hard, not sure whether to pity her or punch her in the teeth. She too got to her feet.

"I love you, I want your baby. I want *you*," she said, the first salty tear sliding down her cheek.

"I'm sorry," he said. "Look, I think a lot of you, you're a good kid, fun to be with. . ."

She cut him short, her own anger now overriding his.

"And an easy fuck," she growled.

"I just don't love you," he told her, almost reluctantly.

She stood quivering for a moment, trying to hold back the flood of tears which she knew would come any minute. Her voice was cracking.

"So what's *your* answer then?" she demanded.

He stepped away from the table.

"I think it'd be simpler if we just didn't see each other again," he said.

"As easy as that? Forget the relationship. Nine months down the drain. Is that all it meant to you? Is it?" She was shouting now, the tears flooding down her cheeks. "A good screw when you wanted it? What was I, just a convenient piece of equipment when you got fed up with wanking?"

"I think I'd better go," he said, quietly.

"Yes, go on. Go. Fuck off." She started to tug the sweatshirt off, despite his pleas for her to stop. Eventually she pulled it free and threw it at him, standing there naked in that smoke filled kitchen, the odour of fried food heavy in the air.

"I'm sorry, Lynn," he said.

"Get out," she screamed at him, hurling the sauce bottle in his direction. It hit the wall close by him and exploded, splattering the sticky red liquid all over the place. Lumps of glass skittered across the lino.

She sat down at the table, sobbing, her head resting on her arms and she heard the front door close behind him as he left.

Naked, she sat alone in the kitchen her tears falling onto the paper table cloth and spreading out like transparent ink on blotting paper.

She remained like that for at least thirty minutes before wiping her face and shuffling upstairs to dress. She pulled on a pair of drain-pipe jeans and hauled a khaki coloured T-shirt over her head. She went back downstairs and cleaned up the mess in the kitchen.

At 10.03 a.m. she phoned her doctor and made an appointment to see about getting an abortion.

Thirteen

"Well, this is better than standing under a fucking tree isn't it?" said Keith Todd, adjusting the volume control on the Dolomite's cassette.

Penny Walsh giggled and moved closer to him, gazing out through the windscreen at the rain clouds which were gathering ominously. It was already dark but the impending storm seemed to bring a heaviness to the air, gripping the small car in a black velvet fist. The headlamps were off and the only light came from the sodium lamp about ten yards behind then down the lane. Flanked on both sides by trees and high bushes, it had wide grass verges on either side and it was on one of these that Keith had parked the car.

"And you're really going to buy this off your dad?" Penny said, patting the passenger seat.

"Once I get a job, yeah," Keith reassured her. "He doesn't mind me borrowing it until then."

Neither of them had jobs, both Keith and Penny had left school at sixteen, just two years earlier. The ritual of signing on had become, as it had to hundreds of thousands more of their generation, a way of life. But Keith was an eternal optimist and, tonight, in particular, he felt lucky. That feeling proved to have foundation as he felt Penny slide one hand onto his thigh. He responded by pulling her towards him, their mouths locking, tongues darting feverishly back and forth, each anxious to taste the other.

Keith felt her hand clawing its way up to the growing bulge in his jeans. He responded by squeezing her left breast feeling the nipple stiffen through the thin material of her blouse.

She turned in her seat, one leg now drawn up beneath her. His rough hand found the buttons on her blouse and undid them, moving more urgently now as

90

he massaged her plump breasts. For her own part she managed to undo the zip of his jeans, coaxing his stiffness free, running one finger along the shaft from tip to base before enveloping it with her warm hand.

Keith grunted and reached beneath her short skirt. As her hand began to move rhythmically up and down, he felt her part her legs slightly and his probing digits pulled the slinky material of her panties aside in an effort to reach the moist warmth beyond. He slid two fingers into her eager cleft and she stiffened in response.

Paul Harvey was less than ten yards from the car.

He crouched in the bushes, the sickle held firmly in his hand, watching the young couple inside the vehicle, his expression a mixture of disgust and bewilderment. The first spots of rain began to fall but Harvey ignored them, his attention riveted to the car. The windows were steaming up and it was becoming difficult to see inside from his present vantage point. The two young-sters inside were merely indistinct blurs before him. He gripped the sickle tighter.

During his own teenage years he had never known the pleasure of a companion, male or female. He had tried to make friends, when his father had allowed it but Harvey's self-consciousness and naivety had let him down until at last, he resigned himself to being a loner. Not that the people of Exham did anything to help him overcome those shortcomings. Fate, and the towns-people, seemed to be conspiring against him, trying to ensure that he would never know what it was like to be a part of society. And, in truth, perhaps Harvey didn't want to be a part of it.

He moved slowly towards the car.

Penny bent her head and closed her mouth over the bulging purple head of Keith's penis, flicking some drops of clear liquid from its tip. He gasped as he felt her warm tongue curling around his erection, the sensations which he felt becoming stronger by the second. He, himself, continued to move his fingers within her, using his thumb to tease the hardened bud of her clitoris. Keith allowed his head to loll back onto the head-rest, closing his eyes as he felt her pushing more urgently against his hand. He could hear her rasping breath, feel its hotness on his slippery shaft.

There was a thunderous roar as the first rumble of thunder broke like a wave on a rock and the sound make Keith open his eyes.

He almost screamed.

Glaring in at him through the side window, his face distorted by the swiftly flowing rain, was Harvey.

Keith, pulling Penny upright, withdrew his fingers and reached frantically for the ignition key. The girl sat back, dazed and confused.

"Keith, what. . ."

The engine roared into life and the young lad looked once more out of the side window.

The face had gone. Of Harvey there was no sign.

Keith slumped back, shaking uncontrollably and, high above them, a powerful fork of lightning tore open the clouds.

Fourteen

The eighth foetus had been buried, its tiny body now lying beneath the slippery mud with the others. Harold dried his hair with a towel and checked on the milk bubbling in the pan on the hot-plate.

Eight of them in that shallow grave. He yawned and glanced across at the alarm clock. It was 1.45 a.m. It hadn't taken him so long to bury the last one. The constant rain had transformed the earth into a quagmire. Indeed, it had been raining for the past two days on and off and that, at least, made his task easier. The clods came away easily.

He lifted the saucepan just in time to prevent it boiling over, poured the milk into a mug and tossed the pan into the sink.

Outside, there was a particularly loud growl of thunder which seemed to roll across the land like an unfurling blanket. The little hut shook and Harold stood still for a moment, wondering if the entire flimsy structure was going to collapse around his head. The rumbling died away to be replaced by a whiplash crack of lightning which seared across the bloated, mottled sky and, for brief seconds, left a brilliant white afterburn on Harold's retina as he watched it. Mesmerized by the sight of nature's fury at its most potent, he crossed to the tiny window and stood looking out as the storm gathered for its furious onslaught on Exham and the countryside round about. Black cloud, buffeted by the wind, came rolling in to empty its load while lightning split the heavens with blazing white forks of pure energy. The thunder grew to a crescendo, like a thousand cannons being fired at once. The little hut shook once more as the storm intensified. Harold watched in awe, recoiling every now and then from the particularly violent flashes of lightning or the seemingly endless volleys of thunder. And, through it all, came the persistent pounding of the rain as it hammered against buildings and turned the ground into sticky slime. On the tarmac around the hospital entrance, the water puddled in pools ankle deep, each droplet exploding on the black, saturated surface. Even inside the hut, Harold could detect the strong smell of ozone as the sky was torn open by the powerful fingers of light which rent the thick black clouds like hands through wet tissue paper. Thunder roared menacingly and, in one or two places in the hospital, windows rattled in their frames. For those patients still awake, the world outside became a blur as they squinted through the rain-drenched windows. There was no steady trickle of tear-like droplets this time but a massive deluge which seemed to strike the windows and cascade down in one liquid flow, as if there were many men standing out there throwing buckets of the stuff at the panes. The few lights that burned outside were diffused into mere blurs through the rain-battered windows.

Harold sipped at his milk and watched the celestial fireworks, drawing back slightly as each blinding burst of forked or sheet lightning exploded across the sky, to be followed by a deafening blast of thunder. It sounded like some gigantic animal roaring in pain, the lowing of a massive steer lashed by a whip of ferociously undiluted force.

In the field behind Harold's hut, the pylons swayed ominously in the high wind, their normally stable structures looking suddenly vulnerable. They crackled loudly and the thick power lines hummed as they were rocked back and forth by the onslaught. The metal groaned as it was bent and blasted by the wind and, beneath one of the pylons, less than fifty feet from its base, the shallow grave which Harold had dug was saturated to the extent that some of the top soil began to wash away.

There was a crack of lightning which screamed across the black heavens for a full five seconds, a blast of energy so powerful that for long moments even the thunder seemed to cease. The crackling fork hit the pylon nearest to the hospital fence, striking it at the very point where the huge power lines were attached. There was a blinding flash of blue and white sparks and an angry sputtering as the thick cable, twice as thick as a man's torso was wrenched free of its housing by the fury of the impact. Then, it simply fell to earth, the other end of it still attached to the preceding pylon. But the severed end twisted and writhed on the wet earth like some kind of gigantic snake, showering the sodden mud with sparks and pumping hundreds of thousands of volts into the sticky ooze. The pylon itself shook violently as the cable twisted at its base, contorting madly like an eel on a hot skillet as it poured its immense reservoir of energy into the earth. The grass nearby was immediately blackened by the furious discharge, the mud even bubbling in places as the endless supply of electricity continued to gush into the ground. The cable twisted and whiplashed for what seemed like an eternity as it unleashed its pent-up power in a display which even overshadowed the mighty forks of lightning still flashing across the sky. The power line poured seemingly endless stores of crackling volts into the wet earth which, itself, acted as a conductor, further aiding the explosive exhibition.

Fifteen

The picture on the TV broke up into a maze of static and Judith Myers looked up as she heard Andy Parker curse.

"I knew we should have got a different set," he grunted, thumping the TV with the flat of his hand.

"It's the storm," said Judith, gazing out of the bedroom window at the forks of lightning that rattled across the sky. She lowered her book and ran an appraising eye over Parker who stood naked before the television as if daring it to start playing up again. The picture gradually gained clarity and he nodded appreciatively, but still waited defiantly. Judith giggled.

"What's so funny?" he asked, without turning to look at her.

"You," she said. "Get back into bed or at least draw the curtains. Someone will be calling the police. They'll lock you up for indecent exposure." She chuckled again. Parker remained where he was.

Slowly, almost reluctantly, she slid the sheets down a little way to uncover her stomach, stroking a hand over its firm flatness. Gone was the bulge she had hated so much. The abortion had been successful and she had been out of Fairvale for more than a week now and had even been into work for a couple of hours.

A particularly thunderous crack of lightning tore across the sky as the storm reached ever greater heights and Judith winced as she felt sudden, unexpected pain just below her navel. She pressed the area gingerly, as Parker shouted and cursed at the TV which was again hissing at the onslaught of so much static in the air.

Judith sucked in a painful breath, eyes fixed on her abdomen. The flesh seemed to stretch across her pelvic bone, becoming shiny, then, as she watched, a single drop of blood welled inside her navel. It spread outwards until it overflowed and trickled down her side like a solitary crimson tear.

"Oh my God," she gasped, her eyes bulging.

"What's wrong?" asked Parker, still more concerned with the recalcitrant TV. He had his back to Judith.

She opened her mouth to speak but no words would come. The single drop of blood dripped onto the sheet beside her, blossoming on the material. The pain below her navel grew stronger and it felt as if someone had punched her. The flesh suddenly contracted then rose an inch or two, rising and falling almost rhythmically.

96

She threw back the covers and finally, Parker *did* turn round.

He saw the blood, saw the skin on Judith's abdomen stretching and contracting, saw her naked body trembling.

She tensed for immeasurable seconds, her entire body stiff then, with a gasp, she crumpled. He dashed for the phone but she stopped him.

"Judith, for Christ's sake. . ." he said, fear in his voice.

"The pain's stopped," she told him, her voice quivering.

She reached for a tissue and wiped away the blood from her belly. "I'm all right."

He slammed the receiver down.

"All right," he shouted. "It's that fucking abortion. I told you not to have it. I'm getting a doctor, now." He reached for the receiver once more and dialled.

She pressed her abdomen once more but there was no pain. Parker was speaking to someone now, telling them that it was urgent but his words didn't seem to register with her. The blood in her navel had congealed into a sticky red syrup which she wiped away. Parker slammed the phone down and told her that the doctor was on his way.

Outside, another shaft of lightning ripped across the sky, followed a second later by a clap of thunder which threatened to bring the house down around their heads.

They both sat in stunned silence, waiting.

Sixteen

Even in the deep gloom inside the hut, Harold could make out his mother's features. Her skin was peeling away, mottled green in places where it had turned gangrenous. Her hair hung in loose, flame-seared strands, blackened wisps against the pale pink of her scalp. When she opened her mouth no sound came forth, just a swollen blackened tongue which dripped dark fluid over her scorched lips. She moved towards him, her own putrefying odour almost palpable, wrapping itself around his throat like obscene tentacles.

As her stench filled his nostrils, Harold screamed and screamed. . .

He awoke beating at his pillow, the covers thrown off. His body was soaked in sweat and his throat felt raw from screaming. Gradually he realized that it had been yet another dream.

Someone was pounding on the door of his hut.

Harold uttered a small moan of fear then, as he saw the murky daylight flooding through the window, he found the courage to get to his feet. He padded across to the door.

"Who is it?" he called.

"Harold are you all right?" the voice from the other side asked and, after a moment or two, he recognised it. Harold unlocked the door and pulled it open to find Winston Greaves standing there. The senior porter was spattered with rain which was still falling from the banks of grey cloud overhead. He looked Harold up and down, noticing how pale the unscarred side of his face looked. There were deep pits beneath both his eyes and his hair was plastered to his head with sweat.

"Are you OK?" asked Greaves, stepping inside.

Harold nodded.

"Do you know what the time is?" Greaves asked him.

He shook his head, sitting down on the edge of the bed.

"It's after nine o'clock," the coloured porter told him. "You should have been on duty over an hour ago. I thought you were ill or something."

"I'm sorry," said Harold, apologetically. "I didn't sleep very well last night." He got to his feet. "If you give me a minute, I'll get ready."

"If you don't feel well, I can get one of the doctors to come over and have a look at you. You. . ."

Harold cut him short.

"No. I'll be all right. I'm just tired," he explained.

Greaves nodded and sat down on one of the rickety old wooden chairs while Harold padded into the small room which housed the chemical toilet. He emerged a moment later and, after splashing his face with water from the cold tap in the kitchen, he began dressing. The muddy clothes which he'd worn the previous night to bury the foetus were pushed out of sight beneath the bed. Finally, he pulled on his overall and together he and Greaves began the walk across the open ground towards the main building. Harold looked up at the sky which still promised rain but now was falling in small droplets, quite different from the downpour of the previous night.

"I hear there was a blackout last night," said Greaves.

Harold nodded.

"It's the worst storm I can remember," Greaves confessed. "Still, the electricity company should have everything fixed by this afternoon. I heard that one of the cables was brought down." He stopped and looked behind him towards the field where the damaged pylon was. "They're trying to fix it up now."

Harold spun round and his eye bulged. There were indeed men moving about in the field near to the pylon, some climbing on it, others using ladders to reach inac-

99

cessible areas. There was even a small crane crawling through the mud.

"Oh my God," he murmured, softly.

The men were all around the pylon. They were working in *that* field.

Near to the grave.

Harold swallowed hard. If they should find it. . .

Greaves walked on but Harold remained where he was, his gaze fixed worriedly on the men in dark blue overalls who swarmed over the pylon in their efforts to repair it. He saw the crane, the large white and blue van parked nearby and he began to tremble. They would find it. They must do. But, it was at least fifty yards from the base of the pylon he told himself. It should be relatively safe. His ready-made assurances did not have the desired effect and he wondered if the rain might have washed the shallow covering of soil right off exposing the bodies beneath. He hurried on to join Greaves, his mind in a turmoil.

He spent most of the day thinking about the men in that field, expecting at any time one of them to walk into the hospital and tell of the grave that they'd discovered. Then his secret would be there for all to see. His crime would be exposed. For that was what they would call it. A crime. Not understanding, they would punish him, they would not want to listen to his reasons. They would not be able to comprehend the thought behind his actions.

Every chance he got, he stole a look at them, to see how far their work was progressing. To see if they had stumbled on the grave. He could eat no lunch, so knotted with fear was his stomach. He spent his entire break standing in the rain outside watching the blue-clad men repairing the damage to the pylon.

When, at three fifteen that afternoon, they finally left, Harold breathed an audible sigh of relief.

Seventeen

Harold pulled on his shirt, wincing when he felt the damp material touch his skin. He hadn't had time to wash the garment since the previous night and it was still stiff with dried mud. So were the trousers which he put on but, after a moment or two, he grew to accept the cloying feel of the odorous cloth against his skin. He pulled on his coat and tucked the torch into one pocket – he'd taken it from a store-room in the hospital earlier in the day. The fifty watt bulb hung above him. He hadn't put it on since returning to the hut over four hours ago and the hands on his alarm clock had crawled around to 12.26 a.m. Harold knew that he was taking a small risk leaving the hut earlier than usual but, he reasoned, his business in the muddy quagmire was more important than usual and, besides, if someone did see him it would be easy enough to explain away the fact that he was out that late. Also, he was carrying nothing with him tonight. Nothing, that was, except his fear. He realized that the men from the electricity company who had repaired the downed power line could not have discovered the grave of foetuses, he would have known about it by now. However, he was worried that the driving rain might have disturbed the top soil which covered the grave.

He folded the blanket up as small as he could and tucked it inside his coat. It was to be used as an extra covering on the grave. He would drape it over the eight bodies interred there and then build more layers of earth over the blanket, ensuring once and for all that they were hidden from prying eyes. It was cold but, despite that, Harold could feel the beads of perspiration on his forehead and between his shoulder blades. He swallowed hard, checked everything one final time and then headed for the door of the hut.

Harold peered out, making sure that there was no one about, then he slipped around the side of the small building and was swallowed up in the shadows which formed so thickly at its rear. He walked to the low barbed wire fence and clambered over it, nearly slipping on some damp grass at the top of the ridge. It had stopped raining and the night air smelt crisp, filled with the aroma of wet grass. His hot breath formed small white clouds every time he exhaled and Harold was pleased when he finally reached the bottom of the ridge, almost slipping half way down. He walked across to the pylon and felt his feet sinking into the mud at its base – a testament to the comings and goings of men and machinery earlier in the day. He flicked on the torch and shone it over the ground, seeing the outline of heavy footprints in the soft soil.

There was not enough natural light for him to find his way so he kept the torch on.

Above him, the sky was a patchwork of clouds and stars. It looked like a canopy of soggy black velvet that someone had thrown a handful of sequins onto. There was a slight breeze, cold and just strong enough to send the clouds rolling across the dark backdrop.

Harold shone the torch down once more and saw where the fallen power cable had scorched the earth over a wide area. He didn't know how many volts each of those massive overhead wires carried but it certainly had done some damage. The blackened grass and mud seemed to extend as far as thirty yards, perhaps more. He could pick out the tracks of the crane in the mud too and, close by, someone had dropped an empty cigarette packet. He kicked it aimlessly with the toe of his shoe and walked on, the breath now rasping in his throat. He was very close to the grave.

The boot marks and crane tracks ended abruptly and Harold realized that the men had not gone anywhere near to the hole. He moved on, slowing his pace some-

102

what. He sucked in a shaking breath, the frosty air making his mouth and the back of his throat even drier. He tried to swallow but couldn't. It felt as if his heart was trying to smash its way through his ribcage. He played the powerful torch beam over the area ahead of him, his boots creaking on the soft mud as he advanced.

Something pale gleamed in the shaft of light and Harold held the torch on it, moving forward with even more deliberate steps until he was at the spot which he knew so well.

"Oh God," he croaked.

The bulbous head of one of the foetuses had been exposed when the constant rain had washed away the covering of earth. As Harold had feared, the top soil had been almost completely eroded and, as he shone the torch over the length of the grave, he saw that more of the tiny creatures lay virtually in the open, only the tiniest covering of mud hid them from view. He scratched his head in puzzlement. Even if the men from the electricity company hadn't actually come as far as this, surely, he reasoned, they could not have avoided seeing the exposed bodies? The grass round about, what remained of it, was blackened so the cable had discharged its power into this part of the field too. How could they have missed the small grave? However, the important thing was that he was still undiscovered. He knelt, and scooped up a handful of wet earth, ready to cover the corpses once again.

But, looking down at the vile array of abortions which lay before him, something nagged at the back of his mind. He dropped the handful of soggy muck and frowned. It was something about the position of the creatures. Harold had buried them in a straight line and yet, three, perhaps more, were lying sideways now. One even lay spread-eagled across one of its unfortunate companions. The driving rain would have been enough to wash away the top soil but not to move the

103

position of the foetuses. Had the men from the electricity board found them? Had he been reported? His mind suddenly began to race, his heart beat even faster. It would take maybe a day or two for the people at the hospital to discover that *he* was responsible. He would not know immediately that he had been found out. He began to shudder with cold and fear. What would they do to him? He clenched his fists, his confused mind searching for some other answer. *Any* other answer. Perhaps animals had disturbed the grave. A fox? A badger perhaps? He picked up his torch and shone it over the nearest foetus, inspecting the small body for damage. The arms, the legs, the body were all untouched. Harold leaned closer, casting furtive eyes over the head. It looked swollen, mottled red and black in places, it appeared like a huge festering sore. The tiny mouth was open, pieces of mud clogging it. Harold reached forward with one shaking finger and brushed the muck away. The body looked so limp, not rigored as would be expected, but soft and malleable. Harold shone the torch close to it, prodding the skin with his fingers, mildly disgusted by its slimy softness. He was breathing hard now but his fear had been replaced, to some degree, by an appalling kind of curiosity. He prodded the tiny body with his fingers, even touching the torn, putrescent umbilicus for a second before returning his attention to its face. The stench which rose from the grave was almost overpowering, a cloying odour of decay which couldn't even be driven away by the fresh breeze which sprang up but Harold didn't seem to notice it. He shone the torch over the other bodies, some of which were in an advanced state of decomposition. Harold looked on them with a feeling akin to pity and, for long moments, he crouched in the mud gazing at the bodies, then, he took the blanket from his coat and laid it beside him. He decided to lay the foetuses back in their original position before completing the burial so he lifted the one nearest to him and placed it gently between two smaller specimens, one of which had already had its sightless eyes devoured by worms. Harold shuddered and hurried to complete his task. The smell, which he had not noticed before, suddenly seemed to be unbearable to him, filling his nostrils and making his head ache.

Each foetus he touched felt similarly cold and soft, the touch of their flesh on his fingers making him quiver violently. But, nevertheless, he completed his task, finally reaching for the body which he had first inspected. Puzzled once more by its position in the grave, Harold lifted it gently in order to replace it in the original space he had made for it. It seemed heavier than the rest and he guessed that it must have been aborted at a much later stage than the others. He lowered it gently into place and shone his torch over it one last time.

The foetus opened its eyes.

Harold's body stiffened, his hand almost crushing the torch. It was as if thousands of volts of electricity were being pumped through him, the shock making him rigid. His single good eye bulged madly in the socket, he shook his head gently from side to side.

The foetus moved one arm, raising it slowly, as if soliciting help and Harold heard a low sucking sound as its mouth opened. A blob of black fluid appeared on its lip and trickled down its chin. The tiny chest heaved once then settled into a more rhythmic motion.

He kept the torch aimed at the thing, his entire body shaking uncontrollably.

To his left there was another low, liquid, noise which reminded him of asthmatic breathing only it was thicker, more mucoid and Harold swung the torch beam around. He began to mouth silent words as he saw a second foetus slithering awkwardly in the sticky ooze.

105

It was smaller than the first one, its umbilicus moving tentacle-like, as it struggled in the slime.

Harold felt his heart beginning to pound. He felt as though his head were swelling. The execrable stench filled his nostrils, hanging in the air like an almost palpable cloud of corruption. He dropped the torch but it fell to the ground with its light pointing into the grave and, in that light, Harold saw a third creature begin to move. It rolled onto its side, yellowish fluid so viscous it was almost jellied, oozing from the hole in its belly where the umbilicus should have been. Part of its body was blackened and rotted, one arm mottled, two of the tiny stubby fingers missing. It clambered up and fixed Harold in a hypnotic gaze, the twin black orbs which were its eyes holding him immobile.

He pressed both hands to his head and screamed but no sound would come. His mouth was stretched open as far as it would go, the shriek of terror and revulsion waiting to be released but he could not summon it. That ultimate exclamation of disgust remained deep within him. He tried to stand, to get away but his knees buckled and he fell face down in the mud, close to the edge of the grave, watching helplessly as the three living foetuses crawled towards him. He felt as if someone had laid a huge weight on his body, for when he tried to rise again he felt an intolerable pressure pinning him down as surely as if he'd been skewered to the mud with a long knife. He could only watch, mesmerized, as the trio of abominations drew closer to him. He was babbling incoherently now, his words unintelligible even to himself. His mind struggled to accept what his eye saw but could not, *would* not. He fought against the pressure above him and managed to rise, dragging himself to his knees, eyes still locked on the monstrosities before him.

"No," he murmured, his entire body trembling.

The leading foetus had reached the edge of the grave and was trying to crawl up the side.

Harold shook his head violently. He heard voices.

Was there someone else with him?

He spun round, searching for the source of the voice.

Had someone discovered him?

"Who's there?" he gasped, his gaze still riveted to the trio of creatures beneath him.

Again the voice came only this time it was joined by another, and another. Soft, hissing words which he could barely understand seemed to flicker inside his head like a dying candle flame. He stopped trying to back away and watched the three foetuses writhing in the grave. He tried to tell himself that he would awake in a moment, safe, in his hut. He would leave this nightmare behind him, wake up to find that it had all been a figment of his imagination.

He bowed his head and tears began to flood down his cheek. Kneeling like some kind of penitent, he remained where he was, his body racked by sobs, his vision blurring as he cried like a child. Gradually, the spasms subsided and he stared down at the three creatures which lay in the sticky mud, pinned in their collective gaze. Then, very slowly, he unrolled the blanket and lifted the first of them out, putting it gently onto the soft material. He repeated the procedure with the other two. They lay before him, grotesque parodies of human babies – living nightmares. The third moved slightly and Harold reached forward and wiped some of the thick yellow discharge from its belly, rubbing his hand clean on the wet earth.

"Yes, the grave," he said, nodding blankly, as if speaking to some invisible companion. He began scraping huge clods of reeking soil onto the other five bodies in the grave, sweating with the exertion. It took him nearly half an hour to fill it in then he turned back to the three creatures who lay on the blanket.

"I will find you shelter," he said. He smiled crookedly. "Gordon." He looked down at them.

"Gordon."

The word echoed inside his head, swirling around in a fog of confusion that seemed to be thickening by the second. A mist made of nightmares from which there was to be no escape.

Harold sat on the edge of his bed, looking down at the three foetuses on the blanket before him. He had left the light off in the hut and, in the darkness, the hands of his clock glowed dully. Harold noted that it was approaching 2.23 a.m. His head was throbbing and his body felt stiff, every muscle crying out for rest but he could only sit. Sit and stare at these. . .

He didn't even know what they were. He realized that they were abortions but, more than that. . . The thought trailed off once more.

Words. Soft, sibilant, came hissing inside his head once more and Harold wondered if he was imagining them. Were they really his own thoughts? He swallowed hard. The voices seemed more distinct now, as if they were speaking directly to him.

He nodded in response to the silent question.

"Yes," he said, softly. "I am afraid of you."

A pause.

"Because I don't know what you are." If not for the fact that he was constantly pulling at the flesh on the back of his right hand, he might still have thought that this was some horrendous nightmare from which he would be hurled screaming at any second, to wake up sweating and trembling in his bed with the daylight streaming in through his window. As it was, all he heard were the voices again, echoing, resonating like whispers in a cave.

He gave answers to unspoken questions.

"Food? What can *I* do?"

108

Hissing inside his head.

Harold shook his head and stood up.

"I can't."

The whispers became louder.

"No." He backed off until suddenly he felt a searing pain explode inside his head. White light danced before his eyes and he felt something warm and wet trickle from his nostril. He put a finger to the orifice, withdrawing it to see dark fluid on the tip. The blood looked black in the darkness. Harold swayed drunkenly. It felt as if someone had clamped a vice on his skull and were twisting the screw as tightly as possible.

"All right," he yelled and the pain receded. He leant against the nearest wall, panting. "Tell me how," he sobbed.

The words came slowly and, at first he recoiled again but remembrance of the awful pain when he disobeyed forced him to listen. Tears streaming down his face, he sat motionless, hands clasped together, head bowed until finally he got to his feet and walked into the tiny kitchen. He pulled open one of the rotting wooden drawers and rummaged through until he found a butcher's knife. It was a heavy bladed implement, rusty in places, its black handle missing a screw but, as Harold pressed his thumb to the cutting edge he found that it was still wickedly sharp. He shambled back into the other room and sat down on the bed, the knife held in one unsteady hand. The ghostly voices spoke to him once more and he put down the vicious blade in order to undo his shirt. As each successive button was unfastened, he could hear the soft sucking sounds which the foetuses made echoing around the room. They moved only occasionally on the blanket but, all the while, their black glistening eyes were fixed upon him. One of them, the smallest of the trio was gurgling thickly, a stream of fluid spilling from its mouth which it kept opening and closing rather like a goldfish. Harold looked at it and then across at the knife.

Perhaps he should kill them now, destroy these foul things. Cut. . .

He groaned once more as a white hot burst of agony seared his brain. He imagined his head swelling then exploding into a thousand sticky pieces. He undid the final button and pulled his shirt off then, with shaking hands, he reached for the long bladed knife. His own body looked pale in the gloom and his skin was puckered into goose-pimples. He held the knife before him, looking at the wicked weapon then, with infinite care, almost without looking, he pressed the sharp edge to his chest. It felt cold and he held it there for what seemed like an eternity then, with one swift movement, he drew it across his pectoral muscle, opening the flesh, slicing through veins. He moaned in pain, felt the hot bile bubbling up in his throat but he fought it back, hacking at himself once more until a bright stream of blood gushed from the torn breast. His second cut was more random and he was fortunate not to carve his left nipple off. His chest felt as if it were on fire and he swayed for a second, some of his blood splashing the bedclothes and, all the time, the voices inside his head urged him on.

He bent forward and lifted the first of the foetuses, cradling it in his arms for long seconds, allowing some of his blood to drip onto the tiny body, then he raised it to his torn chest. He felt its jellied, putrescent flesh in his hands, he smelt the stench which it gave off and he allowed it to press its bulbous head against his wounds. Harold was shaking uncontrollably as he felt the thing's lips on his chest, probing the ragged edges of the twin gashes, burying its small mouth inside the bleeding maw as it swallowed his life fluid. It bucked violently in his hands and he felt that familiar wave of sickness sweeping over him again but the pain in his

110

chest kept him conscious. Tears streamed down his face, dripping from his chin to mingle with his blood and the odorous fluid which the foetus itself seemed to exude.

He heard the voice deep within the darkest recesses of his mind and he laid the creature back on the cover where it lay still, its face slick with blood, its body bloated and immobile.

He repeated the procedure with the second monstrosity, opening a third wound on the other breast to satiate it. He moaned once more, feeling the thing grip his flesh with stubby fingers as it pressed itself tightly to the weeping wound. It too signalled its satisfaction and Harold completed the vile ritual by lifting the third foetus to his torn pectoral.

When the task was over, Harold got to his feet, unhindered, and staggered into the kitchen. He hung over the sink and vomited violently, remaining there for a long time afterwards, finally spinning both taps and washing the foul mess down the plug-hole. Then he sponged down his chest wounds with a wet towel, pressing it hard against the wounds in an effort to seal them. When he withdrew it, the material was stained orange and red. He was bruised black in some places where the creatures had fed. Harold held the towel in place until he was satisfied that the bleeding had stopped then he dried himself and sought out some adhesive strip which he had in the bedside cabinet. He carefully cut some lengths of it and placed it delicately over the wounds. It still felt as if someone were using a blow torch on his chest but the pain was diminishing somewhat.

Bleary eyed, he looked down at the three abortions.

Where the hell was he going to hide them?

He inhaled deeply, wincing as his torso began to throb once more, looking around for a suitable place. There seemed to be just one.

There was a large cupboard beneath the sink which appeared to be ideal. He carried them, one by one into the kitchen and knelt before the cupboard door, a sliding effort with a metal handle.

"I have to hide you," he said. "Someone might come here."

Silent questions.

He nodded, pulling open the door. A strong odour of mildew wafted out, taking Harold's breath away momentarily. He looked inside and saw that, but for a couple of old saucepans and a plastic bucket, the cupboard was empty. He hastily removed the offending articles, pushing them to one side. A silver-fish scurried from the dark confines of the enclosure and Harold crushed it beneath his foot, gazing down at the shapeless mess for a second before lifting the blanket into the cupboard. This done, he carefully laid the foetus' onto it, finally pulling it over them. He gazed into the darkness, heard the vile mewling sounds which they made, the soft mucoid snortings and gurglings and he closed his eyes. Then, the voices came to him again, soft but full of menace. Full of power. He slid the cupboard door shut and stumbled back into the other room where he collapsed on the bed. Immediately, he was overcome with the welcome oblivion of unconsciousness but whether it was sleep or a blackout he was never to know. Either way, he sprawled on the blood-speckled bed, the odour of the creatures still strong in the air.

Outside, the rain had begun to fall again, pattering against the window, thrown by the wind which rattled the glass in its frame. Inside, the steady ticking of the clock was the only sound.

It was 3.17 a.m.

PART TWO

". . . death could drop from the dark
As easily as song."
                    – Isaac Rosenberg

Eighteen

Inspector Lou Randall pushed two coins into the vending machine at the end of the corridor and pressed one of the buttons. A plastic cup dropped down but no tea followed it. Randall muttered something to himself and pressed the reject button but the machine had swallowed his money and obviously didn't intend parting with it. The Inspector swore and kicked the recalcitrant contraption, smiling when he saw a stream of tea suddenly gush forth into the waiting cup. Grinning, he retrieved the tea and retreated back to his office, closing the door behind him.

He crossed to his desk and sat down, lighting up a cigarette before flipping open the first of half a dozen files spread on the work-top.

They were statements from four residents of Exham, all of whom claimed to have seen Paul Harvey in the past two days. Randall read each one slowly, shaking his head every now and then. Every one gave a different description and at least two of the sightings had happened at exactly the same time but on different sides of town. He closed the file and dropped it amongst the others. He sat back in his chair, the plastic beaker in one hand, the cigarette in the other. His office was already full of smoke and an empty packet of Rothmans lay at his elbow. He put down his tea and massaged the bridge of his nose between thumb and forefinger, trying to assess what little he knew of the investigation so far.

He ticked the items off mentally, as if striking them from some kind of psychological shopping list.

1. Harvey escaped six weeks ago.
2. Four sightings so far, all unsubstantiated.
3. All possible hiding places searched.

Randall sat forward in his chair. If the escaped prisoner *was* in or around Exham then where the hell was he hiding? He reached for a green file and opened it. It was a psychiatric report on Harvey, something which the Inspector had read before but now scanned yet again in an effort to glean some insight into the man he was hunting.

Harvey was dangerous – there was no doubt about that – but, as far as he could tell, the man was no idiot. A number of tests had been carried out on him by the prison psychiatrist. The results showed that he was prone to bouts of manic depression. His IQ was below average, his faculties not quite spot on but he wasn't crazy. That was what made him more dangerous, thought Randall. Harvey was unpredictable.

Randall shut the file and closed his eyes for a moment. So far no one had been harmed and the Inspector was becoming more and more convinced that the prisoner was nowhere near the town. Nevertheless, somewhere, nagging at the back of his mind was the conviction that eventually he would meet Paul Harvey face to face and it was a prospect he did not relish.

Lynn Tyler hauled herself out of bed, wincing slightly at the pain from her abdomen. She straightened up and the pain receded. The doctors had told her to expect a little discomfort after the abortion and, after all, she had only been home for a week. She stood up and looked down at her pale body, noticing how her stomach had begun to fill out. She was surprised at this, expecting that it would flatten after the operation. She drew in a breath and held it, pulling in her belly for a moment. It didn't flop forward when she exhaled, the skin remained taut across her pelvis and stomach and she ran both hands over it. It felt hot, as if she had been standing next to a radiator and Lynn pressed the tight skin cautiously, puzzled by its feel. There was no pain, just the peculiar sensation of heat. She sat down on the edge of the bed once more, one leg hooked beneath her, both hands still pressed to her belly. She lay back, letting her hands slip to her sides and, gradually, the burning seemed to disappear. When she replaced her hands she felt only the familiar coolness of her skin. She gazed at the ceiling, tracing the many cracks, her thoughts rerunning the events of the last couple of weeks, as if she were rewinding a piece of cine-film – with each frame a memory.

She thought of how happy she'd been when she first discovered she was pregnant but of her fear at telling Chris. And how well that fear had been founded. She could still remember that morning he walked out on her, the morning she had decided to have the abortion.

As she lay there, a feeling of bitterness swept through her. Not only had she lost Chris, the one man she had ever loved, she had also lost the child she wanted. She had been forced out of necessity to have the abortion, knowing she would never be able to bring up a child alone.

The tears came suddenly and unexpectedly and she rolled onto her stomach in an effort to stifle them in the pillow. She wanted to forget him, tell him to fuck off, that she didn't need him. She wanted to yell it in his face. Tell him that there were plenty more men around. Her mind was in a turmoil and, as she rolled back onto her side, the tears dripped onto the sheets and soaked into the material. She wiped them away, smearing her mascara, wincing slightly when she felt the peculiar burning sensation return, the skin stretching across her stomach and pelvis until it seemed it would tear.

She gasped at the stab of pain below her navel.

But, as quickly as it had come, it vanished and, tentatively, Lynn Tyler got to her feet, her hands gently stroking her belly.

There was no more discomfort.

She crossed to the wardrobe and began to dress.

Nineteen

Harold leant on the edge of the sink and gazed at the pale, ghost-like image which stared back at him from the mirror. There were deep, dark pits beneath both his eyes, his eyelids looked crusted and heavy and, when he exhaled, it came out as a deep sigh. There was no one else in the hospital toilet to see him and, for that, Harold was thankful.

God, how the day had dragged. It seemed more like eight years not eight hours since he'd started work. He'd been in on time and had done his best to disguise the fact that he felt so wretched. The three vicious cuts on his chest ached beneath the plaster and his joints seemed to groan in protest every time he moved.

His efforts to disguise how he *felt* might have been successful but there was no hiding his appearance. He looked, in the tradition of that time-honoured phrase, like death warmed up. He'd only eaten a small lunch and a couple of chocolate biscuits and even they had made him feel sick. His stomach rebelled at each new intrusion and, at one point, he had thought he was going to vomit.

117

He pulled the plug in the sink and shuffled over to the towel-roll, tugging hard on it to find a clean piece. Then he dried his face and hands, took one last look at his drawn visage and walked out into the corridor.

The wall clock opposite him showed 7.30 p.m. He still had another two hours before he was finished for the day. Harold sighed, thankful, at least, that it was time for a break. He made his way to the lifts and found an empty one. He punched the five button and leant back against the rear wall as the car rose swiftly. He would have preferred to have spent his break alone but Winston Greaves had insisted that he come to the office so that the two of them could talk. As the lift reached five and the doors slid open, Harold decided that talk was the last thing he needed but, nevertheless, he had to keep up appearances as best he could. As he walked towards the door of Greaves's office he felt his legs go weak and, for long seconds, he thought he was going to faint. Thankful that no one was around, he stood still for a moment, supporting himself against a wall. His head was spinning, the floor swimming before him. That ever-present pulse of pain at the back of his neck had now developed into a series of hammer blows to his skull and, once again, he fought back the urge to be sick. Sucking in deep breaths of stale, antiseptic air, he walked on.

Greaves had the kettle on when Harold entered the small office. The coloured porter looked up and smiled and Harold managed a thin grin in return. He sat down heavily, leaning back in the plastic chair. Greaves eyed him appraisingly. He too noticed the pallor, the milkiness of Harold's unscarred skin. The dark rings beneath his eyes looked as if they had been made by soot. The one good eye was bloodshot, the glass one sparkled with its customary unsettling brilliance. It looked all the more incongruous set against the drawn quality of the rest of his face.

118

Greaves waited for the kettle to boil then made the tea, handing Harold a mug. He watched as his companion struggled to remove the tea bag, scalding his fingers in the hot liquid. Greaves handed him a spoon and Harold finally succeeded in lifting the tiny bag out. He dropped it into a nearby ashtray and sat gazing down into his mug.

"Are you all right, Harold?" asked Greaves, sitting down opposite him.

"Yes."

The answer came a little too quickly, full of mock assurance.

"You look a bit under the weather," Greaves told him. Actually, Harold, he thought, you look half-dead.

"I'm OK," Harold told him, sipping at his tea.

"The job isn't getting you down is it?" Greaves asked. "I mean, I know it can be depressing sometimes."

Harold ran a hand through his hair again.

"I didn't sleep well last night," he confessed.

"That's not the first time is it? Why don't you ask one of the doctors for some sleeping pills?"

Harold shook his head.

"I'll be all right. I've just got a bit of a headache."

"There's nothing worrying you is there?"

Harold looked up.

"Why?" His voice was heavy with suspicion, perhaps a little over-cautious.

Greaves caught the inflection.

"I just asked," he said, smiling, trying to sound calm.

When Harold raised his mug to drink again, his hands were shaking, something which did not go unnoticed by his companion. Greaves regarded him warily over the rim of his own mug. Harold certainly looked rough, he thought, and he was unusually jumpy. Still, if he hadn't had any sleep. . .

He sat up as Harold swayed uncertainly in the chair. The coloured porter was on his feet in an instant, moving around the desk towards his companion. Harold put one hand to his head and leant forward, taking the weight on his other elbow.

"Harold," said Greaves.

The older man waved him back.

"I'll be all right," he said. "I just felt faint."

Harold was shaking all over and a fine film of perspiration had greased his skin. He sucked in deep lungfuls of air and gradually straightened up but Greaves remained where he was.

"I think it might be best if you went back to your hut for half an hour or so, just for a lay down," the coloured porter said. "And while you're there, get something to eat. That's half of your trouble, you don't eat enough." He put out a hand which Harold grasped, allowing himself to be helped up.

"Come on," said Greaves. "I'll help you."

Together, the two of them made their way to the lift, descending to the ground floor. They headed for the main entrance without Harold speaking a solitary word. He stopped twice, worried that he was going to pass out but Greaves supported him. The senior porter suggested they see a doctor but Harold resisted the offer with a determination bordering on panic. So, slowly, they made their way out of the main building and towards the stretch of grass which led to Harold's hut. As they drew closer, perhaps a hundred yards from the flimsy structure, the older man pulled away and stood, swaying uncertainly, his good eye looking as glazed as the false one.

"I'm all right now," he said.

Greaves looked puzzled.

"I'll just see you inside," he said. "Make sure –"

Harold cut him short.

"No."

There was a note of near pleading in the word and Greaves wrinkled his brow.

"Don't come inside," said Harold, then he managed a weak smile. "I'm OK. Really."

Greaves did not move but he remained unconvinced.

"I'll be back on the ward at quarter past eight," Harold promised, nodding vigorously. "Quarter past eight."

He turned and headed for the hut, tottering drunkenly until he finally reached the hut. Greaves watched him through the darkness his eyes fixed to the small dwelling, waiting for the light to be put on inside. The hut remained in darkness. The coloured porter stroked his chin thoughtfully. Perhaps he should go and check on Harold anyway.

He began walking towards the hut.

Less than ten yards further on, he slowed his pace then finally stopped. No, he told himself, Harold must be allowed some privacy and, after all, he had promised to be back at work in less than forty-five minutes. Greaves stood a moment longer, his eyes riveted to the hut. Still no light came on. The senior porter sucked in a deep breath then turned and headed back towards the main entrance. His mind was full of unanswered questions the main one being, why would Harold not let him inside the hut? What was he hiding? Greaves administered a mental rebuke for himself. Harold probably had nothing to hide. He was probably just ashamed of the fact that the hut was a bit of a shambles. Nevertheless, as he reached the main entrance to the hospital, Greaves looked round once more, expecting to see a light coming from the hut and he was mildly disturbed when he saw nothing.

His curiosity was aroused and, as he made his way back up to his office, he became more and more convinced that Harold was hiding something. Perhaps he'd been stealing? Greaves swiftly dismissed that particular notion. For one thing there was nothing worth nicking in the hospital and, secondly, Harold probably wouldn't have the intelligence to pass for a thief. It was probably a quite innocent reason, Greaves told himself as he reached his office. He sat down and sipped his tea which was now stone cold. He put the kettle on to make a fresh cup, glancing at his watch.

It was 7.46. Harold would be back in half an hour.

Greaves waited for the kettle to boil.

Harold stood in the darkness, his back to the door of the hut, his eyes closed. He finally crept across to the window and, squinting out, he could see Greaves as he stood and watched and then finally turned and left. Harold had breathed an audible sigh of relief at that point. He didn't reach for the light switch but moved furtively in the gloom, making his way into the kitchen. He stood staring at the cupboard door for long seconds, the cupboard beneath the sink with its sliding door. With a shaking hand he reached out to open it then swiftly withdrew, the breath catching in his throat. The cuts on his chest began to throb and he took a step backward.

The hissing began.

He placed both hands to his temples as his headache seemed to intensify, the voices fluttering inside his mind like dialogue from a half remembered dream.

He moved towards the door.

Harold knelt and opened it, sliding the cupboard opening back an inch at a time, recoiling from the rancid odour of mildew and something stronger. Something more pungent and cloying. The stench of decay. It wafted out of the cupboard in an almost visible cloud making Harold cough.

He had covered the three foetuses with the blanket and now he could see their dark shapes moving slowly beneath the material.

Words came into his head, words which he had heard before. Mutterings and commands which he knew he must obey and which, now, he found himself wanting to obey.

The kitchen knife was still lying beside the sink, its blade dull with rust and dried blood and Harold's groping hands closed around the handle. He swallowed hard, listening to the words which whirled around inside his head, making him dizzy. His ears were buzzing and he was finding it difficult to focus on the three writhing shapes beneath the blanket but, finally, the feeling diminished somewhat and he reached for the loose corner of the material, pulling it back to expose the trio of creatures beneath.

Harold gaped at them, the breath rasping louding in his throat as he inhaled the rank air. At first he thought he was mistaken but, on closer inspection he realized that his first reaction had been correct. There was *no* mistake.

All three of the foetuses were growing.

Twenty

Winston Greaves glanced at his watch, drumming on his desk top with his free hand. It was almost 8.35 p.m. Where the hell was Harold? He had promised to be back on the ward by quarter past eight. Greaves chewed his bottom lip contemplatively. Perhaps the other porter had just returned and gone back to work without letting him know. Greaves pushed the thought to one side. No. Harold would have come up to the office first, to let him know that everything was all right. Greaves stared at the bottom of his own empty mug. Perhaps everything *wasn't* all right. Harold had looked ill, maybe he'd been unable to return to work. He might even need medical attention of some kind.

Greaves sat for five more anxious minutes then he got to his feet and headed out of his office towards the lifts. He reached the ground floor asking a number of other staff members if any of them had seen Harold. None had. Greaves exhaled deeply. Obviously he had not returned to the main building. Not sure whether to be angry or anxious, Greaves headed for the main doors, intent on finding Harold. He must still be in his hut after all. Perhaps he'd just fallen asleep. Was he really ill? These and other thoughts passed through the coloured porter's mind as he crossed the expanse of grass which led to the small dwelling where his companion lived.

There was still no light on in there.

Greaves wondered how Harold would react to his appearing at the hut this way. Would he refuse him entry as he had done earlier? Maybe he *did* have something to hide. If that was the case, Greaves told himself, he would find out what it was.

As he drew nearer the hut he became aware of how quiet it was. The darkness seemed to envelope the tiny hut like a black velvet glove, shutting out all sounds too. Greaves slowed his pace as he approached the door, straining his ears to pick up the slightest hint of movement from inside. It remained as quiet and forbidding as a tomb. For the first time, Greaves became aware of the cold, not just the ever-present chill in the air but a deeper more numbing cold which seemed to seep into his bones. He shuddered and glanced around him. Trees nearby swayed gently in the breeze, the beginnings of a mist swirled in the hollows of the field beyond the hospital grounds.

Greaves knocked hard on the door of the hut.

No response.

He knocked again, tapping his thigh with the flat of his other hand.

Nothing. Just silence. And the cold.

"Harold," he called, knocking again.

This time he knelt and tried to see through the keyhole but it was too dark inside the hut. He clambered to his feet and moved across to the window, cupping both hands over his eyes as he pressed his face to the soiled pane. He narrowed his eyes and could just make out a dark form on the bed. He banged the window but the shape on the bed remained immobile. He returned to the door and twisted the handle.

It was locked.

Perhaps he should go back and get help. For a moment he considered the idea but then decided that he should deal with it himself if possible. He didn't want to get Harold into trouble unnecessarily. Greaves put his hand on the door knob and twisted it again, this time throwing his weight against it. The lock was old and rusted and it came away with relative ease. The subsequent momentum sent Greaves stumbling into the hut itself. He almost fell, only retaining his balance by hanging onto the door. Then he gently pushed it shut behind him, immediately aware of the appalling stench which filled the hut – a pungent, nauseating odour which made him gag. It seemed to have no source but to be permeating the entire hut, oozing from the woodwork like sweat from pores.

He flicked the light switch. The bulb flickered, buzzed irritably then blew out. Greaves fumbled in his overall pocket for his lighter. He flicked it on and held the small flame above his head. It cast a pool of weak orange light and, in that sparse illumination, the porter saw the shape on the bed was Harold.

Greaves crossed to the prone body, his mouth dropping open.

Harold lay on his back, one leg drawn up foot resting

on the bed, the other stretched out so that the heel of his shoe was touching the floor. One arm lay across his stomach whilst the other hung limply at his side. Greaves stepped closer, seeing the dark stains on the floor, on the bedclothes. He realized that it was blood and, as he leant over the older man his foot brushed against Harold's outstretched arm. The knife fell with a dull clatter and Greaves almost shouted aloud. The blade was slick with blood too. There were pieces of plaster lying on the bedside cabinet and some soaking cotton wool. The crimson gore on it looked black in the darkness. But it was Harold himself who gave Greaves the biggest shock. The coloured porter leant as close as he could, staring at the vicious cuts on his companion's chest, one of them still weeping blood. The others were in the process of sealing, their ragged edges held together by congealing gore.

"Oh God," murmured the porter and he reached out to touch Harold's shoulder. He could see the man's torn chest rising and falling but he could solicit no reaction from him. Greaves prised open the unconscious man's eyelids and held the lighter close. Its flame sparkled in the glass orb. The pupil of the good eye contracted. Greaves pressed a tentative index finger to the older man's jugular vein and felt it pumping.

I've got to get help, he thought. He flicked off the lighter and headed towards the door.

Something fell with a crash in the kitchen and Greaves spun round.

"Who's there?" he said.

Silence.

He moved towards the other room, once more flicking the lighter on, using its meagre light as a guide. His own footsteps sounded heavy and conspicuous on the wooden floor as he advanced.

He heard breathing. Faint, mucoid breathing which seemed to grow louder as he paused in the doorway of the kitchen. He held the lighter higher. It was beginning to get hot and he changed hands as his eyes scanned the tiny room. A plate lay shattered close by. There were drops of dark fluid on the enamel of the sink. Greaves crossed to it, his nostrils once more filled with an unbearable carrion stench. He dipped a finger in the dark fluid and sniffed it.

It was blood.

There was more of it on the door of the sliding cupboard opening beneath and Greaves knelt, pulling the door back as far as it would go. A blast of almost palpably rancid air gushed out and he had to fight hard to prevent himself from vomiting. He saw the blanket inside the cupboard, the dried blood caked on it. He reached out to touch it.

The first foetus seemed to roll into view from a darkened corner of the cupboard.

Greaves opened his mouth to scream, his eyes bulging as he saw the monstrosity. It pinned him in a hypnotic stare, its own black eyes glinting with a vile lustre. There was blood around its mouth and on its chest – even on the minute, shrunken genitals.

Greaves tried to back away, the lighter falling from his grasp, but he was unable to tear his horrified gaze away from the foetus's twin black orbs. He saw the second one drag itself into view, its own eyes focusing on him too. He reached back to grip the door jamb in an effort to pull himself away but his hand closed over something soft and jellied. He shrieked and looked down to see the third of the creatures. Greaves had grabbed its arm. He hurriedly pulled his hand away, noticing the trail of blood which the thing had left behind when it had dragged itself from beneath Harold's bed.

He was trapped. Pinned by their gaze, he was a prisoner of his own crippling terror. Now he felt the pain begin to build behind his eyes and at the base of

127

his skull as the three abominations concentrated their fearful powers on him. It felt as if their eyes were burning into his head, like black laser beams they bored through his skull to his brain. He moaned and put both hands to his head in an effort to stop the pain which was growing more intense by the second. He tried to shut his eyes and blot out the insane vision before him but he couldn't and now he felt blood running from his nostrils. Filling his ears. Even his tear ducts seemed to swell and burst until he was weeping crimson. The pain in his head reached unbearable heights. He felt his legs go numb. He opened his mouth to scream but his tongue felt thick and useless, as if it had been injected with novocaine. Blood gurgled in his throat. His hands dropped from his head as he lost the use of them and finally he could only sit and watch, through a haze of red as the three creatures made one more concerted effort against him. Both his temporal arteries seemed to swell, pulsing madly for agonising seconds. His eyes seemed to swell and protrude as if pushed from the inside. But, somehow, Greaves managed to roll onto his belly and, using his legs as a means of propulsion, he pushed himself away from these nameless monstrosities. Into the other room he crawled, past the still motionless form of Harold, until he reached the door, the pain now reaching heights beyond endurance. Greaves managed to haul himself upright and, with a despairing moan, he flung the door open and staggered out, tottering drunkenly towards the beckoning lights of the main building.

He was almost there when, in a blinding moment of incredible agony, the veins and arteries inside his brain ruptured with so much force that most of the frontal and temporal lobes were destroyed. Winston Greaves collapsed but his body continued to jerk spasmodically for a few moments even after his death.

His body was found the next morning by an ambulance driver and the autopsy revealed that Greaves had died as the result of a massive cerebral haemorrhage.

Harold took the news of his friend's death badly. So badly that he spent his day off lying in bed but he did not sleep because, all the time, inside his head, the voices whispered.

It was to be a long time before he recovered from the news of Winston's death and the loneliness which he had thought banished now returned with numbing intensity.

Twenty-one

The onset of night brought about contradictory feelings within Paul Harvey. He welcomed it because it hid him and cloaked his furtive excursions from the farm. But he feared it too because it brought memories. Night had, in the past, always been a time of fear for him. The time when his father and mother would fight or when, in later years, he would be dragged from his bed and beaten, forced to bear that reeking stench of stale whisky and tobacco in his face as his father shouted at him.

Harvey hated to be shut in. It was another legacy of his childhood. His bedroom door was always locked from the outside, and this practice continued right up until his father died. There was no chamber pot in his room and, more often than not, he would be forced to urinate out of the window if he awoke during the night. Before he understood that trick he would simply wet the bed or do it into one of the drawers. Consequently,

129

the clothes inside stank most of the time. However, whichever course of action Harvey had taken it had brought savage retribution from his father. During his troubled years at school, Harvey had been quizzed by teachers and taunted by his fellow pupils about the cuts and bruises which he bore almost all the time but, of course, he never dared to divulge the truth of how he sustained them.

His hatred of enclosed places had intensified during his stay in Cornford prison. The fact that he was kept in solitary, for the sake of the other prisoners, made things worse. But now, to a certain extent, he was free to wander the open fields and hillsides of Exham for the first time in his life and, with night now draped across the countryside like a shroud, he did just that.

As he stood at the top of a hill, the lights of the town glittered invitingly below him and Harvey gripped the sickle tightly as he made his way down the incline. An owl hooted close by but Harvey ignored its cry.

The town beckoned and Harvey did not refuse its call. He felt no fear, just a peculiar feeling that was something like exhilaration.

The woods on the outskirts of town swallowed him up.

Twenty-two

Ian Logan pulled up the zip on his leather jacket and shivered. He stood beneath the swaying sign of "The Black Swan", fumbling in his pocket for the packet of Marlboro and a box of matches. Thanks to the gusting wind, it took him three attempts to light the fag but finally he succeeded and, hands dug deep into his pockets, he started walking.

Other staff members, another barman included, were also leaving and Logan muttered cursory farewells to them. They all seemed to have cars except him and nearly all of them were going in the opposite direction. Even the one vehicle that was going his way sped past without offering him a lift. Logan exhaled deeply, his breath clouding in the night air.

He glanced at his watch and saw that it was approaching 12.15 a.m. He was usually home by half past eleven at the latest. He could imagine Sally's reaction now, almost hear her whinings as he walked in the front door. Moaning that his supper was spoiled, asking him where he'd been. He worked six nights a week, the only other day he spent at home listening to Sally moaning about how he should get a better job so that they could move into a *decent* house.

He decided to take a short-cut. There was bound to be an argument when he got in anyway so he might as well get it over and done with.

He cut down the lane to his left, knowing that he could be home in ten minutes. He quickened his step, the cigarette bouncing up and down between his lips as he walked.

The lane was dimly lit at the best of times but now, with the witching hour twenty minutes old, all but three of the lamps had been extinguished. There was the odd porch light on outside one or two of the cottages but, apart from that, the lane was wreathed in a heavy gloom. Visibility was made all the worse by a writhing mist which seemed to have settled over the fields. Blown by the wind, it seemed to ooze over the hedges like some kind of ethereal sea whose waves moved in slow motion.

Logan glanced at the white-washed cottages as he walked. Each one had its own drive and there was

131

hardly one which did not boast two cars. These private dwellings stood out in marked contrast to the estate on which he lived. It lay a mere few hundred yards down the lane and the staid uniformity of the council houses offered a marked contrast to the gleaming individuality of these expensive properties. Perhaps Sally was right, he thought, it would be nice to live in a place like that. He was contemplating that thought when something moved away to his right.

He glanced round, slowing down only slightly, squinting into the blackness in an attempt to see what had made the sound. He heard a shuffling, scratching noise and, a moment later, a hedgehog scuttled out from beneath one of the hedges and trundled across the lane. Logan smiled to himself as he watched it disappear into one of the gardens opposite. A few yards further on another of the tiny creatures was splattered across the road. Cars sometimes drove down the lane and, obviously, this one had squashed the unfortunate hedgehog. It had been there a long time for, even in the gloom, Logan could see that its flattened remains were stiff, giving it the appearance of a spiky frisbee. He smiled at his analogy and walked on.

There was a farmhouse on the right. Painted black, it was almost invisible in the darkness but, from inside, he could hear the barking of a dog. The bloody thing had gone for him a couple of times in the past and he passed by hurriedly despite the fact that the animal was safely penned in the building. He walked another few yards and came to a rotting wooden stile. Beside it a bent and battered sign declared:

FOOTPATH

The so-called footpath led across a field and came out right opposite his own house. He decided to risk the many cow-pats which littered the field and cross it in an effort to get home quicker. He put his foot on the bottom plank of the stile and hoisted himself up. It creaked ominously under his weight and for a second he thought it was going to collapse but, as nimbly as possible, he swung himself over and landed with a loud plop in the mud on the other side.

"Sod it," he said, aloud, scraping some of the glutinous muck off on the bottom plank. That done, he set off across the field.

The light from the lane diminished to a point where his only guide was the odd light burning in the houses which backed on to the field. It was virtually impossible to see more than fifteen or twenty feet ahead. The crispness of the night air made the smells around him seem all the more prominent and he winced at the strong odour of cow dung. The ground was soft despite the frost and he almost slipped over twice, the second time shooting out a hand to grasp the fence which ran alongside him. He yelped in pain as his groping fingers closed over some barbed wire. Logan stopped dead, fumbling in his trouser pocket for a handkerchief, dabbing at the small cuts and muttering irritably to himself. He reached into his coat pocket for his fags and lit one up, puffing at it for a second before moving on.

The field was separated from the nearest house by a double row of trees, the ground in between each one thick with underbrush. Gorse and blackberry bushes grew in rampant abundance, in many places reaching shoulder height. There was a powerful smell of rotted vegetation in the air and Logan muttered to himself as he walked.

A twig snapped close by and, instinctively, he stepped back, the noise sounding thunderous in the stillness of the night.

His foot sank into something soft and he realized that it wasn't mud.

"Bloody cows," he groaned, shaking his foot.

However, his complaints were cut short when he heard another sound – the low rustling of bushes being parted. Logan squinted into the thick underbrush but he could see nothing. There was a moment's silence then the sound came again, closer this time.

A fox perhaps? Probably another hedgehog.

He swallowed hard and walked on, quickening his step for reasons he himself was not sure of. The other stile which marked the far end of the footpath was less than a hundred yards away and Logan could see the light from a nearby house beckoning him. His feet made squelching sounds in the mud and, as he walked, he glanced towards the trees nearby.

There was a loud scratching sound in the bushes less than two feet from him and he opened his mouth, allowing a small gasp to escape his lips. A sibilant rasping sounded so loud in the stillness and, at last, Logan broke into a run. He kept his eyes firmly fixed on the light ahead of him but it seemed to be a million miles away.

Beside him, the snapping of twigs seemed to grow to deafening proportions and he realized with horror that whatever was in the bushes was keeping pace with him.

His mind sought an explanation. It wanted to find a logical answer but all he could think of was getting to that bloody stile and clambering out of the field.

It was fifty yards away and he was still running, the bushes actually moving beside him now, some pushed over by his invisible companion. He could not bring himself to look for fear of what he might see.

Thirty yards.

The light ahead gleamed brighter and Logan found renewed strength in his legs as, beside him, he heard a low whining sound.

His breath was rasping in his lungs, his mouth dry.

Ten yards and he could see that stile. It was broken

134

in two places and for that he was grateful, because it meant he wouldn't have to waste time clambering over it.

Five yards.

He almost fell, slipping in another cow-pat. His arms pinwheeled wildly for a moment but he retained his balance. The perspiration was now heavy on his face, his breath harsh and almost painful. His legs ached from running and he could feel his heart hammering against his ribs.

There was a loud screech and a snapping of wood to his right, so close it seemed that it was coming from inside his own head. Something burst from the under-bush and flew at him. He tried to scream but couldn't find the breath. He went down, face first into the mud, rolling over quickly, his eyes bulging and terror winding icy tendrils around his throat.

The cat which had leapt out of the bushes at him was already scampering off into the darkness, a mouse held firmly in its jaws.

"Jesus Christ," he gasped, wiping his face and dragging himself to his feet. For long seconds he stood there, trying to regain his composure. He closed his eyes and sucked in a deep breath, holding it for a second before exhaling in an audible sigh of relief. His clothes were splattered with mud and cow dung and he tried to brush it off with his hands. What the hell would Sally say about this? He suddenly found that he could smile and, as he watched the cat loping off across the field, he began to laugh.

"Bloody idiot," he said to himself and, still chuckling, he clambered over the stile.

The dark shape which loomed behind him seemed to grow from the blackness itself. Where gloom and night air had swirled around, there was suddenly something tangible.

Ian Logan thought he had heard a gust of wind but

135

what he did hear, *all* he heard, was the arc of metal as
the weapon descended. The scream was locked in his
throat. His eyes bulged wildly as he saw something
metallic glinting above him. The dark outline of. . .

Before he had time to discern the shape, his throat
was slashed open.

Darkness became eternal night.

Twenty-three

Despite the fact that the sun was shining, there was a
harsh chill in the air and Randall shivered involuntarily
as he stepped out of the Panda car. He yawned and
rubbed a hand across his face. Behind him, the radio
crackled and Constable Higgins reached for it; Randall
didn't hear what he said because he was already making
his way up the small incline that led to the footpath. A
piece of rope had been tied across the entrance to the
footpath and another uniformed constable stood there.
The Inspector recognized him as Chris Fowler, the
youngest man on the force. Yet to reach his twenty-sixth
birthday, the constable looked fresh-faced and alert and
seemed to remind Randall of his own weariness.

"Morning, sir," said Fowler.

Randall smiled thinly. The youngster was still
nervous, only having been on the force for six months
and he was still somewhat in awe of his superior. The
Inspector patted the younger man on the shoulder as
he passed. He swung his leg over the piece of rope and
started up the narrow path. There were houses on
either side of it, both separated from it by high hedges
and a welter of rampant wild plants which seemed still

136

to be flourishing despite the onset of the cold weather. Clumps of stinging nettles grew thickly on either side, spilling over onto and into the cracks in the broken concrete in places. Long fingers of blackberry bush clutched at the policeman's jacket as he passed. Muttering irritably to himself, Randall tugged the jacket free and walked on. The heady aroma of wet grass and damp wood filled his nostrils and he reached for a cigarette, lighting it hurriedly as if trying to dispel the fresh natural odour of the countryside. He sucked hard on the filter and walked on.

Ahead of him, tall trees were dotted with black clumps which signalled the presence of crows' nests. Most of them were abandoned by the look of it. Just one solitary bird hovered in the crisp blue sky, as if casting an eye over the proceedings beneath it. Randall glanced at the houses on either side of the path. They were all simple red-brick buildings, with neatly kept gardens and suitably gleaming windows. Nothing seemed out of place on the estate, for every building appeared similarly immaculate.

Opposite him at the moment, in the house across the street, Sally Logan was being comforted by her mother while a perplexed police-woman tried to make some sense out of her hysterical blubberings.

Yes, everything was in its place on the estate. Even the corpse in the field just ahead.

Randall clambered over the wooden stile at the end of the footpath and eased himself down, trying to avoid the glutinous pools of mud. There was a powerful smell of rancid muck and, Randall suspected, cow shit. His suspicions were well founded when he nearly stepped in a pat. He glanced around, at the trees and undergrowth which ran alongside the barbed wire fence marking the boundaries of the field to his right. To his left ran another fence which separated the back gardens of nearby houses from the expanse of field and, straight

137

ahead, he saw a group of three men standing around a blanketed shape. All three turned to face him as he drew nearer.

Two were on his force, Constable Roy Charlton and Sergeant Norman Willis. The third man looked like a midget placed beside the two burly policemen. He nodded a greeting to Randall and the Inspector returned the gesture. Dr Richard Higham stepped back from the shape at his feet and took off his glasses, polishing them enthusiastically with the monogrammed handkerchief he took from his trouser pocket. Randall exhaled deeply, looking down at the grey blanket. All around it, the mud was stained a deep rust colour, the dried blood mingling with the thick, oozing slime. The Inspector sucked hard on his cigarette and blew the smoke out in a long thin stream.

"What have we got?" he asked, his question addressed to no one in particular, his gaze riveted to the shapeless form at his feet. A hand protruded from beneath the blanket, the fingers curled and rigored.

Sergeant Willis handed the inspector a wallet and watched as his superior flipped it open. It contained about twenty pounds, mostly in pound notes, an Access card which bore the embossed name Ian J Logan and a couple of small photos. The photos showed a young woman, the man's wife Randall reasoned, and the other had her smiling out at the camera, a dark-haired man beside her. Randall held the photo before him and then looked down at the shape beneath the blanket.

"We haven't been able to make positive identification yet, guv," said Willis. "But we're pretty sure it's him."

Randall looked puzzled and handed the wallet back to his sergeant.

"What's the problem with identification then?" Randall wanted to know. He looked at Higham who knelt down and took hold of one corner of the blanket.

138

"The bloke under there is the one in the picture, isn't it?" He took a final drag on his fag.

"You tell me," said the doctor and pulled the material away to expose the corpse.

"Jesus Christ Almighty," murmured Randall, quickly clenching his teeth together, fighting to control the somersaults which his stomach was performing.

Willis lowered his head, Charlton looked away. Only Higham glanced first at Randall and then at the corpse.

The head was missing.

Randall wiped a hand across his face and sucked in several lungfuls of air. His stomach was still churning and he could almost feel the colour drain from his cheeks. Yet, somehow, he managed to keep his gaze fixed on the decapitated body. Blood was caked thickly all down the front of Logan's coat and for many yards around the body. The dark stains were everywhere. Randall felt a bead of perspiration burst onto his forehead as he studied the hacked and torn stump of the neck, a portion of spinal cord visible through the pulped mess. The head had been severed very close to the shoulders and apparently with some difficulty because there were a dozen or more other equally savage gashes at the base of the neck and even on the shoulders themselves. At first sight however, the damage seemed to be confined to that particular area, the blood which covered the body having come from the severed veins and arteries of the neck rather than from any wounds in the torso.

"Put it back," said Randall, motioning to the blanket and Higham duly obliged. The Inspector reached for his cigarettes and hurriedly lit another.

"The ambulance is on its way," Willis told him. "They'll take the body to the hospital."

"How long has he been dead?" asked Randall, looking at the doctor.

"It's difficult to say without the benefit of a thorough

post-mortem," Higham told him. "The pathologist at Fairvale will be able to tell you that more precisely than I can."

"Try guessing," said Randall, taking a puff on his cigarette.

Higham shrugged.

"There's very little surface lividity," he pulled back the blanket once more and indicated the pale hand with its clawed fingers. "Although the massive loss of blood may well be a cause of that." He sighed. "I'd say he'd been dead about eight or nine hours."

Randall looked at his watch. The hands showed 9.06 a.m. He nodded.

"Who found him?" he asked.

"A couple of kids," Willis said. "On their way to school."

"Christ," muttered Randall. "Where are they now?"

Willis explained that both children were being treated for shock at their homes close by.

The Inspector walked around the corpse and ambled over towards the thick bushes close by. A portion of the fence had been broken down and some of the underbrush crushed flat.

"Have you checked this out?" he asked, indicating the overgrown area.

Willis joined him.

"We found footprints in there and in the field over here," he motioned for Randall to follow him. He motioned to the single set of deep indentations in the mud. The Inspector knelt and examined the imprints more closely.

"Looks as if he was running," he said, blowing out another stream of smoke. "But why the hell are there only one set of tracks? It doesn't look as if anyone was chasing him."

"Whoever did it must be a right fucking maniac,"

140

said Willis. "I mean, who the hell cuts off a bloke's head and. . ."

Randall cut him short.

"By the way, where is the head?" he asked.

"It was taken, guv." The words came out slowly. "We can't find it anywhere."

Randall raised one eyebrow questioningly, his mind suddenly preoccupied with another thought.

"Paul Harvey," he said. "How long is it since he escaped?"

Willis shrugged.

"It must be going on for eight weeks, maybe longer," the sergeant said. "We haven't been able to find hide nor hair of him. He's probably in another part of the country by now, guv." The two men looked at each other for long seconds, the gravity and drift of Randall's suspicions gradually dawning on the older man.

"Get all the cars out. I want this bloody town searched again," Randall said.

"But guvnor, we hunted high and low for him for over a month," Willis protested. "There's no way he can still be in or around Exham."

"I want that search initiated, sergeant." The Inspector paused. "Look, there's been two murders in the history of this town, both committed by Paul Harvey. In the last two days, four people reckon to have seen him. Now we've got this," he pointed to the covered remains of Ian Logan. "Doesn't it seem just a little *too* coincidental?"

Willis shrugged.

"So you reckon Harvey killed Logan?"

"I'd lay money on it and, once the pathologist's report is in, then I'll have an ever clearer picture." The Inspector walked over to the fence. "The footprints you found in the bushes, can you get casts from them?"

Willis shook his head.

"There's too many and, what with the rain last night. . ." He allowed the sentence to trail off.

"Shit," muttered Randall. He turned to see a couple of uniformed men clambering over the stile, one of them carrying a furled stretcher. They made their way across to the body and, under the careful supervision of Higham, lifted the corpse onto the stretcher. Randall watched them as they carried the headless body away, struggling to get back over the stile with their recumbent load.

"I want that coroner's report as soon as it's completed," he said to Willis. "Send one of the men over to the hospital to pick it up as soon as it's ready."

The sergeant nodded. The two men walked back towards the waiting figure of Higham and Charlton, then the four of them made their way back down the footpath behind the two stretcher bearers. The ambulance itself was parked behind one of the Pandas, two of its wheels up on the grass verge to allow cars easy passage in the narrow street. Randall watched as the body was loaded into the back of the vehicle and he could see people peering from their front windows to see what was happening. Some had even opened their front doors and were standing there quite unconcerned in their efforts to get a better view of the proceedings. A handful of people already knew that something sinister had happened in the field. By lunch-time probably the entire street and half the estate would know what was going on, such was people's fascination with the macabre, Randall had found. Anything even slightly out of the ordinary was a source of endless curiosity to them and, in a way, he felt a curious kind of pity for these people whose hum-drum existences were only brightened up by the occasional death or break-in on the estate. A murder would no doubt fuel their coffee time chats for months to come as they speculated and fabricated, each teller adding his or her own particular

142

brand of exaggeration until the tale would eventually become local folk-lore. It was something to be mulled over in years to come – and perhaps even laughed about.

As he climbed wearily into the waiting Panda, the last thing Lou Randall felt like doing was laughing.

The afternoon grew dark early and, at four o'clock, Randall found that he had to switch on the lights in his office at Exham's police station. The building itself was a two storey, red brick edifice about five minutes walk from the centre of the town. Its ground floor comprised an entrance hall, the complaints desk (where Willis now stood doing a crossword) and, beyond that, a type of rest room which doubled as a briefing base for the small force. A flight of steps led down to the basement and its six cells whilst the upper floor was made up of offices and store-rooms. There was a vending machine at the head of the stairs and Randall had managed to coax a cup of luke-warm coffee from it by the simple expedient of kicking it. The bloody machine was playing up and force seemed to be the only thing it responded to. Usually, one of the men popped in his twenty pence and the machine swallowed it gratefully without offering a drink in return. There'd been numerous complaints about it and Randall had decided it was time to get in touch with the manufacturers to see about getting it replaced. However, his thoughts lay on matters other than vending machines as he sat at his desk tapping his blotter with the end of a pencil.

Thoughts raced through his mind at break-neck speed, not allowing him to focus on them.

The murder of Ian Logan. The hunt for Paul Harvey. Even now, men were out searching for him, retracing ground which *he* knew they had already covered in the first early days when the maniac escaped. Randall sipped his coffee but found that it was cold. He winced

143

and put the cup down. Harvey. Harvey. Harvey. The name rolled around in his mind like a loose marble. He thumped his desk irritably and got to his feet. There *had* to be a link between Logan's murder and the escaped maniac. He walked to the window of his office and gazed out. From his vantage point he could see the small railway station which served Exham. A train was just pulling out, heading for London. The people of Exham were lucky in so far as they were able to reach the capital direct. Just a few stops up the line, in Conninford, lay Regional HQ and Randall's superiors. They had already been on to him about his failure to find Harvey, once they discovered that the wanted man had committed a murder they would probably try and nail Randall to their office wall.

He sighed and ran a hand through his hair. He felt so helpless, so frustrated. He looked out over the town.

"Where are you, Harvey?" he muttered, aloud.

He knew he would return home that night, the problem still on his mind. It was always like that now. He had many sleepless nights sifting through problems, unable to divorce work from home any longer. Home. He smiled bitterly at the irony of the word. It wasn't a home any longer, not without Fiona and Lisa to welcome him. The house was still and lifeless without them and had been for the past five years. There was no warmth any more, just the harsh white greeting of the walls and their glass smiles beaming out at him from behind carefully framed photos. When it had happened, Randall had wondered whether or not he would ever recover. It had felt as if something had been torn from inside him, as if a part of his being had ceased to exist, robbed of their love and companionship. He had seen the change in himself over the past few years. He had his work and that was something but it was precious little substitute for a wife and daughter. He had become, against his own will, a cynical and embittered man. To a certain extent the cynicism had always been present – it went with the job someone had once told him. The bitterness, however, and the feeling of desolation which sometimes bordered on anger, was something which he had only recently learned to live with and even, in his worst moments, to nurture. He had allowed the seeds of resentment to blossom into blooms of hatred and fury. He closed his eyes, feeling as lost and lonely as he had ever done in his life.

The knock on the office door brought him back into the real world so fast that the thoughts vanished from his mind.

It was Constable Stuart Reed, a tall, gangling individual with a heavily pitted complexion. He was in his mid-thirties, perhaps two or three years younger than Randall himself. The constable was carrying a thin file.

"Coroner's report on Ian Logan, guv," he announced, waving the file in the air.

"Thanks," said Randall, taking it from him.

The PC turned to leave but the Inspector called to him.

"See if Norman's got any coffee or tea on the go will you?" he asked. "The stuff out of that bloody machine tastes like cat's piss."

Stuart nodded and, smiling, left his superior alone. Randall flipped open the file and found that it contained just three pieces of paper. The coroner's report, another report on the possible murder weapon and a carbon headed:

FAIRVALE HOSPITAL/NOTICE OF DECEASE

All three were signed with the same sweeping signature – *Ronald Potter*.

Potter was chief pathologist at Fairvale, a fact born out by the legend below his name stating that in block letters.

Randall ran a close eye over each of the three docu-

145

ments in turn, pausing here and there to reread certain sections. He fumbled in his jacket pocket for his cigarettes and took out the packet muttering irritably to himself when he found it was empty. He picked up his biro and chewed on the end of that instead. The initial report ran for four pages much of which was comprised of medical jargon but, by the time he put it down, Randall understood how, if not why, Ian Logan had died.

"Eight lateral wounds on the shoulders and neck," he read aloud. "The head was severed by a single edged weapon. Depth of wounds ranges from a quarter of an inch to two and a half inches. No other external damage."

Randall dropped the report onto his desk and leant forward in his seat, glancing at the second sheet. It was a short piece on the possible nature of the murder weapon. Once more he read aloud.

"Traces of rust found in all but one of the wounds." The Inspector drummed softly on the desk top with his fingers.

"Rust," he murmured. He pulled a notepad towards him and scribbled on it:

1. Rusty knife?
2. Strong man (depth of cuts)?
3. No motive?

He pulled at one eyebrow as he considered his own scribblings. It would take someone of extraordinary strength and savagery to sever a man's head without the aid of a serrated tool. The implement appeared to be straight-edged. He checked back over the first report. No, there was no mention of any straight blade. A single edge, yes. He ringed the word knife and drew three question marks beside it. An axe maybe. He quickly dismissed the thought. The wounds would be much deeper if an axe had been used. Even so, the deepest had penetrated two and a half inches. To Randall, that implied the weapon had been used in a swatting not stabbing action. Ian Logan's head had been hacked off, not sliced off. He glanced back over the report and noted that portions of chipped spinal cord had been found, something which further indicated that the head had been cut off by repeated powerful blows. Where the severed appendage was now remained to be seen.

Randall exhaled deeply and sank back in his chair. He tapped on the arm agitatedly, wondering if any of his men had found Paul Harvey yet. It had to be Harvey, he reasoned. Everything pointed to that. The bastard was still in or around Exham somewhere. The Inspector gritted his teeth. He had to be found, even if it meant tearing every house and building down brick by brick. He glanced at the pathologist's report a last time and felt the hairs prickle on the back of his neck. He had the unshakeable feeling that it would not be the last such report he read.

Twenty-four

The staff canteen at Fairvale seemed more than usually crowded and Harold Pierce found that he had to move carefully with his tray of lunch. The mug of tea lurched violently and threatened to spill and, twice, the plate which bore his beans on toast slid dangerously near to the edge of the laminated board. Harold eventually found a seat alone and set his lunch down, almost grateful to have reached the haven of a chair. He sat, exhaling heavily. His stomach was rumbling and he felt hungry but the sight of the food made him feel nauseous. He picked up the knife and fork and held them before him, gazing down at his steaming food but, after a moment or two, he put the cutlery down and contented himself with sipping at his tea.

His head ached, something not helped by the constant hum of conversation which filled the canteen. All around him, groups of nurses, doctors, porters and other hospital staff chatted and laughed, complained and swore. Harold sat alone, the sea of sound washing over him like an unstoppable current. It had seemed like a loud buzzing at first but, as the day wore on, the buzzing had diminished until it became words. Admittedly they were fuzzy and indistinct, but they were words nevertheless. Harold could not make out what the voices said but they persisted. He closed his eyes and put one hand to his ear as if he thought it possible to pluck these ever-present sounds from inside his head with his finger-tips. But the noises continued, mingling with the cacophony of sound in the canteen.

Harold sipped his tea, wincing as he picked up the mug. He raised it to his lips with effort, almost as if it were made of lead instead of porcelain. The brown liquid tasted bland on his furred tongue.

Someone asked him to move his chair and Harold turned to see a very attractive woman standing behind him. She was dressed in a white coat, open to reveal the full swell of her breasts beneath the blouse she wore. The skirt hugged her slender waist and hips and as Harold looked into her face he found himself captivated by a pair of the brightest blue eyes he'd ever seen. Her thin face was framed by short, brown hair. She was smiling.

For long seconds, Harold gazed at her, realizing from her attire that she was a lady doctor. He woke up to the fact that he was blocking her way and hurriedly pulled his chair in, allowing her through. She smiled again and thanked him, and he watched her as she made her way up to the food counter and began picking things out, talking happily to the women there. Harold touched the scarred side of his face with a shaking hand, his one good eye still riveted to the woman in the white coat. All the other sounds in the canteen seemed to fade as his attention focused exclusively on the doctor. She had carried her tray of food to a table where a number of other doctors sat and he could see her laughing and joking with them. He lowered his head again, once more aware of the pain which gnawed at the back of his neck and head. The voices in his mind continued to mutter and mumble their incomprehensible dialogue and Harold gritted his teeth until his jaw ached.

Finally, he got to his feet but as he did so he felt his knees buckle and he shot out a hand to steady himself. His flailing hand caught the edge of the plate and, before he realized what was happening, it had fallen from the table and smashed on the floor. Those nearby turned to see what had happened and Harold coloured beneath their curious gaze. He looked down at the mess of broken porcelain and baked beans and shrugged apologetically as a large woman in a green overall waddled across the canteen carrying a mop and bucket.

"I'm sorry," mumbled Harold.

"That's all right, love," said the woman. "It happens all the time. But if you didn't like our cooking you could have told us. You didn't have to chuck it all over the floor." She looked up at him, laughing loudly.

Harold swallowed hard, his body trembling.

"I'm sorry," he repeated, not seeing the joke. He hesitated for a moment then turned briskly and made for the exit door, imagining all eyes were on him.

"Who is that man?" asked Dr Maggie Ford, running a hand through her short brown hair. She watched

Harold's rushed departure with a feeling akin to pity. "I don't remember seeing him around the hospital before."

Frederick Parkin drained what was left in his coffee cup and dabbed at the corner of his mouth with a handkerchief, paying particular attention to the thick white moustache that overhung his top lip.

"His name is Pierce as far as I know," he told Maggie. "He was a patient at the old mental hospital until recently."

Maggie nodded slowly.

"I wonder how he got that terrible scar? Poor devil."

"No one seems to know too much about him," Parkin told her. "A fire I would think, looking at it." His tone brightened and he smiled broadly at Maggie. "Why the sudden interest?"

"You know me, Fred," she said. She pointed to her nose and winked. Both of them laughed. "I just feel sorry for him," she added finally. "It must be an awful burden going through life like that. He's got guts to walk about in that state."

"Your compassion is overwhelming, Maggie," said Parkin, good-naturedly. "Sometimes I think you're in the wrong job. You should have been a social worker."

"There's nothing wrong with taking an interest in people," she said, defensively. "After all that's what we're all paid for isn't it?"

Parkin smiled.

"I bow to your superior logic," he said. He got to his feet, said a few words to another man at the end of the table and then made his way out. Maggie sipped her coffee, her mind still unaccountably fixed on Pierce.

She was thirty-two and had been a consultant gynae-cologist at Fairvale for the last four years during which time she'd built up an enviable reputation for herself. She had not, as might have been expected, encountered any resentment from her male colleagues – rather the opposite in fact. They had welcomed her eagerly into their midst, impressed by her abilities and also, she thought with a smile, by her female assets. She was the sort of woman who exuded that peculiarly ambiguous demeanour that combined sensuality with innocence; although, with a handful of lovers behind her, Maggie could scarcely claim the word innocent in its literal sense. She was a dedicated woman, single-minded to the point of obsession about her work, something which had caused conflict in many of her relationships but it was not a matter on which she was prepared to compromise. Her mother was always telling her that she should be married but, for Maggie, a career was the only thing which mattered. Men, when she found the time for them, were little more than a brief interlude. At the moment, she lived alone in a small flat about twenty minutes drive from the hospital and she went back to an empty home every night. She said this did not bother her and, on the surface, it appeared that she was telling the truth. However, somewhere inside her was a need which had to be fulfilled and fulfilled by far more than the occasional brief relationship or one night stand. Maggie harboured a brooding fear of loneliness. Some nights, lying alone in her bed she would contemplate the idea of sharing the rest of her years with a partner who cared for *her* above all else. But that thought was always tempered by the fear that she would not be able to reciprocate that bond no matter how hard she wanted to. If many people struggled with the problem of wanting to *be* loved, Maggie Ford was trying to come to terms with the fact that she wanted *to* love. It seemed as if that pleasure were to be denied.

She sat in the canteen and finished her coffee then, finally, she got to her feet. Glancing at her watch she remembered she had a patient to see in ten minutes.

It was almost 1.55 p.m.

Harold pushed the trolley out of the lift into the eerie twilight of the basement. He guided it over the polished floor, past the pathology labs, towards the furnace room. His head felt as if it were swelling and then contracting like some bulbous extension of his pulse. The voices inside his head continued to hiss but they were gaining a startling clarity now. Harold listened to his own footsteps echoing in the corridor as he approached the furnace room, surprised to see that the door was open.

He hesitated, his hands suddenly trembling and he gripped the handrail of the trolley until his knuckles turned white. The noise inside his head grew to a fresh crescendo and it sounded as if someone were holding two gigantic sea-shells against his head such was the roaring in his ears.

He could see the furnace through the open door, its great metal door yawning open to reveal the blistering flames within, competing with the ever-present hum of the generator. Harold's world had become one of noises and he closed his eyes momentarily before walking on towards the room. He could already feel the heat from inside. He bumped the door open with one end of the trolley.

Brian Cayton turned as the door opened. He recognized Harold and smiled.

"Hello, Harold," he said, reaching for a pair of forceps which lay on the trolley which he himself stood next to.

As Harold watched, he saw Cayton grip the forceps and clamp them around the limp and dripping form of a foetus which he took from a receiver. Its head lolled back as if the neck had been snapped and Harold saw blood running from its tiny mouth.

"What are you doing?" he demanded, stepping towards the other porter who was still holding the tiny body before him, trying not to inhale the rank odour which it gave off.

"You know what I'm doing," said Cayton, a little impatiently. "I've just come from pathology."

He held the foetus closer to the hungry mouth of the furnace.

"You're going to burn that child," said Harold, flatly.

The smile faded from Cayton's face.

"Yes. Of course I'm going to burn it." He paused, fixing his gaze on Harold's good eye. "Besides, it isn't a child."

The words inside Harold's tortured mind finally burst through the fog of indecision like diamond bullets.

"Stop it," he said, moving closer.

Cayton raised a hand to ward him off.

"Look, Harold, I know it's not very pleasant but it's got to be done," he said, forcefully. "Christ, you've done it yourself, what's the big deal?"

Harold felt searing pain inside his head and he blundered towards the other porter who stepped back, bewildered. Then, suddenly, he turned and tossed the foetus into the flames.

Harold screamed. A high keening wail torn raw from his throat, the wild ululation of a creature in pain. He crashed to the ground heavily, pulling the trolley over with him. His last conscious thought and sight, one of the foetuses being devoured by the ravenous fire. He rolled onto his back, vaguely aware that Cayton was heading for the door.

"I tried to stop him."

Words pounded in his ears, low guttural raspings, thick with power.

"I tried, I. . ."

Pain. Agonizing, white hot pain, filled his head for interminable seconds. Mercifully, Harold Pierce blacked out.

153

Maggie Ford yawned and reached up to massage her neck, allowing her head to rest against the rear wall of the lift. There was no one else in it and Maggie slipped one foot out of her shoe, flexing her toes. Her feet were killing her. Come to think of it, she ached all over.

"A good hot bath when you get home," she said aloud, suddenly embarrassed with herself when the lift doors slid open, the car having bumped to a stop without her even noticing.

She saw Brian Cayton standing there, his face flushed, a thin film of perspiration on his face.

"Doctor," he gasped, jumping into the lift. "Can you come down to the basement straight away? One of the other porters has collapsed."

She was going to protest but the concern on the young porter's face was such that she decided to remain silent. He jabbed the basement button and the lift dropped the remaining floors. When it came to a halt at its appointed place, Maggie found herself running behind Cayton, so infectious was his anxiety. She followed him to the furnace room, immediately struck by the foul odour of soiled linen and the blistering heat which poured forth from the still open metal door. She saw Harold lying prone beside the overturned trolley, arms outstretched.

"Go and get help," she told Cayton. "Get someone to help you, we've got to get him up." Even as she spoke, she slid back the lid of one eye and shone her penlight on it mildly repelled by the feel of the cracked skin beneath her fingers but she administered a swift mental rebuke to herself at her reactions, now more concerned when she realized that Harold's pupil didn't react to the light. She tried again, feeling mildly foolish when she realized that it was the glass eye she was gazing into. She repeated the procedure with the good eye, relieved to see that this time there was pupilary contraction. Even as she pocketed the penlight, he

154

began to stir. He tried to sit up but Maggie restrained him.

"Just take it easy," she said, softly and the initial look of fear on Harold's face was replaced by one of pained bewilderment.

He found himself looking into the face which he'd seen earlier. That beautiful thin face framed with the brown hair. *Her* soft hands were touching his wrist, feeling for his pulse.

"Why do they do it?" he croaked.

"Do what?" she wanted to know, checking his pulse against the second hand of her watch.

"Burn the children."

She looked puzzled.

"They burn babies in there," Harold said, tearfully, motioning towards the furnace.

Maggie understood and was thankful that, at that precise moment, Cayton arrived with another porter. On her instructions, they helped Harold to his feet and supported him to the lift.

"Shall we take him to casualty?" asked Cayton.

Maggie shook her head.

"No. Take him to my room on the fourth floor. I think it's time someone examined him."

All four of them climbed into the lift and, in seconds, it was rising.

Twenty-five

Harold sat on the edge of the couch, fidgeting uncomfortably. He watched Maggie as she crossed to her desk and selected a number of implements with which she

155

obviously intended to perform the examination. He didn't know what the things were although he had seen one or two of them many times during his spell in the hospital.

It was warm in the office, the gentle hum of the radiator reminding him of the furnace room. The walls were a brilliant white, the snowy expanse broken only by one large picture window to his right which looked out over much of the hospital below. The room itself was sparsely decked out, containing three hard chairs, a large desk and the couch upon which he now sat. There were filing cabinets against the far wall, each drawer marked with red labels bearing letters. On the desk itself there was a small pile of books, a pencil holder and a clock. The ticking seemed unnaturally loud in the silence.

"When was the last time you had an examination, Mr Pierce?" Maggie asked him, turning back to the couch.

Harold smiled weakly.

"I don't remember," he said. "You can call me Harold if you want to," he added, falteringly.

Maggie smiled and asked him to take off his overall which he did. Beneath it he wore a slightly off-white shirt, the cuffs fraying and worn. She asked him to undo his sleeve which he also did, being careful not to pull the material any further than an inch or two from his wrist, ensuring that his forearm was still covered. Maggie took his pulse once again and scribbled something down on a piece of paper.

"How long have you been working here, Harold?" she asked him, reaching for the opthalmoscope, flicking it on and testing the tiny beam of light against the palm of her hand. Satisfied, she peered into his one good eye, adjusting the implement until she found the correct magnification.

"About eight or nine weeks," he told her.

156

As she leant close to him he could smell her perfume. Just a vague hint but nevertheless detectable. She smelt so clean and fresh and, as she peered through the opthalmoscope, her silky hair brushed the unscarred side of his face. He felt a peculiar tingle run through him and his breathing quickened slightly.

"Have you ever had blackouts before?" she wanted to know.

Harold shrugged.

"I don't think so."

She asked him to take off his shirt.

A look of panic flashed across his face, as if she had just asked him to jump from the fourth storey window. He quivered, the breath catching in his throat.

"Why?" he asked, agitatedly.

She smiled, surprised by his reaction.

"I want to check your heart and lungs." She was already reaching for the stethoscope.

Still he hesitated, dropping his gaze momentarily then looking up at her with something akin to pleading sparkling in his eye.

"I'm all right," he told her, his voice cracking.

"Please, Harold," she persisted.

His mind was racing. What would she say when he took it off? Should he leave now, run out of the room? But then, he knew that they would come for him and when that happened. . . He pushed the thought to one side.

"Harold, please take off your shirt."

With shaking hands, he began to undo the buttons, pulling the bottom free of his trousers. Maggie took the sphygmomanometer from its metal case, preparing to test his blood pressure when she'd finished the chest examination. She tugged the cuff open, the velcro rasping noisily in the silence of the room.

Harold pulled his shirt free, balled it up and held it on his lap, his body trembling.

157

Maggie turned to look at him.

She swallowed hard, trying hard to disguise her horror at what she saw. Harold sat impassively, his eyes closed as if ashamed of the sight of his body.

His chest and arms were covered by numerous raw, angry cuts. Some had scabbed over, others were purple knots where the scar tissue had formed, only to be picked or cut away later. Dark, vicious welts covered his arms from the wrist to the elbow and the parts of his torso and limbs not disfigured by the multitude of sores and wounds were milk white. He had obviously lost a lot of blood from the cuts. One or two were festering, a large one just below his left elbow was a suppurating cleft in the mottled flesh. The most striking thing about the wounds, however, was their positioning. Each seemed to be a measured distance from the next, almost like carefully carved tribal scars. His chest was a patchwork of crusted flesh and dried blood, one nipple having been sliced in two. It was so badly bruised it was black. And that was the curious thing about all the cuts. Around each one was a dark area which, if anything reminded Maggie of a love-bite. It was as if the skin on Harold's body had been drawn between someone's lips, the suction causing the resultant discoloration of the flesh.

"Where did you get these cuts?" she asked him, her voice low and full of muted fear. Fear? Yes, Maggie told herself. Spidery fingers were playing a symphony along the nape of her neck and she felt the hairs rise in response.

Harold didn't answer, he just continued gazing down at the floor.

She moved closer, taking hold of his left wrist, anxious to get a closer look at the numerous gashes. He pulled away from her, his breath coming in gasps.

"Did you cut yourself like this for a reason?" she wanted to know.

158

He opened his mouth to speak, thoughts still whirling around inside his head and now, he began to hear the familiar voices growing in volume as he fought to find some kind of explanation for the shocking appearance of his upper body.

"I think I should call Dr Parkin, let him. . ."

"No." He practically shouted at her. "No."

"Something has got to be done about these cuts, Harold," she said. "Now, will you please tell me how you got them?"

"I . . . I dream," he mumbled.

"About what?" she asked him, taking his left arm in her hand and, this time, she encountered no opposition. She probed the edges of the nearest gash with a wooden spatula, withdrawing it when Harold winced.

"I dream about different things," he said, vaguely, gazing ahead as if he were addressing someone on the other side of the room.

"What do you see in these dreams, Harold?" she asked him. She was using the conversation as a means of distraction while she got a better look at the cuts on his body. The one below his elbow was undoubtedly fresh. She wiped some sticky liquid from it with a piece of gauze and prodded the torn flesh but, this time, Harold didn't react.

"Fire," he said, flatly. "I see fire."

"Can you tell me more about the dreams?" she asked.

"I killed my brother and my mother," he said, almost as if it were a confession. "That was why they put me away." The smile that he flashed at her caused her flesh to rise into goose-pimples. Maggie wondered just how deeply Harold's apparent obsession with the disposal of abortions, and his insistence on calling them "children", went. It made her wonder just how much more he could cope with. The wounds on his body were obviously self-inflicted, perhaps, she thought, as some

159

kind of bizarre revenge against himself for the crime which he felt he'd committed.

"How did your mother and brother die?" she asked.

He told her, and the significance of the fire, the destruction of the embryonic creatures, immediately fell into place.

"I dream about them sometimes," he said. "I dreamt about the furnace room once, I. . ."

He felt a stab of pain inside his head and the voices were there, loud and commanding.

"Tell me about the dream," Maggie said. He swallowed hard, his tone lightening somewhat.

"I don't think I remember now," he told her. "It's best if I don't talk about it. I don't like to think about it."

Maggie nodded, pressing the stethoscope to his chest. His heartbeat was slow. When she took his blood pressure she found it was a fraction lower than normal. Harold may have appeared to be anxious and disturbed but none of his bodily signs showed anything to back that up. She told him to put his shirt back on, dressing the worst of the cuts first.

"Can I go now?" he asked.

"If you're sure you're all right," she said. "But I'd still feel better if you'd let me call Dr Parkin in to have a look at you."

He refused, tucking his shirt back into his trousers and pulling on his overall.

"I'd like you to come back and see me in a couple of days, Harold," Maggie told him.

He nodded, still eager to leave.

"Why don't you go and lie down for a while."

"I feel much better, thank you."

Maggie shrugged. They said brief goodbyes and Harold left, closing the door behind him. He walked slowly down the corridor, the voices inside his head buzzing agitatedly.

160

"I didn't say anything. I kept the secret," Harold whispered to empty air.

"Will you hurt her?" he wanted to know.

The voices continued to speak and Harold listened intently.

Maggie sat down at her desk and ran a hand through her hair. Outside, grey rain clouds were gathering and the first fine particles of drizzle were beginning to coat the window like early morning dew on a spider's web. It was gloomy in the office but she did not switch the lights on, merely sat in the deepening shadows, lost in her own thoughts, the vision of Harold's savaged body still vivid in her mind. What could drive a man to inflict such damage on himself, she wondered? She looked at the phone on her desk for a long time, pondering on whether or not to ring Harold's old psychiatrist. Perhaps if she knew more about his background she would better understand why he had done what he'd done. She drummed restlessly on the desk top, her eyes still fixed on the phone then, finally, she got to her feet and crossed to the window, gazing out at the approaching banks of grey cloud.

If he had dreams, nightmares, she reasoned, then maybe the cuts had been inflicted whilst he was in the dream-state. She had heard of people lifting objects in their sleep which they would never be able to move while awake. Perhaps the same principle applied in Harold's case. What he could not bring himself to do in his waking state, he found the subconscious strength to do during his dreams. Namely the self-mutilation. She exhaled deeply. It was too simple an explanation. The cuts seemed *too* carefully spaced, there was nothing random about them. Unlike other psychotics who, given a sharp instrument, would carve themselves up just for the hell of it, Harold seemed to have chosen the spots where he inflicted the damage. It was almost as if he had been guided.

Maggie shook her head, trying to dismiss the thought. For one thing, Harold, as far as she knew, lived alone. He had few friends and certainly no enemies. And, as for the theory of him inflicting the wounds in a psychotic orgy of masochism – well, that didn't tie up because, although he may be mildly disturbed, Harold was certainly not psychotic.

She crossed back to her desk and glanced at the clock. 4.11 p.m.

What really puzzled her was the dark, bruised area around each cut. If Harold was a haematophile and thereby obsessed with the drinking of his own blood then the bruises on his arms could be easily explained but, she thought, that seemed unlikely.

Besides, it still wouldn't explain how his chest came to be in the same state.

Maggie chewed her bottom lip thoughtfully, already determined that if she had not heard from Harold in two days' time, she would personally go to his home and find out just what was happening to him.

Twenty-six

Judith Myers got up from her desk, smiling happily at the other people in the room, anxious to disguise the pain which was gnawing at her stomach and groin. She tried to tell herself that it was muscle strain. She'd been away from work for too long and now bending over a drawing board all day. . .

The idea quickly vanished as she felt a searing jab of

agony in her side. She stood still in the corridor for a moment, leaning against the wall, feeling as if someone had kicked her in the side. She put one hand to the throbbing area and felt it gently, the pain seemed to recede somewhat and she hurried down the short flight of steps which would take her to the toilets.

Once inside, she was relieved to discover that she was alone. She locked herself in one of the cubicles and sat down on the toilet seat, rubbing both sides now, taking short breaths. The pain seemed to be moving deeper into her groin so she stood up and slipped her tights and panties down to her knees, probing gently at the lips of her vagina with her index finger. She withdrew the digit after a couple of minutes, her hand shaking, her eyes half expecting to see it stained with blood. The incident the other night had frightened her but the doctor had told her that slight bleeding was not uncommon so soon after an abortion. Bleeding from the navel however, *was* uncommon but a trip to her own GP had revealed no complications and, despite Andy Parker's protestations, she had returned to work as soon as possible.

Now she pulled up her underclothes and unlocked the cubicle aware still of the pain which seemed to be spreading throughout her abdomen. She felt a sudden wave of nausea sweep over her and just made it to one of the sinks. Bent double over it, she retched until there was nothing left in her stomach. The pain, curiously, seemed to vanish. Judith spun both taps to wash away the mess, cupping some water in one palm and swilling it around her mouth. She looked up, studying her reflection in the mirror. Her face was the colour of rancid butter, the dark brown of her eye-shadow giving her the appearance of a skull. She pulled some paper towels from the dispenser and wiped her mouth, tossing the used articles into a nearby bin. Then, once again, she pressed both hands to her stomach.

"Judith, are you all right?"

The voice startled her and she turned to see Theresa Holmes standing just inside the door.

"It's OK, Terri," she said.

"You look awful," Theresa told her. "Do you want me to fetch the first aid bloke?"

"No, I'll be all right. I just felt sick."

Terri crossed to the sink and stood beside her, the ruddiness of her own complexion a marked contrast to the palour of Judith's. She was two years older and the women had been friends ever since Judith joined the firm.

"A friend of mine, she had an abortion," Terri said. "She had stomach trouble for months afterwards."

Judith smiled sardonically.

"Thanks, Terri, you're a great comfort."

"Sorry, I didn't mean it like that. All I'm saying is, I think it's common to feel bad soon after one."

Judith shrugged.

"It's been over three weeks now," she said.

She went on to describe the incident the other night.

Terri frowned but could offer no helpful information or advice. She asked Judith once more if she felt fit enough to come back to work and the younger woman nodded.

At two o'clock that afternoon, Judith Myers collapsed and was taken home, a slight swelling in her stomach noticed by no one.

Twenty-seven

The doors of the cellar bulkhead rattled in the powerful wind and Paul Harvey grunted irritably, awoken by the sound. He sat, screwing his eyes up in an effort to re-orientate himself with his surroundings. It was dark in the cellar, the only light coming through the slight gap where the two bulkhead doors met. Outside, the moon hung high in the sky, a solitary cold white beam finding its way down into the subterranean gloom. The cellar was large, stretching far away from him on three sides. It ran all the way beneath the farmhouse but he had not ventured far from his present hiding place for some time now. Not during daylight at least.

They had come, as he had expected. Two of them in one of their cars but, he had seen them and he had hidden. Pleased with his own cunning, he had gained entry to the house by breaking one of the small glass panels in the front door and simply wrenching the lock off with one huge hand. He had blundered around inside the empty, dust-choked dwelling until he finally found the cellar door. The rusty key still in the lock. He had unlocked the door and taken the key in with him. *They* had searched the house, he had heard them moving about inside, one of them had even mentioned something about a break-in but, when they had tried the door to the cellar and found it locked, they had gone away. Harvey had remained silent all the time they searched, the sickle held tightly in his grasp just in case. When one of them had tugged at the rusty iron chain on the bulkhead doors, Harvey had thought that they would discover him but his luck had persisted. Through the gap in the doors he had been able to see one of them in his blue uniform, speaking into the box which he carried and which seemed to answer him back. But, after what seemed like an eternity, Harvey had heard them return to their car and drive off. However, determined not to fall into one of *their* traps, he had remained in his hiding place. They would not catch him out again.

The cellar had proved to be far more than somewhere to hole up. Harvey had found that it was full of wooden shelves, each stocked with dusty jars of home-made preserves, pickles and even some bottles of amateur wine. The previous owners of the farm had obviously gone in for that kind of thing and Harvey had been glad to find a seemingly endless supply of food. He'd scooped jam from jars with his bare hands, drunk dandelion wine until his head ached, devoured entire jars full of pickled onions, upturning the receptacle to swallow the vinegar when all the other contents were gone. But his ravenous appetite had proved his undoing. He didn't know how long it was since he'd eaten – three, maybe four days. He'd lost track of time down there in that dank hole. The cellar smelt like an open sewer, splattered as it was with excrement and rat droppings. In the beginning the rodents had competed for the pieces of food which Harvey had dropped but now, as his hunger reached new heights, the rats themselves, as in the barn, had become the prey.

Broken jars littered the floor, their contents now rotting and moulding. Lumps of glass lay everywhere, two of the wooden shelves had been torn down during one of Harvey's frenzied moments. He had tried to eat some rotting marmalade which he scraped up off the floor but it had made him vomit and he sat in one corner now, his trousers damp and reeking of urine. Surrounded by his own excrement, the gnawing in his stomach seemed to fuel the anger which was growing within him. He had left the cellar just once, two nights ago, breathing clean fresh air instead of the fetid cloying odour of putrescence he had come to know so well. He

166

had wandered over the fields, the lights of Exham acting like beacons, attracting him as surely as a candle would attract a moth. He had carried the sickle with him, its rusty blade tucked into his belt.

Now he hefted it before him, running one finger over the cutting edge, pieces of dried blood flaking off along with some minute fragments of rust. He stood up, reaching for the key in his pocket, realizing that he would have to leave this place again. But, the night was his friend, it hid him. Allowed him to move freely. He began climbing the cellar steps towards the door, the gnawing in his belly growing stronger by the second.

Liz Maynard held the book close to her face, peering through her glasses at the print before her. She was holding the paperback in one hand, the other she had balled into a fist beneath the sheet. As she read she would murmur aloud at each fresh development in the chapter, turning the pages with trepidation as the huge flesh-eating creature drew nearer to the hero and heroine who were trapped in a deserted house. She shuddered, lowering the book for a moment when a particularly powerful gust of wind rattled the bedroom window in its frame. After a moment she returned to the book, reading more quickly than usual now. The creature was stalking the young couple and Liz began to tug on the sheet in the anxiousness. The dull glow of the bedside lamp added even more atmosphere to the proceedings and she was completely caught up in her horrifying read. So caught up that she didn't notice she was pulling all of the sheets and covers to her side of the bed.

The creature in the book had found the young couple and was now chasing them.

A hand reached up and grabbed her wrist.

Liz yelped and dropped the book, looking down to

167

see her husband glaring up at her, trying to claw back some of the covers which she had pulled off him.

She let out a sigh of relief and glared down at Jack.

"You frightened me to death," she said.

"You were pulling all the bloody clothes off," he protested. Then he smiled, picking up the book which she'd dropped. He glanced at the cover. It showed a creature with glowing red eyes and huge teeth, dripping blood. "How the hell can you read this sort of rubbish?" he asked, grinning.

She snatched back the book indignantly and placed it on the bedside table with half a dozen others like it.

"It's very good actually," she said, defensively. "Besides, reading this sort of book is good for you. It's a medical fact, and so is watching horror films. It does you good to have a fright every now and then."

Jack nodded.

"Well, the bloody tax man frightens me, without having to read about monsters from hell and things with two heads." He exhaled deeply. "You know I don't know what's more disturbing, the fact that people part with good money to buy the damn things or that there's someone somewhere who dreams them up. I mean, what sort of mentality must a bloke have to write a book like that?"

"You've got no imagination, Jack, that's your trouble," she told him. "You should let yourself go every once in a while. Try reading one of these."

He snorted indignantly.

"I should think so. There's enough horrors in the real world without having to make them up."

She blew a raspberry at him and they both laughed. Married for twenty-eight years, they ran a small shop on the outskirts of Exham selling everything from fresh vegetables to newspapers. They were a rare and welcome commodity in the age of the supermarket and had a large and loyal clientele to prove it.

Liz leant over flicked off the bedside lamp, pulling the covers up around her neck as she settled down.

She was in the process of adjusting her pillows when she heard a distant crash. It sounded distinctly like breaking glass. She sat up, ears straining to pick up any other noise. The window rattled frenziedly in the frame for a second then the powerful gust seemed to ease and silence descended once more. Liz lay down again, ears pricked, heart thumping just that bit faster. She closed her eyes. Jack was already snoring softly beside her, he took a short course in death when he went to bed.

The noise came again and this time she was sure it was breaking glass. Liz sat up, simultaneously shaking her husband. He grunted and opened his eyes.

"What's wrong?" he said, thickly.

"Listen," she said. "I heard something."

Jack Maynard hauled himself up the bed and propped his head against the board at the top.

"I know I heard something," she repeated.

"What was it?"

She told him.

"Probably the wind, love." He smiled. "Or your imagination running away with you after reading that bloody book."

She was just about to agree with him when they both heard a much louder crash. This time it was Jack who reacted. He swung himself out of bed and walked to the bedroom door, opening it as quietly as he could. There was no light on in the landing and it was like looking out into a wall of blackness. A couple of yards ahead lay the staircase which led down into their sitting room. Beyond that, lay the shop itself. As he stood there, he heard unmistakable sounds of movement from below him. Hurriedly, he closed the door and padded back towards the bed.

"I think there's someone in the shop," he said, quietly.

"Oh God," Liz murmured. "We'll have to call the police."

Jack nodded.

"I know," he said, cryptically. "But just in case you'd forgotten, the bloody phone is in the living room. I'll have to go downstairs anyway." Even as he spoke he knelt, reaching beneath the bed and pulling out a long leather case. He lifted it up onto the bed and unzipped it, pulling back the cover to reveal a gleaming double-barrelled shotgun which he hurriedly loaded.

Liz reached across and flicked the lamp switch.

Nothing happened.

She got out of bed and crossed to the main point, flicking it on. The room, however, remained in darkness.

"Oh Christ," muttered Jack. "The wind must have brought a power line down."

"Or someone's been at the fuse box," Liz said, ominously.

He nodded, touching her cheek with his free hand, noticing how cold it was.

"Jack, please be careful," she whispered.

"It's probably just somebody larking about," he said, reassuring neither Liz or himself. "I'll give them a bit of a fright." He hefted the shotgun in front of him. "You close this door behind me."

She nodded, watching as he moved cautiously out onto the landing, immediately enveloped by the inky blackness. He motioned to her to close the door which she did, resting her forehead against it for long moments, her heart hammering against her ribs.

The wind swept around the shop, growling at the windows like some beast of prey.

Jack Maynard could hear it too as he padded stealthily across the landing, moving with surprising agility for a man of his size. He paused at the top step and peered down into the gloom. The darkness was like a thick,

170

clinging blanket wrapping itself around him as he stood there, breathing softly. He gripped the shotgun tighter but, he reasoned, with it being so dark he wouldn't even be able to see the intruder if he decided to come at him. The bloody gun was useless in such impenetrable gloom. It was like trying to teach a blind man to shoot bottles.

Cursing the power failure, Jack began to descend the stairs.

The third one creaked beneath him and he stood still, a thin film of perspiration greasing his face. He could still hear some distant scrabblings from beyond, now certain that the intruder was in the shop. He moved more quickly down the stairs, the shotgun held across his chest, ready to swing up to his shoulder at the slightest hint of movement. As he reached the bottom of the stairs he flicked the light switch there.

The room remained in darkness.

Jack swallowed hard and moved cautiously through the living room, narrowing his eyes in an effort to make out the dark shapes before him. Some light was coming in through a window but most of that was masked by the large tree which towered outside. To his left lay the door to the kitchen. Straight ahead the door which would take him through into the shop.

He banged his shin against the coffee table and almost overbalanced, stifling a yelp of surprise as he struggled to remain upright. He cursed silently and rubbed his injured leg, ears still alert for any sounds. Other than the howling of the wind, he could hear nothing. His heart jumped a beat and he strained his ears for the noises which he'd heard just moments earlier.

Something cracked against the window pane and Jack swung round, bringing the shotgun up, his thumb instinctively jerking one of the twin hammers back. He saw that it was a tree branch which had struck the glass, the bony fingers of low branches clawing at the window as if seeking entry. He breathed an audible sigh of relief then, turning, decided to check the kitchen before progessing into the shop itself.

It too was empty.

As Jack stepped back into the sitting room the lights flashed on momentarily but the welcome illumination was all too brief and, seconds later, the house was plunged back into darkness.

He reached the door which would take him through into the shop, his hand quivering as he reached for the key. He glimpsed the phone out of the corner of his eye. Should he call the police now? He inhaled deeply. Sod it, he'd have a look for himself.

The lights flickered once more as he reached for the key and turned it.

Paul Harvey heard the door open slightly as Jack Maynard entered the shop. He had heard the other man moving about in the sitting room moments earlier and so he had ducked down behind one of the three counters inside the main room. The one behind which he sought shelter was topped by tin cans and through those Harvey could see the man edge his way cautiously forwards, towards the front door. A small pane in the door had been broken and, as Jack touched it, the wooden partition was blown open by a particularly violent gust of wind.

The shopkeeper jumped back, the gun at hip height.

Harvey saw the weapon and touched his chin thoughtfully. He looked up and saw the door through which the other man had come. Moving as swiftly and silently as he could, he scuttled towards it and disappeared inside the sitting room.

Liz Maynard paced back and forth beside the bed listening for any sounds of movement from beneath her. She looked at the clock on the bedside table, then

172

checked it against her own watch. Jack seemed to have been gone an eternity. The lights flickered on briefly yet again and she gasped aloud at the suddenness of it. What the hell was he doing down there? She hadn't heard his voice. Why wasn't he phoning the police? Perhaps whoever it was that had broken in had attacked him down there in the dark, he could be lying there now with his throat cut. Thoughts tumbled wildly through her mind. She sat on the edge of the bed but her entire body was trembling so she took to her pacings once more. Another glance at the clock. She would give him one more minute then, warning or not, she would go down after him. Her own anxiety about Jack had to a certain extent overcome her fear. She watched as the second hand swept round, marking off the minute.

"Bastards," muttered Jack Maynard.

He was standing before one of the shelves in the shop. The jars had been taken down, the tops wrenched off and some of the contents spread over the floor of the shop. Remnants of half eaten fruit also littered the dusty floor. A can of soup had been gashed open with something sharp, the cold contents now gone. Jack frowned, whoever had broken in must have been *really* hungry if they were prepared to drink cold soup. He hefted the riven can before him, the shotgun cradled over his other arm. Other cans and jars had been taken, one of the shelves all but empty. Sweets, kept on the counter to his right with the newspapers, had also been taken by the handful. Kids? He shook his head. Kids wouldn't do this. He put the can down wondering just who the hell would?

Liz Maynard could wait no longer. She opened the bedroom door and peered out onto the landing, her heart pounding. It was still pitch black out there and she moved somewhat nervously towards the hand-rail.

173

There was no sound from the sitting room below or the shop itself, only the ever-present roaring of the wind. She placed one hand against the wall and took the stairs tentatively, one at a time. As she reached the third one, the lights flashed on and continued to fill the house with their glow for a full minute and a half.

Liz Maynard screamed.

Harvey was already half way up the stairs, the sickle gripped in his fist.

She turned and ran back to the bedroom, hearing the heavy footsteps thudding up the stairs behind her. She screamed again as she threw the door shut and pressed her pitiful weight against it, expecting at any second for him to launch his huge bulk against it. Instead, she heard the loud thud and the splintering of wood as he buried the sickle's vicious curved blade in the door. The point protruded a few inches through it and, as Harvey tore it free, a panel was ripped loose.

She screamed again.

Jack heard her and dashed into the sitting room, looking up to see the large figure of Harvey poised before the bedroom door, the sickle swinging back and forth as it made matchwood of the partition. Jack raised the shotgun to his shoulder simultaneously yelling something at the madman who turned to face him. Harvey moved with lightning speed and, slobbering like a rabid animal, threw himself to the ground.

There was a thunderous roar as the shotgun barrel exploded in an orgasm of fire and lead, the sound amplified by the enclosed space. The deadly load struck the wall just above Harvey's head. Paint and lumps of plaster were blasted away by the impact and Jack cursed aloud when he saw Harvey scramble to his feet, running across the landing towards the solitary window there.

He hit it with the force of a steam train, crashing through the glass and wood, heedless of what lay

174

below. Shards of crystal sprayed out in all directions as Harvey hurtled through. He clutched at empty air for a second before plummeting to earth. He crashed into a privet hedge, the wind knocked from him, but, other than that, he was unharmed. He rolled clear and got to his feet.

Jack Maynard ran to the window and looked out in time to see Harvey loping off into the darkness. Then, the shotgun still gripped tight in his hand, he dashed into the bedroom where he found Liz on her knees beside the bed sobbing uncontrollably. It took him fully fifteen minutes to calm her down then, that done, he made his way downstairs and dialled three nines.

Twenty-eight

Inspector Lou Randall skimmed the file once more then threw it down onto his desk.

"Jesus Christ," he growled. "Doesn't anybody ever see this bastard? What is he a man or a fucking ghost?" He leant back in his chair and rubbed his face with both hands, feeling the stubble on his cheeks and chin as he did so. He'd been called out at six that morning and had driven to the police station without shaving or eating. His stomach rumbled disapprovingly and his mouth felt like the bottom of a birdcage.

"Who found this one?" he asked, wearily.

"A milkman," Norman Willis told him. "He said the body was lying in the road. No attempt to hide it." The sergeant studied his superior's worried face. "He wasn't making much sense when Charlton took the statement from him." He paused. "He's still badly shaken up."

Randall grunted.

"I'm not surprised," he said. "Finding a headless body at half past five in the morning lying in the middle of the street is enough to give anyone the bloody shakes." He glanced at the report again. "Same murder weapon?" It came out more as a confirmation than a question.

Willis nodded.

"Everything about it is the same as Ian Logan's murder. Rust in the wounds, a single-bladed weapon and the head was taken."

Randall fumbled in his pocket for his cigarettes, finding them with some difficulty. There was only one in the packet and he tossed the empty receptacle away, not really bothering whether it reached the waste-bin or not. He lit the fag and drew hard on it.

"What about this other incident?" he said, picking up Jack Maynard's statement regarding Harvey's attack and break-in. Willis told his superior about it while Randall quickly read the statement himself.

"The break-in happened at half past one," said Randall. He flipped open the file in front of him. "The pathologist's report puts the time of death at around two." He tapped on the desk top with his index finger as if seeking some kind of magical inspiration, a clue to what the hell he was going to do next. "He didn't kill anyone at the shop where he broke in, maybe he lost his rag and decided he owed himself one anyway. This poor sod just happened to be the first one he came across." He took another drag on his cigarette. "Where was the body found? Which side of town?"

"Going out towards the main road into Mayford. There's lots of fields out that way," Willis explained.

"Is it being checked?" Randall wanted to know.

"Not yet, we're spread a bit thin at the moment trying to find him but as soon as a car calls in I'll send them out that way."

The Inspector nodded.

"I just don't get it," he said, wearily. "How the hell can Harvey just keep disappearing like he does? He must be hiding somewhere around Exham and yet we've already checked it over once." The Inspector smiled sardonically. "Perhaps he's not as mad as everyone seems to think he is."

"They always say that it's the brains who are locked up and the lunatics who are free," added Willis, shrugging.

"I'm beginning to agree," said Randall. He ground out his cigarette, watching the plume of grey smoke rise mournfully into the air.

"We'll get him, guv," said Willis.

Randall raised an eyebrow, questioningly.

"Can I have that in writing?" he said, humourlessly. The phone rang and, as he picked it up, Willis turned to leave. Randall picked up the receiver, quickly cupping his hand over the mouthpiece. "Hey, Norman, a cup of tea would go down a treat."

Willis smiled and left.

Randall pressed the phone to his ear.

"Inspector Randall speaking."

"I'm not going to beat about the bush, Randall," said the voice at the other end, one which the Inspector immediately recognized as belonging to Chief Inspector Frank Allen. There was a harsh, cold quality to the CI's voice which made it unmistakable. The younger man stiffened in his chair.

"Yes, sir," he said, wondering what his superior wanted. He glanced across at the wall clock opposite him and saw that it was almost 9.05 a.m. Whatever the miserable old sod wanted must be important, Randall mused.

"I understand you're having some problems down there," said Allen. "This escaped maniac, Harvey isn't it? How long has he been free now?"

177

Randall swallowed hard.

"Just over nine weeks, sir. Everything possible is being done to apprehend him. My men. . ."

"And how many has he killed. One or two?"

Randall paled.

"Two, sir." It came out almost as a confession.

Allen exhaled deeply, his voice taking on an even harder edge.

"I see," he said. "Well, look Randall, you don't need me to tell you how serious this whole business is. Your inability to find the man in the beginning was bad enough but now this. For Christ's sake put the lid on it and find Harvey quickly." There was a pause, during which time the CI's mood seemed to lighten a little. "Do you need any help?"

"A couple of bloodhounds I think, sir," he japed.

"Don't be facetious, Randall," Allen snapped. "This series of events is not going to look very good on your record. Now, I asked if you needed any help."

The Inspector clenched his fists until the knuckles were bloodless, trying hard to control his anger.

"Some extra men wouldn't go amiss, sir," he said, brusquely.

"Very well. But catch this bastard. Quick."

"Yes, sir."

Allen hung up.

Randall held the receiver in his hand for a second, listening to the persistent drone then, angrily, he slammed it down onto the cradle. He had the uncomfortable suspicion that someone was keeping tabs on him. Christ, he wanted a cigarette but, as he peered at the empty packet nearby he could only mutter irritably to himself. "Catch Harvey". He shook his head. Any ideas where we should start, big head? He thought, glaring at the phone, the anger still boiling inside him. He got to his feet and looked at the map of the town on his office wall. It bore two red crosses, each marking the scene of the murders. Both were in different parts of Exham. At least two miles separated the scene of each crime. Randall stood gazing helplessly at the map.

"Come out, come out wherever you are, you bastard," murmured the Inspector.

Twenty-nine

The windscreen wipers of the Audi swept slowly back and forth across the glass, brushing away the rain which had been falling steadily for the past three hours.

"I need a new set of blades," muttered Mick Calvin, jabbing a finger at the area on the windscreen which was still rainsoaked.

"You always need something, Mick," said his wife, Diane, firmly belted into the passenger seat beside him. "I think it's about time we had a new car."

Calvin snorted.

"Well, my darling," he said, sarcastically. "As soon as we get home you write me a cheque for six thousand and I'll nip out and get us one."

"You know what I mean," she said, irritably. "*You've* been saying the same yourself for months."

"I just wish your bloody mother didn't live so far away," he added.

Diane studied his profile for a second.

"I suppose it's her fault that the car's falling to bits?" she said, acidly.

"Did I say that? I just said that it's a long drive to where she lives."

Diane smiled impishly.

"She could always come and live with us, that would save the journey."

She laughed aloud at the expression which crossed her husband's face.

"I could get to like long journeys," he said, smiling.

"She wouldn't be any trouble."

"That's what they said about Hitler."

Diane punched him playfully on the arm.

"Dad, can we stop?"

The voice came from the back seat where Richie, their eldest son at eleven, was dressed in a pair of freshly pressed jeans and a Spiderman sweatshirt. He was on his knees, pulling at his crutch agitatedly. Beside him sat his brother, Wayne, two years younger, his face round and red as if he'd been holding his breath for a long time.

"Dad."

"What?" said Calvin.

"Can't we stop? Wayne and me both want to go for a wee," he protested.

"Can't you hold it? We're nearly home now," said Calvin. "And it's Wayne and *I*," he added as an afterthought.

The oldest lad was bouncing up and down now.

"Dad," he persisted, clutching his groin with both hands, as if letting go would release a flood tide.

"Oh, pull over, Mick," Diane said. "They can nip behind a hedge."

"It's wet out there you know," said Calvin, as if trying to deter his two sons.

Diane looked at Wayne who was going ever redder in a monumental effort of self-control which he was obviously going to lose at any minute.

"It's going to be wet in here if you don't pull over," she said.

Calvin nodded and glanced ahead for a suitable place to stop. There were fields all around them but few

180

seemed to be blessed with bushes. He saw the massive edifice of Fairvale hospital towering above a row of trees and remembered that there was a lay-by just beyond. The fields that backed onto the hospital itself would offer plenty of cover for the two kids. He could see the electricity pylons towering over the field, their cables swaying in the breeze. Checking his rear-view mirror, he swung the Audi across the road and into the lay-by. Immediately, the two kids were fumbling for the door locks in their efforts to get out and Calvin couldn't resist a smile as he watched them both scramble out of the car.

"Go behind those bushes over there," he said, pointing towards some bare gorse bushes which masked a sizeable hollow in the field. The hollow ran from the base of one of the towering pylons.

He and Diane watched as the kids clambered over the low fence which separated the lay-by from the field, then both of the boys were racing towards the bushes. They disappeared behind the bushes and Calvin grinned broadly.

"Do you want to go as well?" he asked Diane. "There's plenty more bushes in the field." He laughed.

"No," she whispered, leaning closer. "But I'll tell you what I do want." She pulled him to her and their mouths met eagerly. She spoke something into his ear, kissing the lobe as she did so, one hand straying to his thigh.

"Now that *will* have to wait until we get home," he said.

They both laughed.

The screams which they heard made them both sit bolt upright, but it was a matter of seconds before Calvin was unhooking his seat belt, pushing open the car door. He slipped as he leapt out onto the wet tarmac but regained his balance and hurried towards the fence. Diane was close behind him, her high heels sinking into the mud as she reached the low wooden fence. She struggled over it, seeing that her husband was already racing towards the bushes where the screams were coming from.

He was panting madly, the high pitched screams of his sons ringing in his ears as he ran. The rain plastered hair to his face but he ignored it and ran on, his only concern to reach his children. As he drew closer, he saw Richie staggering from behind the bushes, his face colourless, his mouth open. Behind him came Wayne, his jeans wet around the crutch, his flies still open. By now, Diane could see them. She called their names but no sound seemed to come, she was mouthing the words but only silence escaped her.

Calvin reached his eldest son and held him by the shoulders, gazing into his eyes that were bulging wide and red-rimmed. He was motioning behind him, his breath coming out in deep, racking sobs. Wayne merely stood where he was, apparently oblivious to the rain. Calvin hurried across and lifted the boy into his arms. He seemed limp, like a puppet with its wires cut and, but for the fact that his eyes were open and blinking, he had the appearance of a waxwork model.

"What's wrong?"

It was Diane's voice, trembling and full of fear.

"Wayne, Richie, what is it?" she repeated.

Calvin himself held the eldest boy close to his chest while Diane took over the responsibility for Wayne.

"There," gasped Richie, once more motioning behind him.

"Take them both back to the car," said Calvin but Diane hesitated, watching as he walked behind the bushes and along the depression in the field, stopping at one point. He turned to face Diane, her hair now hanging in dripping coils.

"Take them back," said Calvin, waving Diane away.

"What is it, Mick?" she demanded.

182

"Take them back to the car," he shouted and the vehemence in his voice startled her. She turned and led the two children back across the field towards the shelter of the Audi.

Calvin watched them, waiting until he saw them reach the vehicle before returning his attention to what he had found. He bent, squatting on his haunches, peering at the rain-sodden earth. The grass had been dug over in an area he guessed measuring about twelve feet by six. The mud was sticky and oozing, like reeking gravy and, through this thin film of muck, he could see a face. It was the face of a baby although the definition was questionable. The head, uncovered by the torrential rain, was bulbous with two large growths over the holes where the eyes should have been. In the black pits of sockets worms writhed, one of them disappearing into the open mouth of the putrescing body and it was all Calvin could do to stop himself from vomiting. One rotted, mottled arm protruded from the earth nearby, the fingers stubby, two of them missing. Close to that an entire tiny corpse had been uncovered by the elements. What remained of it had been gnawed in places, maybe by rats or a badger. The stomach had been torn open to reveal a seething mess of mouldering viscera. The stench rising from the grave was overpowering and Calvin took a handkerchief from his pocket to cover his nose, his head swimming. He counted at least half a dozen pieces of human debris and one complete corpse. What lay deeper he could only guess at. He stood up, swaying slightly, the realization that he was indeed standing beside some kind of grave, sweeping over him as surely as the choking stench which wafted from it on invisible clouds. He stood there for long seconds, his eyes fixed on the worm-eaten, ravaged body of one of the foetuses then, as he saw one of the slimy creatures wriggle from a hole in the

183

corpse's stomach like some kind of animated umbilical cord, he finally lost control and vomited violently.

Diane, watching from the back seat of the car, where she was doing her best to comfort the two boys, saw her husband tottering drunkenly back across the field. He finally reached the wooden fence and swung himself over it, supporting himself against the Audi before pulling the driver's side door open. He flopped heavily into the seat and sat motionless, gazing ahead. Diane could hear his laboured breathing.

"We've got to report this," he said, falteringly, reaching for the ignition key and turning it.

"What did you find, Mick?" she demanded. "For God's sake tell me."

He lowered his head momentarily.

"There's . . . something buried." He coughed and, for a moment, thought he was going to be sick again. He gritted his teeth and the feeling diminished somewhat. "Something . . . embryos. There's a grave in that field." He sucked in a deep breath. "We've got to report it, now."

He started the car, swung it round and headed back towards Fairvale's main entrance.

Within an hour he had made a full report to a senior doctor and, thirty minutes later, Mick Calvin led that same doctor and three porters, Harold Pierce amongst them, to the spot where he'd found the grave. And there, under the watchful eyes of both men, five aborted foetuses were uncovered. The bodies were put into a sack and carried back to the hospital where they were disposed of in the usual way. Cast into the mouth of the furnace as they should have been weeks before.

Harold watched as the tiny bodies were born away for disposal his body shaking.

The voices inside his head had begun to chatter once more.

184

Thirty

Harold sat nervously in the outer office, his hands clasped on his knees. The room was large, a white-walled enclosure which he shared with just three leather chairs and a secretary who sat across from him hammering away at the keys of an old Imperial type-writer. The constant clacking sounded like dozens of tiny explosions. The secretary herself was a woman in her forties, a plump lady with greying hair swept back from a face coated with far too much make-up. It seemed to shine beneath the banks of fluorescents set into the ceiling. There was a mug on her desk with a slogan written on it in large red letters. Harold wond-ered if it was her name as he saw the word June on it. She glanced up at him every now and then and when she did, he would self-consciously touch the scarred side of his face as if trying to shield it from her gaze. She smiled at him warmly and he returned the gesture sheepishly. He shifted uncomfortably in his seat which made a sound like someone breaking wind, as is the wont of leather chairs. Harold tried to sit still but it was a difficult task. He glanced up at the wall clock above the secretary's head. It showed 4.26 p.m. Below it was a painting which Harold could not make out. It was just squares, all painted different colours, forming no pattern or shape. Not unlike the paintings Harold himself had done in occupational therapy.

The memory of those days seemed so distant now. Then he had felt as if he belonged at the hospital. He had friends and, more importantly, he was not burd-ened with responsibility as he was now. It seemed like a million years ago. Now he sat in the outer office, waiting, remembering back to just a few hours ago when he had helped to disinter the foetuses which he had spent so much care saving in the first place. Saving was the word to describe his actions but now he feared that they would punish him for it. He closed his eyes and allowed his head to rest against the wall. Immediately, the buzzing in his ears became the rasping voices which he had come to know so well.

Harold sat up, his eyelids jerking open. He looked around, as if expecting to see someone sitting next to him but then he realized that the voices were inside his head.

He swallowed hard.

There was a loud bleep and a green light flared on the console beside the secretary. She flipped a switch and Harold heard her say something into the inter-com. When she'd finished speaking she looked up at Harold, smiled and told him to go in. He nodded, got to his feet and made for the varnished door to his right. It bore a nameplate:

Dr Kenneth McManus, R.C.S.

Harold knocked and received the instruction to enter. He walked in to find Brian Cayton in there as well as McManus who was shielded behind a huge mahogany desk. He motioned for Harold to sit down and brief pleasantries were exchanged. McManus was a big man, tall but muscular with sunken cheeks and lustrous black hair which was brushed back, accentuating the widow's peak he had. His eyes were set close together, rather like fog lamps on the front of a car, only these particular lights glowed with a pale grey hue as Harold found himself pinned beneath their gaze.

"Pierce, isn't it," said McManus, smiling thinly.

Harold nodded.

"How long have you been with us?"

"Two months, sir," said Harold, lowering his head, slightly. "Perhaps a bit longer."

"And you were entrusted with the disposal of aborted foetuses on a number of occasions during this time.

186

Correct?" The words had a harsh, almost accusatory ring to them.

Harold nodded.

"Did you in fact complete the disposal procedure?" McManus wanted to know.

"I did as I was told, sir," Harold insisted, a slight pain gnawing at the back of his neck.

McManus nodded in the direction of Cayton who was sitting to Harold's left.

"Mr Cayton tells me that you tried to prevent him from disposing of a dead foetus," said the doctor. "Is this true?"

"I didn't feel well that day," Harold said, blankly, his one good eye staring right through McManus. He appeared to be in a dazed condition, his mouth forming words which his mind had not formulated.

"How many other times have you tried to interfere with the disposal procedure?"

"I haven't done . . . I didn't try to stop anyone else." The words were coming slowly, monosyllabically. As if each one were an effort. Something not unnoticed by either the doctor or Cayton.

"Are you all right, Pierce?" asked McManus.

"Yes, sir," Harold insisted.

Doctor and porter exchanged puzzled looks.

"Did *you* bury those bodies in the field, Pierce?" McManus wanted to know.

Harold hesitated, closing his eyes for a moment.

He shook his head.

"Why do the children have to be burned?" he asked, looking straight at the doctor with a stare which made the other man recoil.

McManus sucked in a troubled breath.

"Could you wait outside for a while please, Pierce?" he said, watching as the porter got unsteadily to his feet and walked to the door, closing it gently behind him.

"Pierce was the only one who could have prevented the disposal of the five foetuses we found in the field. Correct?" said McManus.

Cayton nodded.

"Yes, sir, but God knows how he did it," the porter confessed.

"I think it's more to the point, *why* he did it? Although his past would go some way to explaining that I suppose." The doctor exhaled deeply. "I don't see that we have any alternative other than to dismiss him. It's unfortunate but I'm just grateful the papers didn't find out about it."

"Wasn't there a similar case in Germany a few years ago?" said Cayton. "Only there, they'd been making soap out of the remains."

McManus raised one eyebrow.

"He lives on the grounds doesn't he?"

"Yes," Cayton told him. "In that old hut."

"Well, I'm afraid he'll have to leave there too."

"What if he's got nowhere to go, sir?"

"That's not our problem, Cayton. The man is obviously unbalanced in some way. He'll probably end up back in an institution. Probably the best place for him. I just don't want him in *my* hospital." The doctor was already reaching for a switch on the console before him. He flipped it up.

"Send Pierce back in will you, please," he said, settling back in his chair, hands clasped across his lap.

Harold re-entered and sat down, listening unconcernedly as McManus explained that he was to lose his job. It wasn't until the doctor mentioned leaving the hut that the older porter showed any trace of reaction. His one good eye seemed to bulge momentarily but the moment passed and he sat in silence as the reasons for his dismissal were reeled off. But Harold wasn't listening to McManus, his attention was focused on the voices which spoke to him from within. The doctor finally finished and leant forward in his chair, glancing first at Cayton and then at Harold.

"I'm sorry things turned out like this, Pierce," he said. "I realize your problems. Perhaps you would be better off. . ." he was struggling to find the words, rummaging amidst the welter of bluntness for a few morsels of tact. "It might be best if you returned to the institution. I can contact doctor Vincent, I'm sure, if you have nowhere else to go, he would understand."

"Thank you," said Harold, blankly, absently touching the scarred side of his face. It felt dry beneath his fingers.

"Do you have somewhere to go, Harold?" asked Cayton.

"Yes." The word came out almost angrily. "I have somewhere to go." He got to his feet, a new found strength filling him. "I have somewhere to go."

A hissing, sibilant command sounded so loud inside his head that he almost winced but he turned and walked towards the door, moving as if each step were an effort.

"Goodbye," he said and left them.

It was a long time before either McManus or Cayton spoke.

As Harold stepped into the lift he looked straight through Maggie Ford. She smiled at him but the gesture provoked no response. His one good eye looked as glassy as the false one, his skin was the colour of rancid butter.

"Harold." Maggie put out her hand to touch his shoulder.

He looked at her again, some of the mistiness vanishing from that blank stare. He touched his face and swallowed hard.

"Harold, are you all right?" she asked him, as the lift doors slid shut.

He opened his mouth to speak, his lips fluttering noiselessly.

The words inside his head became warnings.

Harold looked squarely at Maggie, his brow furrowing slightly. She released her grip on his shoulder, much as someone would let go of a dog when they'd just discovered it was liable to bite them at any minute. The doctor regarded Harold warily, somewhat relieved when his expression changed to its customary calm blankness.

"I'm leaving here," he said, softly.

Maggie looked puzzled.

"Leaving? Why?"

"They told me to leave. Because of the children."

"What children, Harold?" she demanded. "And who asked you to leave?"

"Doctor McManus told me to leave." He gazed at her with that seething vehemence once more, his face darkening.

"They kill the children," he hissed.

Maggie was almost relieved when the lift reached its appointed floor and she could step out and away from Harold. She glanced back at him, watching as the doors slid shut on his disfigured visage. She waited a moment then took the stairs up to the fourth floor and Doctor McManus's office.

Maggie didn't time how long she was in the senior consultant's office but she guessed later that it couldn't have been more than five minutes. She tried to persuade her superior that Harold was in a bad way both physically and mentally.

"He's ill," she insisted. "He should be taken into care, not thrown out onto the streets."

McManus was unimpressed.

"He committed a breach of hospital regulations," the

190

older man said. "He's lucky he's not being prosecuted never mind dismissed."

When she asked what he meant, he explained about the foetuses, the grave in the field, how Harold had hidden the bodies and then interred them in secret rather than incinerating them.

"Oh God," murmured Maggie.

"*Now* do you understand why he has to go?" said McManus, irritably. "The man's disturbed. I should never have taken him on in the first place."

"Well then that's all the more reason to take him into care," Maggie insisted.

"He needs psychiatric help, not medical help."

She told him about the cuts on Harold's body but McManus was obviously tiring of the conversation and it showed in the sharp edge which his words acquired.

"As far as I'm concerned, Miss Ford, the matter is closed. Pierce will be out of the grounds by tomorrow morning." He looked at his watch, tapping the glass. "Now I suggest you return to *your* duties. I presume you have patients to attend to?"

"Yes, doctor," she said, her face flushed.

She left the office, closing the door just a little too firmly behind her. There was something badly wrong with Harold and she was determined to find out what it was. She glanced at her watch. It was 5.30 p.m., in another two hours she would be off duty. When that time came, she decided she would go to Harold's hut and speak to him.

Thirty-one

Harold moved slowly about the hut collecting what few possessions he had, bundling them into the battered old suitcase he'd been lent. Every now and then he would stop still and glance towards the kitchen, as if trying to catch sight of something. The voices whispered insistently inside his head, like the wind rustling paper.

He heard scuffling sounds coming from the cupboard in the kitchen. There was hessian laid out before it and, when the last item was dropped into the suitcase, Harold passed into the other room and knelt before the door, his hand quivering slightly as he slid it open.

A vile, cloying stench billowed from the hiding place and Harold recoiled at the ferocity of the odour. He gazed into the cupboard, mesmerized.

All three of the foetuses had doubled in size.

Maggie Ford glanced at the clock on the wall of her office and noted that it was approaching 7.40 p.m. She sat back in her seat, slipping the cap back onto her pen. Her neck and shoulders ached and she reached up with both hands to perform some swift massage. Outside, the sky was mottled with rain clouds and a thin film of drizzle covered the office window like a gossamer shroud. Maggie yawned and got to her feet, remembering that she'd promised herself a visit to Harold's hut before she went home that night. She took off her white coat and hung it up on the hook, pulling on a lightweight mac in its place. She glanced at a chart on the office wall and noticed that she was due in surgery at eight-thirty the following morning. Maggie took one final look around the office then flicked off the light and left.

She took the lift down to the ground floor, mumbling

a few hasty "goodnights" on her way to the main entrance. When she reached it she paused, pulling up her collar to protect herself from the worst ravages of the icy wind. The chill in the air was turning the drizzle into particles of sleet and Maggie shivered, turning to her left, heading towards the open stretch of ground which would take her to Harold's hut. Almost invisible in the gloom, she could see that no lights burned inside and she wondered if perhaps he'd gone to bed. As far as she knew he didn't go out at nights so it was more than likely that he was in the small dwelling. She muttered to herself as her heels sank into the soft earth but she struggled on towards the still and black shrouded hut.

She found herself shivering but the movements were not merely a product of the cold weather. She felt an unaccountable fear rising within her as she drew nearer to the building. Perhaps it had been Harold's reactions in the lift which had unsettled her, she thought, angry with herself for feeling the trepidation she now experienced. It was pity she should be feeling for Harold, not fear.

Maggie found that the door of the hut was slightly ajar. She knocked all the same, simultaneously calling the older man's name. When she received no answer, she cautiously pushed the wooden door which swung back on its hinges with a high pitched shriek. Maggie called Harold's name once more then stepped inside.

The smell of damp was almost overpowering but mingled with it was a more pungent odour which she had difficulty identifying. She looked around the interior of the place. The bed had been stripped, the sheets and blankets gone but, on the mattress she noticed a dark stain. Now dried and powdery, the substance seemed to crumble beneath her probing fingers. She wet the tip of her index finger and on withdrawing it from the mysterious patch she found that it was congealed blood. Maggie swallowed hard and looked around. The door to her right, the one which led through to the kitchen, was closed.

"Harold," she called, moving towards the door.

The hut greeted her with silence.

She pushed the door but found that it was stuck.

Maggie tried again and, this time, it budged a few inches. She put her weight against it, realizing that the door was a fraction of an inch too large and was sticking. Eventually, she succeeded in opening it and found herself standing in the tiny kitchen.

The door of the cupboard beneath the sink was open, the handle splashed with blood.

Maggie squatted before it and squinted through the gloom at the crimson liquid. It glistened in the half-light and she could see that it was fresh. There was a fetid stench coming from the cupboard and Maggie paused for long seconds before deciding to look inside. She gripped the handle, trying to avoid the blood, and pulled it open.

There was something inside the cupboard, something which she couldn't see in the blackness. Something moving.

She could hear a faint scratching too, an agitated skittering which stopped abruptly. The cupboard was large, large enough for a fully grown man to climb into but Maggie certainly had no intentions of crawling inside to see what was making the noise. She coughed, her eye suddenly caught by something which lay on the wooden floor beside her. She picked up the matted strands, turning them over in her fingers.

There was a sudden movement from within the cupboard and Maggie screamed as something soft and furry brushed against her leg. She dropped the stiff fur, almost overbalancing.

The mouse scampered away, past her and disappeared through a hole in the wall.

194

Maggie sucked in a deep breath, held it for a second then exhaled.

"God," she murmured and got to her feet.

She ran both hands through her hair and blew out a troubled breath. Harold Pierce was gone, no doubt about that. But exactly where, she had no idea.

The old Exham Mental Hospital now stood deserted and already dust had begun to accumulate in thick layers on the floors and window-ledges. Some of the windows had been broken, the dirty glass lying in the wards which were now empty of beds. It was as black as pitch in the empty building and Harold blinked his one good eye repeatedly, as if the action would somehow give him the power to see through the darkness. But he had lived at the hospital for so long he knew every inch of it and he moved with assurance through the long corridors, his tired footsteps echoing loudly in the silence. He was aware of nothing but the musty smell of the place and the aching in his legs where he had walked for so long. He had no idea what the time was but, outside, a large watery moon gave him some light and illuminated his stumbling progess somewhat.

He had left the three foetuses in a room on the first floor while he himself explored the remains of the deserted asylum. For the first time in months he actually felt happy. It was like a homecoming for him. He belonged here in this place, in this empty Victorian shell which smelt of damp and was thick with dust. It had been his home for so many years before and now it would be his home again.

He paused at the foot of the staircase which would take him up to the first floor, the voices hissing in his ears again. They were calling him and Harold made his way almost eagerly to his room where they waited.

Thirty-two

Lynn Tyler grunted as she felt the weight of the man's body on top of her. She sucked in a deep breath but it slowly subsided into a groan of pleasure as she felt his swollen penis slide into her. He bent his head forward, his unshaven cheek scraping her.

"Don't you ever shave?" she murmured, her complaint dissolving away into another exclamation of pleasure as he began thrusting into her with firm strokes.

She couldn't remember his name. Barry or Gary. Something like that. It didn't matter much to her either way. She'd picked him up at a disco about two hours earlier and was now enjoying the consummation of what, for her, was to be yet another notch on the bedstead.

She ran a hand through his thick black hair, wincing slightly as she felt the slick greasiness of it. His breath smelt of beer and, when he kissed her, it was a clumsy slobbering action, rather like being accosted by a Saint Bernard. However, she weathered his attentions, enjoying the sensations he was creating within her. One of his rough hands went to her breast and squeezed hard. So hard that she yelped in pain but all he did was grin and squeeze the other one with equal force. Her nipples rose to meet his strong advances, her hips now beginning to rotate in time to his thrusts.

She felt a glow around her groin which spread slowly to her belly but it was not the pleasant warmth that signals the approach of orgasm. It was an uncomfortably familiar burning sensation which she had experienced two or three times since returning from hospital. Lynn sucked in a sharp breath as a stab of pain jolted her. Her lover took it to be a sign of her excitement and grunted something but she didn't hear him, her mind was now occupied with the growing pain in her lower region which seemed to be intensifying. The weight on top of her seemed almost unbearable but she gritted her teeth, whispering words of encouragement in his ear, trying by any means she could to drive the thoughts of the searing pain from her mind.

Barry or Gary or whatever his name was, suddenly withdrew his organ, leaving her panting in frustration but that feeling of frustration did not remain long as, a moment later, she felt his hot breath on her left breast then the right. His tongue flicked against her swollen nipples and he drew them between his teeth making them even harder and more erect.

The pain in her abdomen grew more acute. The skin across her belly seemed first to contract and then to stretch, rising in two places in the form of almost imperceptible bumps. Lynn swallowed hard, the burning sensation now even stronger. It felt as if someone had poured a kettle full of boiling water all over her abdomen.

A particularly prominent bulge rose just to the right of her navel, strained against the flesh defiantly for long seconds then vanished.

The man was up on his knees now, looking down at her vagina and she almost screamed aloud as she saw the blood.

Lynn Tyler thrust a shaking hand between her legs and withdrew it slowly to see crimson staining her fingertips. She felt the burning inside her, stared at the blood as it trickled down her quivering digits and, finally, she did scream.

Thirty-three

It was cold inside the pathology lab and Randall dug both hands deep inside his trouser pockets. The smell of chemicals was strong and the inspector wrinkled his nose, peering around the large room with its green painted, white tiled walls. There were three stainless steel slabs set side by side, the last of which bore a sheet covered occupant. There was a small tag attached to the big toe of the left foot. It bore a name and a three digit number. The number coincided with one of the many lockers that ran the full length of the far wall. A storecase for sightless eyes.

Above the slab dangled a scale, beside it there was a tray littered with surgical instruments, one of which, Randall noticed with revulsion, was a saw. He glanced across at PC Fowler who looked even paler than usual beneath the glare of the fluorescents. The young constable was gazing at the covered body on the far slab. He was shivering and, he told himself, it was not solely the product of the chill air.

In one corner of the lab there was a sink and it was there that the hospital's chief pathologist stood. He washed his hands then pulled on a pair of rubber gloves, pressing his fingers together to ensure that they fitted like a second skin. Ronald Potter turned and headed for the slab. He was in his forties, his bald dome hidden by the toupée which he wore. It was a bad fit because flecks of what little hair he retained showed beneath it at the rear but Randall was concerned with more important things than ill-fitting hair pieces at the moment. Both he and Fowler moved forward as Potter reached the slab and pulled back the sheet.

The pathologist eyed the corpse indifferently, leaning over it, inspecting the preliminary damage. He stroked his chin thoughtfully, considering the object before him with the same concentration which a child would apply to selecting a sweet from a chocolate box.

Randall looked at the body for a moment then diverted his gaze towards the pathologist.

Fowler gritted his teeth and looked away, trying to retain his breakfast.

The body was badly mutilated about the shoulders and was, once again, headless. Blood had trickled into the gutter which ran around the rim of the slab, most of it from the torn stump of the neck. The head had been severed much higher up this time, just below the bottom jaw as far as Randall could see. Indeed, fragments of bone and even a tooth also lay on the slab where the head should have been.

Potter reached for a metal probe and began poking about in one of the many gashes that criss-crossed the remains of the neck.

"This is becoming something of a habit isn't it, Inspector?" he asked, plucking a pair of tweezers from the trolley.

"What?" asked Randall, puzzled, his attention riveted to the stomach-turning sight before him.

"Finding headless corpses." The pathologist looked up and smiled, humorlessly. "How many is this now? Three isn't it?"

Randall clenched his fists at his side and glared at the older man.

"Someone somewhere must have quite a collection. I didn't know we had head-hunters in Exham."

"What are you a pathologist or a fucking comedian?" snapped the Inspector, irritably. "I want to know what he was killed with. I don't want Sunday Night at the London Palladium."

It was Potter's turn to glare. The two men locked stares for a moment then the pathologist returned to his work. He laboured in silence for a good ten minutes then straightened up, wiping some blood off on his apron.

"As far as I can see, the head was severed with the same weapon as the one used on the two previous victims." He paused. "A single-edged blade of some kind. There's rust in two or three of the wounds as well." The older man pulled the sheet further back and regarded the remains of the body. "No other external damage. The pattern's the same."

"With the other two you said that there was a lot of blood in the lungs," Randall reminded him. "What about this one?"

Potter smiled thinly and reached for a new tool. He held it before him and Randall saw that it was a tiny buzz-saw, its steel blade glinting beneath the lights.

"Let's have a look, shall we?" said Potter and checked to see if the instrument was plugged in. It was. He stepped on a pedal near his left foot and the buzz-saw whirred into action with a sound that reminded Randall of a dentist's drill. As he watched, the pathologist lowered the spinning blade to a point just below the sternum of the corpse, then, with one expert movement, he buried it in the flesh, allowing the screaming blade to carve a path through dead flesh and bone, opening the rib cage until the lungs were exposed. A foul stench rose from the open chest cavity and both Randall and Fowler backed away.

The high-pitched whine ceased abruptly, to be replaced by a sickening crack as the older man prized open the sawn-through rib cage exposing the vital organs beneath. He picked up a pair of scissors and carefully snipped away at the lining of the chest, finally cutting into the left lung just below the trachea. As the expertly-wielded scissors sliced through the pleura, a clear fluid spilled out to be followed, a second later, by the first dark, almost black, clots of congealed blood. Seemingly oblivious to the thick red cascade, Potter opened the lung from top to bottom finally pulling open the organ with his gloved hands. Randall swallowed hard.

"Exactly the same as the other two," said Potter.

"What exactly does that mean?" the Inspector asked, trying to look anywhere but at the ruined torso of the corpse before him. He wanted a smoke and his fingers anxiously toyed with the packet of Rothmans in his pocket but he kept his composure as best he could and waited for an answer.

Potter shrugged.

"The killer attacked from behind. That's easy enough to see from these wounds here," he pointed to three particularly large gashes on the lower part of the neck. "The blade was used in a type of swatting action. These are cuts, not punctures. The fact that there are no defence cuts on the hands or arms would seem to indicate that the victim was dead after the first or second blow."

"Could the head have been severed with one stroke?" Randall wanted to know. "By a very strong man for instance."

Potter shook his head.

"No,"

"You sound very sure."

"Well, Inspector, for one thing, strength has nothing to do with it." He smiled thinly. "It's technique. When beheading was the accepted form of execution during the Middle Ages, right up to the sixteenth century, there was a certain art to it. The headsmen were trained for their job and even then it was common for them to take two or three blows to sever the head completely. And they used axes or large swords. These wounds were inflicted with a small weapon."

Randall nodded.

"Thanks for the history lesson," he said.

"Besides, in this case," he motioned towards the

201

corpse, "As with the previous two, the head was removed by a series of blows. Chopped not sliced off."

Fowler blenched and decided he needed some fresh air. Randall told him to wait in the car outside. The young constable left, gratefully, his footsteps echoing around the large cold room. The other two men waited until the PC had departed then they spoke briskly, Randall watching as the pathologist completed the autopsy. His mind was brimming over with ideas and thoughts. Harvey. The murder weapon. But, something which Potter had said troubled him, something about strength having nothing to do with it. He turned the thought over in his mind finally dismissing it. The incident at the grocer's shop the other night had confirmed his suspicions once and for all. Paul Harvey was responsible for these killings. It was just a matter of finding him. Randall chewed his bottom lip contemplatively. Find Harvey. That was what he'd been trying to do for nearly three months now and he was still no closer. As he stood in this cold room his men were out searching Exham and the surrounding countryside, covering ground which they'd already searched months before in a vain effort to find the maniac. Randall exhaled deeply and looked at his watch. It was 10.34 a.m. He'd been at the hospital for over three hours, ever since the corpse had been discovered in the front garden of a house on the south side of town. The Inspector had driven to the scene of the crime and then ridden the ambulance to the hospital to await the autopsy report. He had not intended to stay for the actual event but, he had reasoned, there was nothing for him to do back at his office except twiddle his thumbs and lose his temper trying to figure out just where the hell Harvey was. So he had stayed.

Potter completed his work and pulled the sheet back over the body, calling in one of the lab technicians to complete the task of sewing the corpse up again.

Randall watched as the older man washed his hands at the sink, humming happily to himself as he did so. When he'd finished he turned to face the policeman.

"Is there anything else I can do for you, Inspector?" he said, sardonically.

Randall shook his head.

"I do have other work to do," the pathologist reminded him, motioning towards the door.

The policeman shot him an acid glance and headed towards the exit, glad to leave this foul place. He slammed the door behind him and headed for the lift, jabbing the button which would take him up to the ground floor. He closed his eyes as the car rose the short distance to the upper level. It smelt of plastic and perspiration in there and Randall was pleased when he could step out. He fumbled in his jacket pocket and retrieved his cigarettes, hurriedly lighting one up. He'd taken two drags on it when a voice called to him and he turned to see an attractive woman walking towards him. She wore a long white coat, open to reveal a green blouse and grey skirt. But, as she drew closer, Randall found himself captivated by a pair of piercing blue eyes. They gleamed like chips of sapphire but there was a warmth to them.

She pointed to a sign on the wall to his left which said "NO SMOKING" in large red letters. He took the cigarette from his mouth and dropped it, grinding it out beneath his foot.

She had seen him emerge from the lift and, immediately, her curiosity had been aroused.

"You're not a member of staff are you?" It was a statement, not a question.

"No." He smiled, still gazing into those gleaming blue eyes. "You could say I was here on business."

She looked puzzled but Randall fumbled in his pocket for his ID. He flipped the slim wallet open and showed it to her.

"Police," she said.

He nodded.

"It's not a very good photo," she said, indicating the small snap in the wallet. Their eyes locked for brief seconds and Randall detected the hint of a smile on her lips.

"Is it about the murders?"

He snapped the wallet shut, his expression hardening.

"What makes you think that?" he asked, sharply.

"Because we don't have too many policemen calling here at this time in the morning." She studied his face, hard and lined, puffy beneath the eyes from lack of sleep. He still had some stubble on his chin from his hasty shave. "Don't look so alarmed," she told him. "Word does travel you know. Three murders in less than a week is bound to be news."

Randall nodded.

"So who are you?" he wanted to know.

She introduced herself and, as he held her hand he found his gaze drawn once more to those blue orbs. She was, indeed, a very attractive woman. He looked for the wedding ring on her left hand but didn't see one, something which surprised him. They exchanged brief pleasantries then Randall announced that he should be going.

She called him back.

"Have you got any idea who you're looking for?" she asked.

Randall eyed her suspiciously.

"That's police information, Miss Ford," he said. "Why do you ask?"

"Well, it's probably nothing. . ." She allowed the sentence to trail off but Randall's curiosity was suddenly and unexpectedly aroused.

"What is it? If you've heard anything, tell me." There was a note of urgency in his voice now.

204

She explained about Harold. Falteringly, not sure whether she was making a fool of herself or not, she told Randall about the ex-porter's background, about the examination she had carried out, and about Harold's apparent regression. Randall listened but was unimpressed. She mentioned her search of the hut, the discovery of the blood and finally, almost reluctantly, the incident with the foetuses' grave.

"Jesus Christ," muttered Randall. "Where is he now?"

"No one knows," said Maggie.

The Inspector ran a hand through his hair.

"Everybody seems to be disappearing," he said, wearily.

"Maybe it's just my imagination but, well, he was disturbed," she said.

Randall nodded.

"I don't think this. . ." He asked the porter's name again and she told him. "I don't think Pierce is tied up with these killings. The severed heads, they're like Harvey's trade-mark. I can't see that it's anyone but him." He hesitated. "But I'll check out this Pierce anyway." He turned to leave but paused. "Thanks, Miss Ford."

"Maggie," she said.

"Thanks, Maggie," he said, smiling. "You know, if every doctor looked like you the Health Service would have an even longer waiting list." He winked and headed for the exit.

She watched him go, wondering if she had done the right thing. She doubted that Harold was connected in any way with the killings but if Randall could find out where he was she would feel a little easier. She took the lift to her office, the vision of Randall's hard but appealing face still strong in her mind. It was a vision that would not fade easily.

Randall slid into the passenger seat beside Fowler and nodded for the constable to start the car. He told the young PC to drive out to the new psychiatric hospital on the outskirts of Exham and the journey was completed in less than twenty minutes. Neither of the men spoke, each wrapped up in his own thoughts. Fowler still felt queasy at the thought of the autopsy and Randall's mind was trying to digest the information which Maggie had given him. However, there was something else on the Inspector's mind, something not directly linked with police business. It was the doctor herself and, as he allowed his head to loll back against the head-rest he thought about those sparkling blue eyes and that soft brown hair. He even afforded himself a smile.

Messages came through over the two-way as they travelled as other cars reported in. The news was the same every time – not a trace of Harvey. Randall hooked the receiver back into place and looked up as Fowler swung the Panda into the driveway which led up to the new psychiatric hospital. What a contrast to the old place, thought Randall as he got out. Where there had been granite there was now glass. Where there'd been barred windows there was now double glazing. The entire structure looked light and airy, a marked contrast to the forbidding monolithic bearing of the old asylum.

Randall got out of the car, telling Fowler he wasn't sure how long he'd be. The Inspector discovered that Doctor Vincent was with a patient so Randall paced up and down a spacious outer office until the head of the hospital found time to see him. He smoked six cigarettes in the thirty minutes he was forced to wait, gleefully ignoring the sign which asked visitors to refrain from the habit. He ground out the final butt just as the doctor's door opened to admit him.

Randall declined the offer of a cup of coffee, more interested to know what Vincent could tell him about

Harold Pierce. The psychiatrist seemed puzzled at first but then produced a file which included a photo. Randall looked at it, struck immediately by the appalling disfiguring scar which covered half of Harold's face. He asked how the man came to bear it and Vincent told him the whole story.

"Have you seen anything of Pierce since he left the old asylum?" Randall wanted to know.

Vincent shook his head.

"He hasn't been readmitted?"

The psychiatrist looked puzzled.

"Is Harold in some sort of trouble, Inspector?" he asked.

Randall shook his head and asked, "Have you any idea where he might go? Did he have any relatives around here?"

"Look, Inspector Randall, is there something I should know? What exactly *is* going on?"

"Nothing as far as I know," said the policeman. "It's just that Pierce has gone missing. I wondered if you might know of his whereabouts. That's all."

Vincent stroked his chin thoughtfully, looking hurt, as if Harold's aberrations were some kind of personal slight against *him*.

"I haven't a clue where he might be," said Vincent.

The two men sat in silence for long moments then Randall coughed preemptively.

"While Pierce was under your care did he ever display any violent tendencies towards other patients?" he asked.

"Absolutely not," said Vincent, emphatically.

"What about against himself? Self-mutilation, that type of thing?"

Vincent looked shocked.

"No."

Randall nodded, took one last look at the photo of Harold Pierce then got to his feet. He thanked the psychiatrist for his time and walked back out to the waiting Panda.

Fowler was dozing behind the wheel, the unrepaired heater still blasting out its full fury. The PC jerked upright when Randall knocked on the window. The Inspector climbed in and, after rubbing his face with both hands, Fowler started the engine, swinging the car round in the direction of Exham. They were back at the police station in less than thirty minutes.

Randall pulled off his coat and stuck it on the hanger on the back of his office door. He took the cigarettes from the pocket and crossed to his desk, lighting one up as he did so. He slumped into his chair and blew out a mouthful of smoke in a long blue stream. It swirled before him, writhing gently in the still air, forming patterns then dissipating. He sat forward and pulled a pencil and notepad towards him then, with rough strokes, he sketched a passing likeness of Harold Pierce's face somewhat over-emphasising the scarred side. Tiring of his attempts at art he wrote down two names beneath the sketch.

Paul Harvey

Harold Pierce

He considered them both for a moment then crossed out the bottom one, tapping on the pad with the end of the pencil.

Both men had disappeared, apparently without trace. Was there some bizarre link which he hadn't yet thought of? Randall scribbled across the rough sketch, tore the leaf from the pad and tossed it into the wastebin. He pushed the thought from his mind. There was no link between the two men, he was searching for answers where there were none. Clutching at straws had become something of a hobby for him just lately.

The phone rang.

"Randall speaking."

"Inspector, it's me," the voice was immediately recognizable. "Maggie Ford."

Randall smiled to himself.

"What can I do for you, Miss. . ." He corrected himself. "Maggie?" He heard her laugh at the other end.

"It's about what I said earlier, about Harold Pierce. I didn't think at the time but I remember now, when he was dismissed, apparently he said that he *did* have somewhere to go."

"You wouldn't happen to know where that was?" Randall enquired.

She didn't.

"Well, not to worry. I've got some news for you too. After I left the hospital this morning, I went out to the new psychiatric place and did some checking up on your friend Harold. I think you can stop worrying. I spoke to the Chief Consultant psychiatrist there and he assured me that Pierce had never shown any signs of violence. If I had a list of suspects I'd cross him off it right now." He laughed, humourlessly.

"So you're convinced it's Harvey?" she said.

"No doubt about it."

There was silence at the other end for a moment. Randall frowned.

"Maggie."

"Yes," she said. "I'm still here." The pause was a nervous one, both anxious to prolong the conversation but not sure how to progress. Randall felt like a schoolkid and noticed, with amusement, that his hand was trembling slightly.

"What time do you finish work tonight?" he asked.

"I'm off at ten," she said, almost apologetically.

"I know a nice little restaurant that stays open until late. I can pick you up outside the hospital."

Maggie laughed.

"If you're asking me to dinner the answer is no."

Randall felt suddenly deflated, almost shocked at her refusal but his mood rapidly lightened as she continued speaking.

"I know the restaurant you're talking about," she said. "It's too expensive. Besides, I'm a better cook anyway and, my flat's nearer. You wouldn't have so far to drive."

It was Randall's turn to laugh.

She gave him her address.

"Be there at about quarter to eleven."

They exchanged farewells and Randall put the phone down, feeling happier than he'd felt for a long time.

There was a knock on the office door and Randall shouted for the visitor to enter. It was Sergeant Willis.

"Thought you might have brought me a cuppa, Norman," said the Inspector.

"Sorry, guv," said Willis. "Just the pathologist's full report and this." He handed another piece of paper to his superior. It bore the numbers of all the Panda cars belonging to the Exham force. Each number had the driver's name next to it.

"They've all just checked in," said Willis. "The East side of the town is clear. There's still no sign of Harvey."

The smile faded rapidly from Randall's face and the familiar feeling of angry frustration swiftly drove away the fleeting twinge of elation he'd experienced moments before.

"I suppose we just keep looking then?" said Willis.

Randall nodded.

"Yes," he muttered, his voice low. "We just keep looking."

Outside, it was beginning to get dark.

Thirty-four

"Well, I don't think the bus is coming," said Debbie Snell pushing another stick of Juicy Fruit into her mouth.

"If we hadn't been mucking about in maths we wouldn't have got detention and we wouldn't have missed the bloody bus would we?" Colette Hill told her irritably.

"Well we *were* mucking about and we *did* get detention," Debbie said, leaning against the bus stop.

"Why don't you ring your precious Tony up," Belinda Vernon told her. "If you hadn't been going on about him we wouldn't have got told off in the beginning."

"Oh piss off," Debbie said, defiantly. "Anyway, if the bus isn't here soon I might just do that."

All three girls were from Exham Comprehensive School, the largest of the town's three schools and they wore its distinctive maroon blazer. Which, in Debbie's case refused to do up because of her mountainous breasts. All three girls were fifteen but Debbie was a taller, more mature-looking youngster than her two companions. They stood forlornly at the stop glancing agitatedly at their watches or periodically glancing up the road in the hope that a bus would appear from around the corner. The bus stop itself, complete with its glass shelter, backed onto a thick outcrop of trees which, in turn, masked some of the rolling fields that formed Exham's boundaries.

It was from these trees that Paul Harvey watched the three girls.

As a teenager he had always found girls impossible to cope with. Their jokes, their jibes, their little tricks. He had not known how to react and, on one occasion, when one of them had made exaggerated advances towards him, he had been left humiliated – standing alone amidst the jeers and laughter trying to hide an uncontrollable erection. The memory, as did so many of the others, still hurt.

Now he watched the girls from the shelter of the trees, close enough to hear what they were saying. The sickle was gripped tightly in his hand.

Debbie took one more look at her watch.

"Well, I'm not waiting around any longer," she proclaimed. "I'm going to phone Tony."

She rummaged through her pocket for a coin and, with a haughty "Goodbye" set off down the hill towards the phone box. The other girls watched her go until finally she turned a corner and disappeared from view.

Harvey moved swiftly but stealthily through the trees, tracing a parallel path with the lone girl. The dusk was deepening into darkness now, further adding to his concealment and he was content to remain within the confines of the woods, his eyes constantly on Debbie.

She reached the phone box and pulled open the door.

Harvey watched as she dialled. He could see her speaking into the mouthpiece and, a few minutes later, she put the receiver down and stepped back outside.

He watched her for a full five minutes as she paced back and forth then, slowly, he rose to his full height and moved through the trees towards her.

Debbie had her back to him and the growing wind masked the sound of breaking twigs and the big man emerged from the woods.

He was within ten yards of her now, almost clear of the trees.

She looked at her watch, oblivious to his approach.

The black Capri came speeding round the corner, headlamps blazing. Debbie ran across the road to meet it, jumping in happily. The driver a young man in his

212

early twenties, spun the wheel and the vehicle turned full circle, heading back to Exham.

Harvey melted back into the woods, merging with the darkness as if he were a shadow.

Thirty-five

Harold sat up, the nightmare fading rapidly as consciousness swept over him. He blinked in the darkness, rubbed his eyes and, as he did so, he felt the perspiration on his face.

It was almost pitch black in the deserted asylum. He had a hurricane lamp in the room but he dare not light it. He sat shivering in the darkness, listening to the high mournful wailing of the wind as it whistled through the countless broken windows on the lower floor, stirring the dust which coated the floors so thickly.

The foetuses were in one corner of the room, covered by a blanket to protect them from the cold. Harold squinted through the gloom, his ears picking up the sounds of their low guttural raspings. He could see the blanket rising and falling intermittently. For what seemed like an eternity he sat cross-legged on the dirty floor then, slowly, he reached for the hurricane lamp and the box of matches nearby. He struck a match, lifted the housing on the lamp and watched as the wick began to glow yellow then he dropped the housing back into place, the dull light gradually filling the room, spreading out like an ink blot around him, driving back the darkness. Holding the lamp in one hand, Harold crawled towards the dormant foetuses.

His hand hovered over the blanket for what seemed like an eternity, then he slowly pulled it back.

The creatures appeared to be sleeping, their eyes closed, sealed only by the thin membrane of skin through which the gleaming blackness of those magnetic orbs still showed. Harold ran an appraising eye over them, swallowing hard.

One of them moved and its arm flopped limply against his knee. Harold let out a low moan and held the hurricane lamp closer to the outstretched limb. The breath caught in his throat and his one good eye bulged in its socket.

As if pulled by invisible wires, the stubby fingers of the nearest foetus slowly elongated, lengthened into spidery tendrils. The flesh looked soft but leathery. Harold pulled the cover back a little more and watched in fascination as the same thing happened with the creature's other hand.

He backed off, heart pounding hard against his ribs.

They were developing at a faster rate than even *he* had first imagined.

Harold sat gazing at them, his mind in a turmoil. Torn between fear and fascination. There was no revulsion any longer, just foreboding.

He wondered how long it would be before the foetuses completed their growth.

Thirty-six

Randall parked his car and walked across to the small group of flats on the other side of the street. Beneath the sodium glare of the street-lamp he checked his watch.

10.43 p.m.

"Spot on," he said to himself, pushing open the double doors which led into the hallway. There was a staircase ahead of him and a lift to his right. He chose the stairs, walking up slowly, feeling somewhat self-conscious carrying the spray of red carnations. Two kids, about fifteen, bundled their way past him laughing raucously and, minutes later, Randall heard the roar of motor-bike engines as the two of them sped off. They'll probably be wrapped round a tree by midnight, he thought. He'd always wanted a motor-bike when he was a kid but his parents had resolutely forbidden it. Death traps, his father had called them. Over the years, with the number of accidents he'd seen, Randall had come to agree.

He reached the landing and found that it was bright and clean-looking with paintings hung on two of the walls. There was an enormous rubber plant outside one of the flat doors which looked like something out of "The Day of the Triffids". The building consisted of just three storeys, six flats on each floor and it bore a marked contrast to the flats on the larger estates on the other side of Exham. No grafitti here, he thought. No dog shit in the hallway or cat's piss on the landings. Sweetness and light he mused, somewhat sardonically. The small block was quiet, everyone either went to bed early or Maggie was the only one on this floor he thought as he found her number. He pressed the bell and a two tone chime answered him. He held the carnations beside him, finally producing them when Maggie herself opened the door.

She smiled broadly, her face lighting up and, once more, Randall was struck by her extraordinarily sparkling eyes. It was like looking at a June sky – two pieces of heaven captured within those glittering orbs. She was dressed in a crisply laundered grey dress and a pair of high-heeled gold shoes which seemed to accentuate the smooth curve of her calves. Maggie was a small woman, about five-three Randall guessed, but the graceful suppleness of her legs made her appear taller. He ran a quick, appreciative eye over her, thinking how different she looked from when he'd first seen her that morning.

She ushered him in, taking the flowers gratefully.

"I didn't know what sort of chocolates you liked," he said, somewhat self-consciously. "So I thought I'd play safe."

"They're beautiful," she said and went off to find a vase. "Sit down."

He sank into the welcoming luxuriance of the sofa and looked around him. The room was quite large but sparsely furnished with just the three piece suite, a sideboard and a coffee table. A gas fire blazed before him, one of those with mock flames. There was a portable TV perched on a high table in the far corner of the room, a small music centre to his left. Two doors led out of the room, the one which Maggie had disappeared through led into the kitchen, the other one, closed at the moment, led to the bedroom and bathroom.

Behind the sofa on which he sat there was a small dining table set for two and the policeman could smell food cooking. The lights were dimmed and the whole room had a cosy feel to it. Immediately Randall felt relaxed.

Maggie returned a moment later carrying the flowers in a white vase. She set it down on the coffee table. He smelt her perfume as she leant over, a subtle aroma which lingered after her.

She poured him a drink and they talked gaily for a while until Maggie got up, announcing that the supper was ready. Randall got to his feet and wandered across to the table, watching her as she carried the meal in.

Randall savoured the meal. It was indeed a treat to eat something prepared by a woman's hands, especially when she was as attractive as Maggie. He looked up at her and for long seconds he imagined he was sitting opposite his dead wife but the vision hastily vanished.

"I'm not used to cooking for two," she said.

He reached for the wine bottle and poured them both a glass.

"That surprises me," he said.

"Why?"

"You're an attractive woman. It's not usual to find women like you on their own."

"Men don't seem interested in women who can compete with them on the same level," she said. "I mean, as far as a career goes. It seems to frighten them off. A woman anywhere else but the kitchen sink is a threat to their egos."

Randall raised his glass in salute.

"Come back Germaine Greer, all is forgiven," he said, smiling. "Where did you dig that speech up from?"

"I'm sorry," she said.

"It's ok, but, like I said, I'm still surprised you're single."

"I could say the same about you," she said, smiling.

Randall grinned.

"I think there's a compliment in there somewhere but I can't quite find it."

"You do live alone though?" she asked.

His smile faded somewhat. He nodded and sipped at his wine.

"Yeah, I have done for the last five years," he told her.

He returned to his food, aware that her eyes were upon him.

"I *was* married. I had a little girl: Lisa. She was two when it happened." He chewed his food slowly, finally sitting back in his chair, running the tip of his index finger around the rim of his glass. Maggie watched him silently.

217

"My wife, Fiona," he began, "she asked me to drive her and Lisa to her mother's. Well, I was just about to set off when I got a call through, could I come down to the station? They'd hauled a suspect in, wanted me to talk to him. I forget what it was about. Anyway, I told her that she'd have to drive herself, that the case was important." He sipped his wine, the voice which he heard sounded alien, distant, as if it didn't belong to him and he realized that he was speaking about the event for the first time since it had happened all those years ago. It seemed like an eternity.

"She'd only passed her test a few weeks earlier." He smiled thinly. "I remember how pleased she was when she *did* pass. But she didn't fancy driving at night, that was why she asked me to take her and Lisa." He paused again. "A lorry hit the car. Big bastard it was, sixteen wheeler. It took the fire brigade four hours to cut them loose from the wreckage. Of course they were both dead by that time anyway." He took a long swallow from his glass.

"Oh God, I'm sorry, Lou," she said.

He nodded.

"If *I'd* have been driving, it probably wouldn't have happened."

"You can't know that," she said.

"Sometimes I wish I'd have died with them," he confessed.

"You shouldn't blame yourself," she said.

He smiled, humourlessly.

"People used to say that to me all the time after it happened. All except Fiona's mother who seemed to agree that it *was* my fault. She hasn't spoken to me since the day it happened."

There was a long silence finally broken by Randall.

"Well, things are getting a bit morbid, aren't they? Shall we change the subject?"

He suggested they clear the table, offering to help

with the washing up. They carried the plates into the kitchen where she washed and he dried. They talked unceasingly, as if each had finally found some kind of confessor. Someone to whom their life's secrets could be revealed without the risk of scorn or judgement. And, in their openness they discovered just how desolate and empty their lives really were, but the discovery of that fact seemed only to pull them closer until, by midnight when they moved back into the sitting room with a cup of coffee each, they felt as if they'd known one another all their lives.

Randall sat down on the sofa, Maggie kicked off her shoes and sat beside him on the floor, legs tucked beneath her. She rested her coffee cup on the cushion next to him and ran a hand through her hair.

Randall watched her, realizing that he wanted her badly. Maggie felt a similar yearning but there was something nagging at the back of her mind. Something which she had not experienced with the other men she'd known. She wanted him, that much she knew but, for some unknown reason, she was afraid of rejection. She knew that he felt something for her, even if it was only physical, but she could not shake the feeling that she would be betraying the memory of his wife and child if she gave herself up to her feelings. But those feelings were powerful and, even as she sat talking to him, she felt compelled to take his heavy hand in hers, gently stroking the back, tracing the outline of his thick veins, stirring the hair which grew thickly on his hand and wrist.

Randall too was thinking about Fiona, wondering if he should be sitting here with this very attractive young woman wanting so badly to feel his body pressing against hers, to feel her hands on him and his on her. He had lost more than his family when Fiona and Lisa had been killed, he had lost a part of himself. The part that once knew happiness, compassion and optimism, but, in Maggie, maybe he had found someone who might help him to rediscover what he had lost. He gazed down at her as she bent forward to kiss the back of his hand and he could not resist the urge to lay one hand on the back of her neck, kneading the flesh there with his strong fingers. She felt so soft, so pliant and a tingle ran through him. You only met her this morning, he told himself, but that didn't seem to matter anymore. They were together and it seemed so right. As if they belonged with one another. He felt a single tear burst from his eye corner. There was fear there too. It had been so long. So long since he'd allowed himself to share any feelings he wondered if, when the time came, he would be able to.

Maggie climbed up onto the sofa beside him. She brushed the tear from his cheek with her index finger but she did not speak.

She thought of all those men before. Was this one going to be different? Could she actually find someone to love? She felt his arms pull her closer and she rested her head on his shoulder. For long seconds they remained still then she twisted around to face him and, tenderly at first, leant forward and kissed him on the lips. Randall responded and suddenly their kisses were deep and probing, making them both shudder. Almost reluctantly, Maggie broke away, her eyes wide, searching his.

"Does it bother you that I've been to bed with men in the past just because *I* wanted to?" she asked.

"Why should it?" he said. "It's your business, Maggie and, besides, the past doesn't matter."

"I think I've been very naive," she confessed. "I was confusing want with need. I wanted physical relationships but I needed something more."

Randall slid his arm around her, shuddering as he felt her hand touch his thigh.

220

"Do you always get philosophical at this time of night?" he asked, smiling.

"It depends on who I'm with," she said, grinning. "You're a good listener."

They lay down together on the floor and made love in the heat from the fire.

For long seconds afterwards, both of them gasped and shuddered with the intensity of their passion. Coupled together and breathless, they held each other tightly.

She bit his shoulder, drawing the skin between her teeth for brief moments until, when she withdrew her head, there was a small red mark there.

"Ouch," he said and nipped her ear lobe.

Maggie laughed, one hand stroking his hair, her finger finally tracing the outline of his eyebrows and, above those, the deep furrows which creased his forehead. She propped herself up on one elbow, looking down at him. She seemed fascinated by his hard face with its many lines and creases, each of which she seemed to follow with her nail.

"You must worry a lot," she said.

He looked vague.

"Wrinkles," she said, kissing him gently on the end of his nose. He frowned and she giggled.

"Do you know it takes forty-five facial muscles to frown but only fifteen to smile?" she asked.

"Thank you, doctor," he said, gripping her soft hand in his. "I don't usually have much to smile about."

She nodded, her expression softening.

"Will I still be smiling tomorrow, Maggie?" he asked.

"What do you mean?"

"This," he said. "Was this just another one night stand?"

She kissed him softly on the lips.

"I hope not," she whispered.

"The lonely doctor and the cynical, embittered copper

221

eh?" he said and, for a moment, she thought she heard a note of sarcasm in his voice. "Sounds like a perfect match."

She smiled as his tone lightened somewhat. He reached up and pulled her to him, holding her tightly. They gazed into each other's eyes, he, once more captivated by those glittering blue jewels with which she stared back at him.

"Would it surprise you to know that you are the first woman I've had since Fiona died?" he said.

Maggie looked a little shocked.

"Lou, I'm sorry if I've made you feel guilty. I. . ."

He put a finger to her lips to silence her.

"I suppose I can't live in the past forever," he said softly. "Nothing is going to bring her or Lisa back. I've got my memories and I'm grateful for them. I loved Fiona more than I thought it was possible to love anyone, and even more so when Lisa was born. When they were killed, something inside me died with them." He paused, swallowed hard and she could see his eyes misting over.

"Don't talk about it," she said, stroking his face.

"No, it's all right," he reassured her. "For the first time since it happened, I *want* to talk about it. For five years it's been bottled up. Because, until now there's been no one who I wanted to tell."

Maggie felt something stirring deep inside her. A feeling almost of pity for Randall.

Her voice took on a reflective tone.

"You know, all these years I've been calling myself liberated," she said, bitterly, "when all I've really been is a slag."

"Don't say that," he said.

She shook her head.

"It's true. I can't remember how many men I've had or maybe I've been fooling myself there too. Perhaps they've been having me." She kissed him on the cheek.

222

"And do you know what I've missed more than anything?"

He shook his head.

"Kids," she told him. "I've always loved kids but my bloody career came first where they were concerned too. Maybe that's why I work with kids. I'm a frustrated mother. Parent by proxy." She smiled humourlessly. "What I wouldn't give for my own child. . ." She allowed the sentence to trail off.

"I think that's enough soul-searching for one night, don't you?" said Randall, touching her face. He pulled her close to him once again and kissed her. She responded fiercely for a moment then broke away and got to her feet. For precious seconds, she stood, naked, before him and Randall gazed almost wonderingly at the smooth outlines of her glowing body.

"Let's go to bed," she said, flicking off the light.

Once in bed they found their passions roused once again and this time they were joined with an abandoned intensity.

Finally, exhausted, they fell asleep, clutching one another feeling that a shared demon was in the process of being exorcised.

PART THREE

". . . Evil, what is evil? There is only one evil,
to deny life."

– D. H. Lawrence

". . . And after the fire a still small voice. . ."

– Kings 19:12

Thirty-seven

Harold was shaking, his entire body racked by uncontrollable shudders. He knelt over the three foetuses and tentatively reached out a hand to touch the one closest to him. Its skin felt soft and puffy, like the swollen flesh on a blister. It moved only slightly as his probing fingers pressed against its chest. The creature made a low gurgling sound and Harold recoiled slightly as some yellowish fluid oozed slowly from one corner of its mouth. The foetus had its eyes closed, the thin membranes of skin scarcely concealing the dark pits beneath.

Close by, the other two creatures dragged themselves towards it, black eyes shining malevolently. Harold looked round, heard the sounds as they approached, shook his head as if to dispel the sibilant hissing within. The voices gradually took on a sharp clarity. It was like the static clearing from a radio transmitter. First there would be just rasping sounds then the words would come through.

"What's wrong with him?" asked Harold, gazing down at the barely moving foetus before him. The thing lay completely motionless by this time, just its thin lips fluttering, the thick pus-like liquid dripping from its mouth.

"Please tell me," Harold said, almost pleadingly.

Hissing, more loudly now.

Harold shook his head.

"No."

They were more insistent.

"What should I do?"

Commands, which he knew must be obeyed.

Harold looked at the ailing foetus and then at its stronger companions. He hesitated for a moment realizing what must be done. But, his reluctance was momentary. He got to his feet and crossed the room to the blanket where he himself slept. Beneath the rolled up coat which passed as a pillow lay the kitchen knife. Harold picked it up, glancing at the dull blade for a second before hurrying back to the trio of creatures. He could feel a slight gnawing pain at the back of his neck and, when he knelt beside the first foetus again, he found that the other two were glaring at him. They fixed him in that formidable stare, watching as he rolled up one sleeve exposing a forearm already criss-crossed with purple scabs and welts. Taking the knife in his right hand, he extended his left arm, flexing his fingers until the veins stood out. He swallowed hard, the razor sharp blade hovering over his own flesh.

Harold drew the knife swiftly across his arm, wincing in pain as the cold metal cut easily through his skin, opening the bulging veins. Blood spurted from the wound and Harold gripped the top of his left arm, dropping the blade beside him. The gash seemed to burn for long seconds and his arm felt as if it were going numb but he fought back the nausea and slowly lowered the slashed appendage, allowing the crimson liquid to run down. It oozed over his hand and dripped from his fingers and Harold carefully dangled the limb above the mouth of the dying foetus, watching as the blood formed red droplets on his fingertips before falling into the open mouth of the creature. Its lips moved slightly but some of the blood splashed onto its face and chest. It made a low mewling sound as it tried to swallow the blood which was mingling with the yellowish secretion already pumping from its mouth. Harold was shaking, the pain now consuming his entire arm. He held the limb steady, watching as the crimson fluid dripped onto the foetus. A swollen tongue lapped at it hungrily. Harold reached out to touch it with his free hand.

"I did as you said," he croaked, looking at the other two creatures. God, they were much larger now, he thought, and he recoiled slightly, whimpering. He gripped the rent in his arm, his fingers brushing against the hardened skin of the freshly healed scabs elsewhere on his forearm. Blood from the most recent cut was seeping through his fingers.

The voices were chattering once more, accusatory this time.

"I didn't kill Gordon," Harold gasped. "I didn't kill my brother."

The voices grew louder until finally, Harold shrieked. It was a cry which came from deep within him. As he looked down at the foetus, it seemed to metamorphosise, its shape changing, its features altering until it was his baby brother lying beside him. After all those years, Gordon was here in this dank, dark place. Harold began to sob uncontrollably as he reached out to pick up the small body. It felt so soft and jellied, as if his rough fingers would go right through the skin, but he lifted it nonetheless, holding the body to his chest, gazing into its face.

"Gordon," he whispered, tears rolling down his cheeks.

The accusations were there once again, whispered words of contempt from inside his head.

"I didn't kill him," he screamed. "It was an accident." Harold lifted its head, feeling how slack the neck was. Its chest was moving but only slightly and he could no longer hear the rasping, guttural breathing. Harold bent forward to kiss the thin lips and, as he did so, the face seemed, in his mind's eye, to alter shape again until it was no longer his baby brother he held but the familiar form of the bloated foetus. He found his lips pressed to cold, wet flesh. He felt and tasted the blood, his blood. The pus stuck to his lips in oozing gobs and Harold shrieked once more, trying to wipe the vile substance from his mouth. He fell backwards, the body of the creature falling from his arms. Harold gagged as the obscene mixture of blood and pus clogged on his tongue. He rolled onto his side and retched until there was nothing left in his stomach.

When the spasms had finally passed, he hauled himself up on one elbow, his head spinning. He wiped the tears from his cheeks and gazed down at the dying foetus, the bitter aftertaste of his vomit still strong in his mouth.

"Oh God," he murmured.

He felt weak, barely able to support himself as he tried to stand. He managed it with effort, reaching for a filthy handkerchief which he pulled from his trouser pocket. He pressed it to the wound on his arm and held it firmly until the worst of the bleeding had stopped.

"I'll always do my best," he gasped, looking down at the foetal monstrosities. "I promise."

Harold took a step backwards. In the darkness of the room he almost stumbled over some of the other debris. The floor was smeared with excrement and dried blood. It smelt like an open sewer. The pungent odour of decaying, putrescent flesh was also noticeable. He dropped to his knees, exhausted by his sleepless night and also by the mental strain which he had been under for so long. He lay on the blanket but he dare not sleep. If he did, the dreams would come and he could not stand that. How he wished he had the tablets they used to give him, with those he never dreamed. There were no spectres waiting in his subconscious then, nothing to crawl out during sleeping hours to torment his mind.

But the dreams *had* returned now. So vividly at times that it was almost impossible to separate imagination from reality. He glanced across at the foetuses and shivered, pulling the blanket tighter around him.

The voices, now that little bit quieter, still hissed inside his head.

Thirty-eight

Maggie Ford washed her hands quickly and dried them on the sterilized towel before pulling on the surgical gloves. With her hair pinned up beneath her white cap she made her way hurriedly into the operating room where the unconscious body of a young woman lay on the table. Around her stood nurses and the anaesthetist who was checking his equipment. He already had his mask on and Maggie followed suit a moment later, crossing to her patient.

"What have we got?" said Maggie, looking down at the young woman whose smock had been opened to reveal her body. Her pubic hair had been hurriedly shaved and the area looked raw and angry but it was the blood seeping from the woman's vagina which disturbed Maggie most of all. There was a prominent bulge around the left hand side of the patient's abdomen, the skin shining beneath the lights of the operating theatre. It looked as if it were being stretched from inside.

"Suspected ectopic pregnancy," Maggie was told by a nurse standing close by. "The woman's name is Judith Myers, they rushed her in about ten minutes ago. She collapsed at work."

Maggie frowned. She inhaled and took a closer look at the bulge in Judith Myer's abdomen. It seemed to be pulsating.

The doctor wasted no time, realizing that the woman's life could be lost or saved in a matter of minutes. She set to work, something nagging at the back of her mind. She had heard the name Myers before, recently too.

The initial incision was made and Maggie worked as fast as she was able until she finally exposed the bulging Fallopian tube. There were audible gasps about the theatre.

"My God," she muttered. "It's a long way advanced isn't it?" She took the instruments that were handed to her, a bead of perspiration popping onto her forehead. The bulge was very large and, impossibly seemed to be moving even as she watched it. The blip on the nearby oscilloscope dipped violently, the rhythmic high-pitched sound fluctuating alarmingly once or twice. A nurse checked Judith Myers's blood pressure.

"Her blood pressure is falling," she said, anxiously.

Maggie held the scalpel in one hand, realizing what she must do but her hands suddenly seemed leaden, her gaze riveted to that pulsing protruberance which was stretching her patient's Fallopian tube practically to bursting point.

Harold huddled in one corner of the room watching the foetuses. They lay still, only the almost imperceptible rise and fall of their chests signalling that they were still alive. But, as he watched, he saw the veins on their bulbous heads swell and throb and their eyes gradually darken until they seemed to be glowing with some mysterious black light that filled the room, drifting like smoke all around them. Their bodies began to shake.

The blip on the oscilloscope was still diving wildly, the

sound occasionally shutting down for brief seconds. Maggie swallowed hard, noting that the membranous covering of the bulging Fallopian tube was actually beginning to tear. She heard muttered words around her as she worked to cut the tube free. She called for a swab, alarmed at the amount of blood which seemed to be forming in the abdominal cavity. It was lifted, dripping crimson, from the danger area to be replaced a second later by another. Then another.

A second split appeared in the thin wall of the Fallopian tube, the membrane tearing like overstretched fabric.

"We're losing her, doctor," someone called and Maggie looked up to see that the oscilloscope pattern had almost levelled out.

Harold opened his mouth in a silent scream as the entire room seemed to fill with a deafening roar. He clapped both hands to his ears but the sound continued. It was inside his head, it was all around him, filling the room until it seemed the walls must explode outwards. The foetuses continued to shudder violently, the veins on their bodies now turning purple, their eyes glowing red like pools of boiling blood.

Maggie recoiled as the large bulge in Judith Myers's Fallopian tube seemed first to contract and then erupt. There was a fountain of blood, pus and pieces of human tissue as the internal organ literally exploded showering those nearby with viscera. A young nurse fainted. The anaesthetist leapt from his seat and dashed across to Maggie's side. Both of them turned to see that the oscilloscope blip had stopped bobbing and bouncing, it just ran in an uninterrupted straight line now, its mournful note filling the operating room. Maggie worked to remove the ruptured tube, trying in vain to save her patient's life. There was blood everywhere, even on the large light above the operating table. Maggie herself wiped some from her face, gazing down almost in disbelief at the damage before her. The young nurse was being helped to her feet and supported out of the theatre.

While another nurse checked the patient's blood pressure for one last time, Maggie herself listened for any sign of heartbeat. There was none. She pulled a penlight from her smock pocket and shone it into the woman's eyes. There was no pupillary reaction.

Judith Myers was dead.

Maggie untied her mask and turned to the nearest nurse.

"Fetch a porter," she said. "I want an autopsy done immediately."

Maggie, her smock and face spattered with blood, made her way back to the wash-room, her movements almost mechanical. She knew what she had just seen but she did not believe it. The ectopic pregnancy had been too far advanced. If her guess was correct, Judith Myers would have had to have been at least five months pregnant for her Fallopian tube to be in that condition. Myers. Judith Myers. Again she felt that nagging at the back of her mind. She knew that name from somewhere.

She pulled off her blood-stained gloves and tossed them into the bin, washing her hands beneath the swiftly flowing water from the tap.

The realization hit her with the force of a steam-hammer and, for long seconds she stood still. Thoughts tumbled through her mind and she exhaled deeply. She finished washing and pulled her white coat back on, heading out into the corridor. Before she took a trip down to the pathology lab, she intended visiting the records department. She had just remembered where she'd heard the name Judith Myers.

It took the clerk in the records office less than five minutes to find the file on Judith Myers. Maggie took the file gratefully and walked across to the desk on the other side of the room. There she sat down and flipped the folder open.

NAME: Judith Myers. DATE OF BIRTH: 14/3/57.
REASON FOR ADMISSION: Clinical Abortion

Maggie scanned the rest of the sheet, her eyes straying to the date of admission. She looked at it again. Could there have been some mistake? She doubted it. She herself had performed the abortion. She looked yet again at the admission date. Finally, clutching the file to her chest she got to her feet. She asked the clerk if she could take the file with her, promising to return it in an hour or so. Maggie left the records office and headed towards the pathology labs.

It took Ronald Potter less than an hour to complete the autopsy on Judith Myers. Maggie sat in his office drinking coffee until the chief pathologist finally joined her. He sat down heavily in his chair and ran a hand through his false hair, careful not to dislodge the toupée.

"Well?" Maggie said.

Potter sniffed.

"Well, Doctor Ford, I'm sure you don't need me to tell you that it was an ectopic pregnancy. She died of massive internal bleeding."

"Did you examine the Fallopian tube itself?" Maggie wanted to know.

Potter stroked his chin thoughtfully.

"Yes I did." His tone was heavy, troubled even.

"What caused the rupture to be so. . ." she struggled for the word, "so violent?"

"Well, the curious thing is, I don't know," said the pathologist, colouring slightly. "The size and nature

234

of the Fallopian rupture would indicate that she was carrying a foetus of over six months which as we both know is clinically impossible. But there's something else puzzling." He paused. "My examination showed no sign of a foetus, any embryonic life or even an egg. There was nothing in her Fallopian tube to cause a rupture of that size. In fact there was nothing in there, full stop."

"So you're saying that she died of a condition that was not pathological," said Maggie.

"That's correct. There was no evidence of any ferti-lized life-form in the Fallopian tube. It's almost as if the swelling and the subsequent rupture were. . ." He grinned humourlessly.

"Were what?" Maggie demanded.

"It's as if they were psychosomatically induced. There is *no* trace of foetus, embryo or egg in that woman's Fallopian tube." The pathologist exhaled deeply and traced a line across his forehead with one index finger.

"Well, I found something too," said Maggie, holding up the file. "How old did you say the foetus would have to be to cause a Fallopian rupture of that size?"

"Six months, at least," said Potter.

"Judith Myers underwent a clinical abortion in this hospital less than six weeks ago."

"That's impossible," said the pathologist, reaching for the file as if he doubted the truth of Maggie's words. He scanned the admission sheet, his brow wrinkling. "There must be some mistake."

"That's what I thought," she confessed. "But, as you can see from the notes, I did the operation myself."

Potter sat back in his chair and shook his head almost imperceptibly.

"A woman has an abortion six weeks ago," said Maggie. "Then dies of a Fallopian rupture that could only have been caused by the lodging of a foetus at least six months old in her tube and yet you find no trace of any foetus. Not even an egg."

Both of them stared at each other not knowing what to say. The silence in the office was heavy, like a weight pressing down on them and Maggie was not the only one to feel spidery fingers of fear plucking at the back of her neck.

Thirty-nine

PC Stuart Reed brought the Panda car to a halt outside the gate which led into the farmyard. The gate, like the fence it was attached to, was rotting. Pieces of broken, splintered wood jutting out like a series of compound fractures from the untended surround.

The farm buildings themselves looked dark and dirty in the mid-morning sunshine and the slight breeze moved the weather vane atop the barn, causing it to squeak loudly like a trapped mouse.

"Why the bloody hell do we have to check this place again?" groaned Constable Charlton. "I mean we've already been out here twice and there was no sign of Harvey."

Reed shrugged.

"Sergeant Willis said we had to go over everything with a fine toothcomb," said the younger man, glancing out at the collection of buildings. "I'd better check in." He reached for the two-way and relayed their position to the station. Willis's voice acknowledged the call.

"Do you want to toss for it?" said Ray Charlton.

Reed looked blank.

"For the privilege of looking around," Charlton clarified.

"Perhaps we should both go," said the younger man.

"And leave the car? Sod off, if the Sergeant calls through and finds out we've both gone for a walk he'll string us up by the bollocks." Charlton studied his companion's face for a moment then he reached for a walkie-talkie, taking it from the parcel shelf. "I'll go," he muttered, pushing open the door. He stepped out into a pool of muddy water and it was all Reed could do to suppress a grin.

"Shit," grunted Charlton and slammed the door behind him. The younger man watched as his companion trudged across the muddy ground, having to lift the farmyard gate out of the sticky muck before he could open it enough to squeeze through. Reed picked up his own walkie-talkie and flicked it on.

"Why didn't you jump it?" he asked, chuckling.

Charlton turned and raised two fingers in a familiar gesture. He walked on, finding, thankfully, that the ground was becoming firmer. The sun wasn't strong enough to dry it out but the chill wind probably helped to toughen up the top soil. He stood still in the centre of the yard and looked around. It was as quiet as a grave. To his right lay two barns, to his left the farmhouse itself. All the buildings had been searched before. When Harvey first escaped he and Reed had been ordered to scout the deserted farm and, as Charlton had expected, they had found nothing. That had been nearly three months ago and now they expected the bloody maniac to be still holed up here when, in reality, he was probably long gone and had been since the first day of his escape. However, Charlton's cynicism did not take into account the three murders and he, as well as everyone on the Exham force, realized that the decapitations were Harvey's trade mark. The bastard was still in or around Exham somewhere but he doubted if it was here.

He decided to check the barns initially and made his way across the yard to the first of the large buildings. The door was open so the constable walked straight in, coughing as the smell of damp and rotting straw hit him. He peered up towards the loft and, glancing across at the ladder which led to the higher level, decided to check it. He reached for the walkie-talkie and switched it on.

"Stuart, come in."

Reed's voice sounded metallic as he replied.

"Have you found something?" the younger man wanted to know.

"No," Charlton snapped. "And not likely to. I'm just checking the first barn."

He switched off the two-way and clipped it to his belt as he began to climb the ladder which would take him up into the loft. The floorboards creaked menacingly beneath his weight and the policeman stood still for long seconds wondering if the entire floor were going to collapse beneath him but then, cautiously, he made a quick inspection of the upper level. A couple of dead rats and some small bones were all he found. He knelt and picked up one of the bones. It looked like a tiny femur and he surmised that one of the rodents that inhabited the barn had served as a midnight meal for an owl. He tossed the tiny bone away and headed back towards the ladder, pausing long enough to tell Reed that the first barn was clear.

It was the same story in the second of the buildings. It held just a couple of pieces of rusty farm machinery, otherwise the place was empty.

"I'm going to check the house now," Charlton said and started across the yard towards the last building.

Reed, still watching from the Panda, saw his companion approach the farmhouse and was puzzled when he hesitated before it. The walkie-talkie crackled into life.

"The door's open," said Charlton, a vague note of surprise in his voice. "Probably the wind."

"Do you want any help?" Reed asked.

Charlton didn't. He slowed his pace as he drew closer to the house, nudging the door back the last few inches with the toe of his boot. The hinges screeched protestingly and, as the constable advanced, he was enveloped by the overpowering odour of damp once again. The house smelt musty, closing around him like an invisible hand. He coughed and moved further into the room. It was a hallway. Straight ahead was a flight of stairs, now devoid of carpet, some of the steps were already eaten through by woodworm or rising damp. To his right lay a door, to his left another, this one slightly ajar. He hesitated, not sure which way to go first. He decided to look upstairs so, negotiating the rickety steps, he climbed to the higher level. The curtains had been left drawn up there and it was difficult to see in the almost impenetrable gloom.

Three closed doors confronted him.

Pulling the torch from his belt with one hand, Charlton reached for the handle of the first door and rammed it down, pushing the door open simultaneously. It swung back against the wall and he immediately brought the torch beam to bear on the contents of the room. There was an old chest of drawers, obviously too big to be moved when the owners' left but, apart from that, there was nothing. The floor was thick with dust and a quick inspection told the PC that it was undisturbed.

He moved to the second door.

Once more the door opened with no trouble, this time into a cramped toilet cum bathroom. The taps were mottled and rusty, the bath itself crusted with mould.

He closed that door behind him and moved across to the last.

The door knob twisted in his grasp but would not turn. Charlton tried again, this time throwing his weight against it but still the door wouldn't budge. He flicked off the torch and slipped it back into his belt then, taking a step back, he aimed a powerful kick at the handle which promptly dropped off.

The door opened a few inches.

Charlton, feeling unaccountably nervous, pushed the door open and stood motionless in the frame, eyes alert for any movement. As with the other two rooms, things were untouched and, almost gratefully, he reached for the two-way.

"The upstairs is clear," he said. "I'm just going to check the lower floor."

"Any sign of life?" Reed wanted to know.

"There's more life in a bloody graveyard," said the older man and flicked off the set. Feeling somewhat more relaxed, he made his way back down the stairs, his heavy boots clumping on the damp wood.

He looked into the sitting room and found it to be empty then he passed into the last room in the house, the kitchen.

He paused at the cellar door, his hand hovering over the knob. Last time he and Reed had been out here, they had left without checking the cellar but, this time, Charlton knew the job must be done. The lock was old and rusty but nevertheless strong and, at first, resisted even his most powerful kicks as he attempted to break it off. Finally, the recalcitrant lump of rusted metal dropped to the floor with a clang and the door opened outwards a fraction. The constable reached for his torch once more and edged inside the doorway until he was standing on the top step of the flight of stone stairs that led down into the all-enveloping gloom of the cellar.

The smell which met him was almost palpable in its

240

intensity and he raised one hand to his face in an effort to keep the fetid stench away. He shone his torch down, the beam scarcely penetrating the blackness. Cautiously, careful not to slip in any of the puddles of moisture on the steps, he descended, breathing through his mouth in an effort to counteract the appalling stench.

He reached the bottom and shone the torch around, playing its beam over the floor, picking out the broken bottles, the shattered lumps of wood where some of the shelves had been overturned. His heart was beating just that little bit faster as he moved further into the dark recesses of the subterranean hole, the torch lancing through the blackness like some kind of laser beam.

He stepped in something soft and cursed, looking down to see what it was.

"Oh Christ," he murmured.

It was excrement.

He winced and tried to wipe the worst of it off, realizing that it was of human origin. A sudden cold chill nipped at the back of his neck and he stood still, sure that he'd heard something. A low rasping sound came from close by. He spun round, his torch beam searching the darkness.

There was nothing.

A loud crackle ripped through the silence and Charlton almost shouted aloud in fear, his mind taking precious seconds to adjust to the fact that it was the two-way. He snatched it from his belt angrily.

"Found anything?" Reed wanted to know

"For fuck's sake don't do that again," rasped Charlton, his hand shaking.

"What's wrong?" his companion wanted to know.

The other constable recovered his breath, angry with himself too for letting the situation get a hold of him.

"I'm down in the cellar of the house," he said. "We didn't check it out last time we were here."

"And?"

"Someone's been here. Whether it's Harvey or not I can't say but, by the look of the place whoever it was was holed up here for quite a time. The cellar's been wrecked." He described the scene of devastation and filth before him. "Call the station," he added as a post-script. "You'd better get them to send another car out here." He flicked off the two-way. Charlton shone the torch beam around the reeking confines of the cellar one last time then he turned back towards the stairs.

The massive bulk of Paul Harvey loomed before him, silhouetted in the dim light which filtered in from the kitchen and, in that half-light, Charlton caught sight of the sickle as it swept down.

Paralysed, momentarily, by the sight of the figure before him, Charlton was unable to move as quickly as he would usually have done. He tried to avoid the vicious blade but it caught him on the left arm, tearing through the fabric of his uniform and slicing open skin and muscle from the shoulder to the elbow. Blood burst from the ragged wound and, with a shriek, Charlton fell backwards, the two-way skidding from his grasp. He tried to scramble to his feet, blood pumping thickly from the hideous rent in his arm.

Harvey advanced quickly, swinging the curved blade down once more. This time the policeman managed to roll clear and the wicked point embedded itself in a broken shelf. Harvey grunted and tore it free, noticing that Charlton was making for the stairs.

"Ray, are you all right?"

Reed's disembodied voice floated up from the discarded walkie-talkie.

Charlton reached the bottom step and, clutching his torn arm, raced up the slippery steps but Harvey moved with surprising agility for a man of his size. He swiped wildly at the fleeing policeman, the sickle blade slicing through the man's thigh, hamstringing him. Charlton crashed down onto the stone steps, white hot pain gnawing at his leg.

"Ray. Come in. What's happening?"

Dazed by his fall and weak from loss of blood, Charlton rolled onto his back to see Harvey towering over him. The sickle swept down once again, this time to its appointed mark. It pierced the policeman's chest just below the sternum, then, using his enormous stength, Harvey ripped it downwards, gutting Charlton with one stroke. A tangled mess of intestines spilled from the riven torso and the policeman's scream was lost as his mouth filled with blood. His head sagged forward as he plunged both hands into the steaming maze of his own entrails, trying to push them back in.

"Ray, for Christ's sake."

Harvey looked around for the source of the voice but realized that it was the two-way. He headed up the stairs towards the kitchen, stepping over the eviscerated body of the dead policeman.

Reed actually heard the sirens in the distance as he looked up towards the farmhouse and, as he opened the door to clamber out, he heard a familiar voice rasping over the two way in the car.

"Alpha one come in," said Randall.

"Reed here," he answered. "I think we've found Harvey."

"Stop the bastard," Randall ordered. "I don't care if you have to kill him. Just stop him."

The sirens were growing louder as the other two Pandas drew closer but, when Reed looked up he saw Harvey emerge into the daylight, his clothes splashed with blood. The young PC shouted to him to stop but the desperate convict merely slowed his pace, as if waiting for Reed to come closer and, as he drew nearer, the policeman saw the sickle. Blood was dripping from its curved blade.

Reed ran across the muddy yard, tripping on something as he did so. He scrambled to his feet to see that it was a rake. He picked it up, hefting the rusty metal head before him like some kind of ancient quarter-staff.

Harvey remained motionless, even when the first of the Pandas skidded to a halt in the yard. Randall leapt out and moved towards the big man.

It was at that moment Harvey chose to strike.

He lunged towards Reed who managed to bring the rake up to shield himself. The sickle struck the wooden shaft and cut through it easily. Reed fell backwards, trying to crawl away through the mud as the big man came for him.

Randall, who had moved closer by this time, picked up a handful of mud and hurled it into the man's face, momentarily blinding him. Harvey raised a hand to wipe the oozing muck away and Randall took his chance. He launched himself at his opponent, smashing into him just above the pelvis. Both of them went sprawling, the sickle flying from Harvey's grasp. Randall reacted first and, with a vicious grunt, drove two fingers into the big man's left eye. Harvey shrieked in pain and rage and scrambled to his feet as Randall backed off, looking for something to defend himself with. Harvey roared and charged at him, catching the Inspector by the shoulder, pulling him down. Randall gasped as he felt strong hands encircle his throat. White light flashed before his eyes. His face began to turn the colour of dark grapes and it was as if his head were going to burst. Then, through a haze of pain, he saw Reed retrieve the metal topped end of the rake.

With a blow combining demonic force and terrified desperation, the young PC brought the rusty metal down on the back of Harvey's head. There was a dull clang, combined with the strident snapping of bone and Randall suddenly felt the pressure on his throat ease.

The big man tottered, then tumbled forward into the mud, groaning. Randall rolled clear, helped to his feet by PC Higgins. Both of them watched, almost in awe, as Harvey raised himself up on one elbow and tried to get up. Randall stepped forward and, with all the power he could muster, drove his foot into the big man's face. The impact shattered his nose, blood and small fragments of bone flying into the air.

"Bastard," muttered Randall, massaging his throat. He prodded the prone body with his foot then turned to Higgins.

"Get an ambulance for him," snapped the Inspector. "But put the cuffs on the bastard first."

Higgins scuttled off to call an emergency vehicle while Fowler cuffed the unconscious convict.

"He killed PC Charlton," said Reed, motioning towards the house. Randall walked slowly towards the deserted dwelling. He did, indeed, find Charlton in the house, his stomach somersaulting as he gazed at the mutilated corpse. He lingered in the reeking cellar for a moment then walked back out into the yard sucking in huge lungfuls of clean air.

An ambulance was approaching, its blue light spinning frenziedly and Randall watched as Harvey was lifted into the back of it by the dark uniformed men. The vehicle turned full circle and sped off in the direction of Fairvale, its siren gradually dying on the wind as it got further away.

"Thank Christ we found him, guv," said Higgins.

Randall nodded.

"Yeah," he said acidly. "But we were three months too late, weren't we?"

Forty

Randall lit up another cigarette and blew out a stream of smoke which diffused in the warm air. It drifted lazily in the lounge bar of "The Gamekeeper". The pub was quieter than usual but, nevertheless, Ralph the landlord busied himself behind the bar, serving and chatting, dispensing booze and gossip in equal proportions. He was a big man, about four years older than Randall and he carried a bad limp (beneath his trousers he wore callipers). He'd been landlord of the pub for the past eight years, prior to which he'd been in the Scots Guards. The limp was a legacy from one of his spells in Northern Ireland.

Every so often he would look across and nod agreeably at the Inspector who was sitting on the other side of the room beside the blazing log fire which roared in the grate. The hiss and pop of burning wood seemed unnaturally loud in the relative calm of the lounge. From the public bar, the far off sound of a juke-box cut through the subdued nattering. The pub was old but the juke-box was its concession to a livelier, more hectic age, one which was lived out in the public bar, frequented mostly by youngsters. The older regulars were content to down their pints and to play dominoes in the snug. Cocooned within that cosy environment, they were oblivious to all around them.

"Penny for them," said Maggie, studying Randall's expression.

He looked up and smiled.

"Sorry, Maggie," he said. "I was miles away."

"I noticed. What's wrong, Lou? You've been quiet ever since we got here."

"Be thankful for small mercies," he grinned.

"*Is* there something on your mind?" she persisted.

He reached for his pint and took a hefty swallow.

"I was thinking about Harvey," he confessed. "I rang my superior, Frank Allen, to tell him we'd got Harvey. Do you know what he said? 'About time'." He paused. "Bastard."

"What happens to him now?" Maggie wanted to know.

"They'll stick him in Rampton or Broadmoor I suppose. He'll be taken back to Cornford prison in the meantime. Though to be honest, I couldn't give a toss where they put him as long as he's out of the way. I just wish I could have got hold of him sooner than I did. Four people are dead now who might still be alive if I had."

"Come on, Lou, you can't carry the blame for those deaths too." There was a note of irritation in her voice. "Stop shouldering the responsibilities for everything that goes wrong. You did your job. What more could you do?"

He raised his glass to her and smiled.

"Point taken." He wiped some froth from his top lip. "What sort of day have *you* had?"

She considered telling him about Judith Myers but decided against it.

"Routine," she lied. "You wouldn't want to hear about it." She sipped her drink, changing the subject swiftly. "It's my day off tomorrow, can you get away a little earlier?"

Randall smiled.

"Well, with Harvey out of the way, there's just the paperwork to be written up." He reached out and touched her hand. "I should think I can sneak out around five."

Maggie smiled.

"What do you usually do on your day off?" he asked.

"Lie in bed," she began.

He cut her short.

247

"Now that sounds like a perfect way of spending a day."

They both laughed.

"I clean the flat, watch TV, read. Go shopping." She raised an eyebrow. "Really exciting isn't it?"

He smiled thinly, gazing into the bottom of his glass for a moment.

"Maggie, I hope you don't mind me asking but, well, these other men that you had relationships with –"

It was her turn to interrupt.

"I'd hardly call them relationships."

"Well, you know what I mean. Haven't you ever felt anything for any of them?"

"Why does it matter, Lou?" she wanted to know.

He shrugged.

"I'm a copper aren't I? Asking questions is second nature. I'm curious that's all."

She took another sip of her drink.

"No, there hasn't been anyone serious before. As I said to you the other night, I envy you your memories. All I've got is notches on the headboard." She smiled, bitterly. "And I'm sure that to most of the men I've slept with that's all I've been. Just another name in the little black book." She paused. "There was one man who wanted to marry me."

"What happened?" he asked.

She smiled.

"He worked for an oil company. They wanted him to move out to Bahrain for six months, he asked me to go with him. I said no. It was as simple as that. I'd just got the job at Fairvale and I didn't intend letting it go. He said that I wouldn't need to work, that we'd have plenty of money anyway but that wasn't the point. He didn't understand how important it was for me to feel needed. I enjoy the responsibilities I've got at the hospital. It makes me feel. . ." She struggled to find the word. "Accepted." She looked at him. "Anyway, I

248

didn't love him." She drained what was left in her glass and put it down.

Ralph appeared at the table, collecting empty glasses.

"Hello, Lou," he said. "You'd better make sure one of your boys doesn't catch you boozing, you might get breathalized." The Scotsman laughed. He looked at Maggie and smiled.

"Mrs Randall," he said. "How are you?"

Maggie swallowed hard and looked at the policeman, then at the landlord. She smiled thinly in response, colouring slightly as the Scotsman made his way back to the bar.

"I'm sorry, Lou," she said, softly.

"For what?" he asked, smiling.

"The barman . . . he thought I was your wife."

"Nothing to worry about. It's not your fault and Ralph doesn't know about Fiona anyway." He took a hefty swallow from his glass. "Perhaps we look married," he said.

"Who *does* know about your wife?" asked Maggie. "About what happened to her?"

"I think most of the men on the Exham force know," he said. "Word travels fast. Coppers like to rabbit as much as anyone else. But, other than them and you," he glanced up at her, "no one here knows I was ever married or that I had a child." He lit up a cigarette. "That was one of the reasons I came to Exham. After it happened, I put in for a transfer. I thought if I got away from London and the places that reminded me of the accident, then it might help me to forget it. So, they shunted me around for a couple of years until I ended up here."

She touched his hand.

"You still miss them?" she asked.

"Naturally." He touched her hand with his own. "But not as much as I used to."

He squeezed her hand, as if afraid that she was going

249

to somehow disappear and she felt the urgency in his touch.

Forty-one

Sergeant Norman Willis checked that Paul Harvey was securely strapped down in the back of the ambulance before making his way back to the waiting Panda close by. He slid into the passenger seat, watching as the rear doors of the emergency vehicle were pulled shut. The blue light was spinning but the siren was turned off. Willis looked at his watch and saw that it was approaching 10.08 p.m. The ambulance pulled away, behind it PC Fowler started the engine of the police car and both vehicles pulled out into traffic.

Willis and Fowler had both been ordered by Randall to remain at Fairvale while Harvey was treated for his injuries (a hair-line fracture of the skull and a broken nose) and then to ensure that the captured prisoner reached Cornford prison.

Willis yawned and rubbed his eyes, blowing out his cheeks.

"It's bloody hot in here, isn't it?" he said.

"The heater's up the creek, Sarge," Fowler told him, without taking his eyes off the ambulance which was travelling at a steady thirty about forty yards ahead of them.

"I think you'd better wake me up when we get to Cornford," said the sergeant, smiling.

Inside the ambulance itself a uniformed attendant sat on the seat opposite the stretcher where Harvey lay. He was reading an old copy of "Reader's Digest", alternately looking up to see if Harvey was OK. The big man moved occasionally, once even moaning softly and the attendant got to his feet and looked down at the patient. Harvey's head was heavily bandaged and a large dressing covered his nose and most of his cheeks. His mouth, however, was open and there was a dribble of thick saliva coming from one corner. The attendant, identified as Peter Smart by the small blue badge on his jacket, looked at the restraining straps and stroked his chin thoughtfully. Harvey was making even louder gurgling sounds now and Smart was worried in case the big man should choke on his own spittle. He hesitated a second longer then began to undo the first of the straps, intending to roll Harvey over onto his side.

The first strap came loose and Smart set to work on the second, the one which secured Harvey's feet.

With his back to the prisoner, Smart didn't see Harvey's eyes flicker open.

For long moments he tried to reorientate himself with his surroundings, with what was going on. There was a dull ache in his head and it felt as if someone were standing on his face but, as he saw the uniformed man undoing the strap on his legs, Harvey realized what was happening.

As the strap came free, he lashed out with his large foot, catching Smart in the solar plexus. The impact of the blow sent the ambulanceman flying backward and he thumped his head hard against the far wall of the vehicle.

Harvey, meantime, was sitting up, tugging wildly at the third and final strap which was across his midsection.

Smart reached for the small box close by, trying to get to the syringe, desperate to inject the prisoner with the 25mg of Promazine before it was too late. He scrambled towards Harvey who, by this time, had managed

251

to free himself and was in the process of getting to his feet.

Smart brought the needle down in a stabbing action, aiming for the big man's chest but Harvey was too fast for him and he clamped one huge hand around Smart's wrist, squeezing it like a vice until the appendage went white. With a despairing groan, Smart dropped the syringe. Harvey drove a powerful fist into the uniformed man's face, feeling bone splinter under the impact. He held his victim by the wrist for a second longer then, using both hands, hurled him against the other wall of the ambulance.

The driver felt the thump and slowed down.

Fowler, following close behind, saw the ambulance brake lights flare and nudged Willis.

"Sarge," he said, anxiously. "They're stopping."

Willis yawned.

"One of them probably wants to have a piss," he said.

By this time the emergency vehicle had indeed stopped. Fowler brought the Panda to a halt about twenty yards behind, watching as the driver got out and walked to the back of the vehicle. He fumbled with the doors, finally turning the handle.

Harvey came crashing out of the ambulance like a tank through a wall. The door slammed into the driver, knocking him flat and, before anyone could react, he was dashing off into the darkened woods to the left, disappearing like a fading nightmare.

Both Willis and Fowler leapt out of the car, the sergeant dashing after Harvey but it was useless. He saw the big man crashing through the undergrowth in his wild flight but the sergeant knew that he could never catch him. He ran back across the road to check on the injured ambulancemen. The driver was bleeding from a cut on the forehead, his companion inside lay unconscious.

252

"Get on the two-way, quick," Willis told Fowler. "Alert all cars. Tell them what's happened."

Fowler ran back to the car and snatched up the radio.

Within minutes, every man on the Exham force was picking up his frantic message.

Outside the pub, Maggie pulled up the collar of her coat and waited as Randall fumbled in his pocket for the car keys. A slight fog had come down during the evening and Maggie noticed how halos seemed to have formed around the sodium street lamps. Objects looked blurred and indistinct through the thin film of mist.

Randall finally found the keys and unlocked the car. Both of them climbed in. He was about to start the engine when the two-way hissed into life. Randall picked it up.

"Randall here, what is it?" he asked.

"It's Harvey," the voice at the other end said.

Maggie saw Randall's expression darken.

"Harvey's loose," the voice said.

Forty-two

Harold paced the corridors of the deserted asylum agitatedly. The wind was whispering through the many broken windows and it seemed to add an accompaniment to his apparently aimless wanderings. He moved with assurance through the dark avenues, through rooms which he had come to know only too well in the past and with which he was now becoming reacquainted. He could not sleep. It wasn't that he dare

253

not but, for the first time in many years, the welcome oblivion of unconsciousness eluded him.

He pushed open a door and walked into what had once been a dormitory. One or two beds, considered too old to be moved to the new psychiatric hospital, still stood in their familiar places. The iron work was rusted, the old mattresses damp and torn. Harold walked across to one and looked down at it. In his mind's eye he could see himself lying there, sleeping peacefully.

Crossing to one of the windows, he stared out into the night. It seemed a million years since he had been here, the memories now like fading photographs, the images becoming more and more indistinct.

He remained at the window for a long time then finally turned and walked back towards the door of the dormitory, pushing it shut behind him. He made his way slowly along the corridor, one hand absent-mindedly touching the scarred side of his face. Harold reached the foot of the staircase which would take him up to the first floor and the room where the foetuses lay. He paused for a moment, gazing up, as if expecting to see someone standing at the top, then, wearily, he began to climb. His legs and head ached and, as he drew nearer to the room, the stench which he had come to know so well wrapped itself around him like invisible tentacles.

He stumbled into the room and froze, both hands gripping the door frame until his knuckles turned white.

The first, and largest, of the three creatures was standing up.

It wavered uncertainly at first, those black pits of eyes pinning Harold in a hypnotic stare. Then, as if moving in slow motion, it began to walk.

Forty-three

Paul Harvey tore the last of the dressing from his nose and cheeks and tossed it aside. He had already removed the bandages around his head. Now he moved slowly down the lane, sucking in lungfuls of early morning air. He still found it difficult to breathe through his nose and his breathing was harsh and guttural. A persistent pain gnawed at the back of his head where he'd sustained the fracture and, periodically, he would press tentative fingers to it.

Exham had yet to come to life. The town seemed to be sleeping as dawn broke but Harvey knew that, soon, there would be people on the streets, in their gardens, walking their dogs. He had to find shelter. He'd spent the night in a shed at the bottom of a large garden. It was from there he'd picked up the shears which he now held in one huge hand but, as the daylight began to creep inexorably across the heavens, he knew he must find somewhere to hide.

The church stood on a hill, on the very edge of one of Exham's many estates. It was old, its stone-work worn and chipped, the colours in its stained-glass windows now faded somewhat. A weather vane squeaked mournfully in the light breeze and Harvey ran appraising eyes over the building as he approached it. Many of the gravestones were coloured with moss and a good number of the plots were overgrown. Here and there, dead flowers lay like discarded confetti, their petals now brown and wrinkled.

He reached the main door but found it locked. He

slammed a powerful fist against it twice, angry that he could not gain entry. Muttering to himself, he made his way around the building until he found another door. This one was old too, the woodwork the colour of dried blood. It was splintered in many places and the chain which held it shut looked brittle. Harvey tugged hard on it, gritting his teeth as he felt the rusty links give. It snapped with a dull clang and he tossed the pieces away, wedging his fingers in the gap between door and frame in an effort to get it open.

The hinges screamed alarmingly but Harvey persevered, finally opening it far enough to give himself access. He slipped inside. The stench and the impenetrable darkness nearly made him change his mind but, fortunately, due to his broken nose he could not detect too much of the fetid odour and he soon found that there was some light coming into the subterranean room. He descended the stone steps cautiously only realizing when he reached the bottom that he was in a crypt.

Nevertheless, it was shelter. He sat down, the shears across his lap.

He waited for the darkness.

Forty-four

Maggie stood still at the top of the stairs, trying to catch her breath. She considered herself a fit woman but climbing up a long flight of stairs with two armfuls of shopping had all but exhausted her. She walked across towards the door of her flat, wishing that she'd put some lower shoes on. Her feet were throbbing and she decided to run a bath as soon as she got inside. She put down her bags and fumbled in the pocket of her jeans for the key.

The phone was ringing inside and Maggie muttered irritably to herself as she struggled to unlock the door; she pushed it open, snatched up the bag and hurried in, one eye on the phone, convinced that it would stop ringing the moment she picked it up. She made a dash for it and lifted the receiver.

"Hello," she said.

"Doctor Ford?"

She recognized the voice at the other end of the line but could not identify it immediately.

"It's Ronald Potter here."

Maggie wrinkled her brow.

"What can I do for you?" she wanted to know.

Potter sounded anxious, distraught even.

"I've been trying to get hold of you for the last three hours," he said, speaking quickly, not giving her time to ask why. She glanced across at the clock on the mantlepiece which showed 4.35 p.m. "There's been another death. The symptoms are identical to those of that woman the other day." Maggie heard rustling of paper on the other end of the line. "The ectopic pregnancy, Judith Myers."

"I remember," she said.

"There was another one this afternoon and the results of the autopsy are exactly the same. No foetus, no embryo, not even an egg and yet she died of a Fallopian rupture."

Maggie let out a long, slow breath, gripping the receiver until her knuckles turned white.

"Doctor Ford."

Potter's voice seemed to shake her out of her trance.

"Yes, I'm still here," she told him. "Look, I'm coming over to the hospital now. I'll be there in about ten minutes." She put the phone down and, without changing, she rushed out once more. The shopping was left discarded on the sitting room floor.

Maggie sipped at the cup of luke-warm coffee and winced. On the desk before her lay half a dozen different files, including those on Judith Myers but the thing which was holding her attention was the neatly typed sheet headed:

FAIRVALE HOSPITAL: NOTICE OF DECEASE.

The name entered in the appropriate box was one which she recognized:

Lynn Tyler.

Maggie exhaled deeply and ran her eyes over the sheet for the fourth time. She had read the autopsy report countless times too, glancing at that of Judith Myers as well. From the wording, it might have been a duplicate of the same woman's autopsy. *Everything* was the same about the two cases. Both young women, apparently healthy, had died from internal haemorrhage due to the rupturing of a Fallopian tube. But it was not just a rupture, it was the complete destruction of that particular internal organ. There were no warning signs, just the rapid onset of symptoms so virulent they had caused death in a matter of hours.

"No evidence of any embryonic or foetal development," Maggie read aloud. The words were the same on both reports. It wasn't a virus of any kind, that she was sure of. Could it be coincidence? The chances must be astronomical. Lynn Tyler had suffered a Fallopian rupture which would have corresponded to her carrying a foetus of over six months. Even the size of the bursts was the same, thought Maggie, and there was one more thing which made her uneasy.

Lynn Tyler, like Judith Myers, had undergone a clinical abortion just seven weeks earlier.

She swept her hair back and tried to find some kind

258

of explanation for the two deaths in the facts and figures laid out before her. There seemed to be no answers, just the unnervingly exact similarities between the two deaths.

There was another file on her desk, one which she now picked up and glanced through. It was a report by the senior porter on the discovery of the foetuses which Harold Pierce had buried in the field beyond the hospital grounds. She read it once, then twice, this time more slowly. It told of how the grave had been discovered, the remains disinterred and disposed of and ended with a note about Harold's dismissal because of his part in the action. Five foetuses had been dug up and incinerated. Maggie frowned and glanced across at another piece of paper to her left. It was a record of all clinical abortions carried out between the beginning of August and the end of September. There had been eight. The porter assigned to dispose of each one had been Harold Pierce.

Eight abortions but only five foetuses found in the grave.

Perhaps he just missed three Maggie reasoned. She chewed her bottom lip, contemplatively. Harold's obsession with the "burning of children", as he put it, was something which had surprised her but now, as she sat alone in her office, she began to wonder just how deep that obsession went.

"Eight abortions carried out," she muttered. "Five bodies exhumed." She drummed on the desk top with her fingers.

There was a knock on the door.

"Come in," Maggie called and was surprised to see Randall standing there.

"I went to your flat," he said. "There was no answer so I thought I'd try here."

"I'm sorry," she said, "something came up." Then, remembering he had problems of his own she added:

"Any sign of Harvey yet?"

He shook his head, producing a newspaper from behind his back. He held it before him.

"I could have done without this too," he muttered, handing her the paper.

She opened it and read the headline:

Maniac Harvey Eludes Police Again

"Oh Christ," said Maggie, quickly scanning the story that accompanied the headline. " 'Mass murderer, Paul Harvey, already thought to be responsible for four deaths in Exham recently, escaped from the police for the second time in as many days. . .' " She allowed the sentence to trail off. "What are you going to do?" she asked him.

Randall was gazing out of the window into the darkening evening sky. The first droplets of rain were coursing down the pane like silent tears.

"About what?" he demanded. "Harvey, or that fucking article?"

"Both."

"Bloody local papers," rasped Randall. "They're all the same. A bunch of two-bit scribblers. They might as well write on toilet paper because the stuff they write is only fit for wiping your arse on." He banged the window frame angrily.

"And Harvey?" she said.

Randall sucked in a troubled breath.

"My men are out there now looking for him, they've got orders to call me the minute they find anything." He turned, scanning the piles of paper and files on her desk. "What's *your* problem?" He sat down opposite her and Maggie began speaking. She explained everything. About the two deaths, about the autopsy reports, the abortions, even the discovery of the foetuses' grave.

"Christ," murmured Randall when she'd finally finished. "How do you explain it?"

"I can't," she told him.

"And the pathologist has no answer either?"

She shook her head.

He asked if it could be a virus.

"Any infection would have shown up in the examination," she told him.

He reached forward and picked up one of the files, flipping through it.

"In both cases," she said, "there was no *physical* cause for the Fallopian ruptures, that's the most puzzling thing. It's as if they were, well. . ." she struggled to find the words, "induced."

Randall looked up.

"I don't get you," he said.

"Every woman reacts differently to an abortion," Maggie explained. "For some it's a great relief but even the ones who want abortions and realize how necessary they are still feel guilty. It might only be in their subconcious but the guilt is still there."

"So you're trying to say that these two women induced the symptoms of ectopic pregnancy in themselves to compensate for the kids they'd had aborted?" he said.

Maggie raised an eyebrow.

"Does it sound crazy?"

Randall dropped the file back onto the desk.

"It sounds bloody ridiculous, Maggie," he said.

"Well then what the hell do you think happened?" she asked.

"Look, you're the doctor not me but you must admit that theory is stretching things a bit."

"Do you know anything about the power of the mind, Lou?"

"About as much as the average man in the street. What kind of power?"

"Thought projection, auto-suggestion, self-hypnosis. That kind of thing."

261

He sighed.

"Come on, Lou," she muttered, "I know it's clutching at straws but it's all I've got. Both women aborted for non-medical reasons."

"Meaning what?" he demanded.

"Usually abortions are carried out if the baby is found to be malformed, retarded or sometimes even dead. Both Judith Myers and Lynn Tyler would have given birth to perfectly healthy children. There was nothing clinically wrong with the babies they were carrying. They had abortions for convenience not necessity."

"You said there were three bodies missing from the grave," he said. "What about the mother of the third aborted child?"

Maggie flicked through one of the files.

"That abortion was a medical necessity," she told him. "The scan showed that the child would have been malformed."

Randall nodded.

"If your theory about the ectopic pregnancies is right," the Inspector said, "then you realize you're trying to tell me they committed suicide."

Maggie sighed.

"I know it sounds ridiculous, you're right." There was a long pause. "Lou, it's almost as if they'd both still had the foetuses gestating inside their Fallopian tubes despite the fact that they'd undergone abortions just weeks before. I don't know what to think."

"What about this business with the grave?" he asked. "Were the three missing bodies ever found?"

"Not to my knowledge."

Randall frowned, aware that what he was about to say was going to sound idiotic. He coughed.

"Is there any way a foetus could continue to grow once it had been removed from the womb?" he asked.

"No. Even in laboratory conditions it would be difficult. Not impossible but extremely unlikely."

He exhaled deeply.

"Now I'm not sure what *I'm* trying to say," he confessed. "But I know one thing, I'd like to talk to Harold Pierce."

"How could he be linked with this?" she wanted to know.

"Maybe he knows what happened to those other three bodies."

Maggie closed the files and stacked them on one corner of the desk. She got to her feet, switching off the lamp. The room was momentarily plunged into darkness.

"Perhaps we'll both think straighter on a full stomach," said Randall, opening the office door for her.

They walked out into the corridor, heading for the lift. Maggie looked worried and, as they reached the ground floor, she took his hand and held it tightly. The two of them walked out to the car park where Randall's Chevette waited. As he opened the passenger door to let her in, Maggie seemed reluctant to let go of his hand. He touched her cheek gently and kissed her softly on the lips.

Inside the car, despite the warmth from the heater, both of them shivered.

They were back at Randall's place in less than twenty minutes.

Neither of them ate much. They spoke quietly, as if afraid that their conversation would be overheard by someone. Again and again they discussed what had transpired at the hospital, as if repeated examination of the bizarre events would somehow lead to a solution. There was no need for either of them to suspect anything out of the ordinary but nevertheless an atmosphere of foreboding seemed to descend over them as they spoke. In the sitting room, Maggie sat close to

263

Randall, glad to feel his arm around her shoulder. Still they talked and still they could find no answers.

"We could go on like this all night," said Maggie, "and it still wouldn't get us anywhere." She smiled humourlessly. "Now I know what you feel like trying to find Paul Harvey."

"There seems to be more than one needle in *this* haystack, though," he said, taking a drag on the cigarette he'd just lit up. He got to his feet and crossed to a drinks cabinet where he poured them both a large measure of brandy.

Maggie glanced around the room. It was small and tidy. Randall obviously took care of the place. There was a pleasing smell of lemon in the room (from a carpet cleaner, she guessed) which further attested to its cleanliness. On the mantelpiece above the glowing gas fire there were three photos. The first was of Randall and his wife and daughter, the second and third of Fiona and Lisa alone. Maggie was struck by how attractive the dead woman had been. The little girl too, smiling out from behind the glass in the frame, sported two dimples which only added to the cheeky playfulness mirrored in her eyes.

"Your wife was very pretty," said Maggie.

Randall smiled.

"I know," he said, handing her a drink. "Lisa looked a lot like her." He crossed to the mantelpiece and lifted the photo of his daughter. "My little lady," he said, smiling. He replaced the photo almost reluctantly and turned back to face Maggie.

"She would have thought the same about you." He smiled and raised his glass.

He took a long swallow, allowing the amber fluid to burn its way down to his stomach. Maggie sipped at hers.

"So," said Randall. "What else can you do about

these deaths? Is there anything more the pathologist can tell you?"

Maggie shook her head.

"I don't know, Lou," she confessed. She gazed into the bottom of her glass and then up at him. "The only thing that bothers me is, if there's no explanation for these two deaths, what's to stop it happening to other women? Maybe even women who aren't pregnant?"

"Why should it affect them?"

"If there was no foetus or embryo in the Fallopian tubes then, theoretically, it could happen to any woman of child-bearing age."

"You can't say that until you know the cause," he protested.

"That's the whole problem isn't it? We don't know the cause."

They both lapsed into silence, a solitude broken by the strident ringing of the phone. Randall crossed to it and lifted the receiver to his ear.

"Randall."

Maggie looked at him and could only guess at what the caller was saying but, from the expression on Randall's face, it obviously wasn't good news. She got to her feet and walked across to him.

"Yeah. When? Whereabouts?" He pulled a pad towards him and wrote something on it. As he listened, the policeman was drawing small circles on the pad with his pencil.

"What's wrong?" Maggie whispered.

"A murder," he told her, handing her the note which bore the location. "But we've got a witness."

She swallowed hard, watching him as he listened, the pencil still performing its spyrographic rotations on the pad.

"Willis," said Randall. "Did the victim have any ID on him?"

"No, guv." The sergeant's voice sounded strained.

265

"We did some finger-print tests just to be sure. We double-checked. Triple-checked."

"Checked what for Christ's sake?" Randall demanded.

Willis sighed.

"The victim was decapitated."

Randall's pencil snapped with a loud crunch.

"What's that got to do with bloody fingerprints?" he demanded.

"The victim was Paul Harvey."

Forty-five

Randall brought the Chevette to a screeching halt, the tyres spinning for a second on the wet tarmac. Across the street he could see an ambulance, its blue light spinning noiselessly, and two Panda cars. Uniformed men moved around in the darkness and, as he pushed open the door, the Inspector saw that much of the far side of the road was lined with trees. Beyond them was a narrow pathway which led between two houses. The pathway was masked by high hedges on both sides. There were lights on in both of the houses and also in some further down the street. Indeed, some people had even braved the rain to stand at their gates in an effort to see what was going on.

Maggie got out too, slamming her door behind her. Together they crossed to the scene of feverish activity. Randall caught sight of PC Higgins and called him over.

"Where's the body?" he said.

"This way, guv," he said. "We didn't move anything until you arrived." He led them a little way down the narrow path to a sheet shrouded object. Randall knelt and pulled back one corner of the covering, wincing as he did so.

"Shit," he muttered.

Maggie too looked at the headless body, letting out a long, slow breath.

"Where's the witness?" the inspector wanted to know.

"He's in the ambulance. Some old girl from the house next door gave him a cup of tea. The poor sod's in quite a state. He's only a kid."

Randall and Maggie followed Higgins to the ambulance, the Inspector hauling himself up into the back of the vehicle. The youth, no more than fifteen, was milk white and shaking like a leaf. He held a mug of tea in both hands as if not quite sure what to do with it.

He looked up anxiously as Randall joined him in the back of the ambulance. Maggie climbed in behind him.

"What's your name, son?" Randall asked him.

The lad picked nervously at one of the spots on his chin and swallowed hard.

"M-Mark Rawlings," he stammered.

"I just want to know what you saw," said Randall, softly.

The youth tried to stop himself shaking but found it an impossible task. Some of the tea slopped over the lip of the mug and burned his hand. Maggie took it from him.

"Well," he began. "I was coming home from the pictures, I'd just left my girlfriend. She only lives round the corner see. So I thought I'd take a short-cut up the lane. I saw this bloke with a knife."

"In the alley?" Randall asked.

"Yeah. He was bending over something. I just saw him lifting the knife. Then I saw that there was a body there. He cut the fucking head off." The youth turned even paler and clenched his teeth together. "I saw him pick it up. He put it in a sack or bag or something. He didn't see me."

"But you got a look at *his* face? The man with the knife?" Randall said.

"Yeah. I know it was dark but, well he had this great big scar or something all down one side of his face."

Randall shot Maggie an anxious glance, the same thought registering in their minds.

"He looked like something out of a fucking horror film," Rawlings continued. "Like he'd been burned or something."

Randall got to his feet, patted the youth on the shoulder and jumped down from the ambulance, helping Maggie down after him. Neither of them spoke. They didn't have to. Randall had a quick word with Sergeant Willis then led Maggie back to the Chevette. They both climbed in, sitting there for a moment, the Inspector breathing heavily.

"When Pierce left the hospital," he said. "Where did he go?"

"I told you before, Lou, nobody knew," Maggie told him.

Randall banged the steering wheel angrily but then, his initial anger subsided. He looked at her.

"He was locked up in that asylum for more than thirty years, wasn't he?"

She nodded.

"I don't get you."

"It's the only home he's ever known." Randall started the engine.

She suddenly understood.

He put the car in gear and swung it round in the wide road. In a few minutes, they were heading out towards the road which would take them to the deserted asylum.

Forty-six

"How can you be sure he's here?" said Maggie as Randall stepped on the brake and brought the Chevette to a halt.

"I can't," he said, opening his door. "Let's just hope this is one hunch that's right." The policeman clambered out from behind the wheel and walked across to the metal gates which barred the way to the asylum. In the darkness he could just discern three words on the stone archway above him.

EXHAM MENTAL HOSPITAL

There was a padlock on the gates and Randall tugged on it. The rusty gates creaked protestingly but didn't budge. The Inspector looked round. The driveway was the only means of getting a car into the grounds but a man could slip through one of the many gaps in the hedge. Randall scanned the ground around him and finally spotted a large stone. He retrieved it and set about the padlock, striking it with all his strength. It eventually came free with a dull clang and dropped to the ground. The Inspector put his shoulder to one of the gates and pushed. It was heavier than it looked and the exertion made him sweat but he finally succeeded in opening it as far as it would go. He repeated the procedure with the other one then hurried back to the car. Starting the engine he guided the Chevette through the archway and along the drive towards the asylum itself.

Flanked on both sides by leafless trees, he estimated

that the driveway must be at least half a mile long. He drove slowly, eyes alert for the slightest movement in the darkness.

"What are you going to do if Harold is here?" Maggie wanted to know.

"I'll tell you that when I find him," Randall told her, cryptically.

He brought the vehicle to a halt before the main entrance and both of them peered out at the building itself. It was an awesome sight, a Victorian edifice which, in the darkness, looked not as if it had been built with separate bricks but hewn from one enormous lump of granite. Five storeys high, it was built in the shape of an "E", the apex of which rose like a church spire. The figure of the weather vane on the top surveyed the bleak and ghostly scene with indifference.

The policeman climbed out of the car. Maggie also pushed open her door but Randall held up a hand to stop her.

"You stay here," he told her.

"But Lou, you don't know for certain that he's here," she protested. "And, even if he is, at least I know him. I could talk to him."

"The man's a bloody maniac," he rasped. "Now get back in the car, lock both doors and don't move until I get back. If I'm not here in an hour use this." He grabbed the two-way and held it up. "Contact the station and tell them where we are. Right?"

She didn't speak.

"Right?" he said, more forcefully.

"All right. Lou, be careful."

He nodded, slammed the door behind him and waited until he heard both locks drop then he made his way slowly towards what had once been the main entrance. As he'd suspected, the doors were locked so he moved along, peering at all the windows, eyes alert for any sign of a break-in, any tell-tale evidence of

Pierce's whereabouts. He rounded a corner and disappeared from Maggie's view. She sat impatiently, hands clenched on her thighs.

Randall moved cautiously, noticing how many of the asylum windows had been broken but he could tell which had been smashed by kids. Just round holes in the panes showed where stones had been hurled. As yet, there was no sign of forced entry. He sucked in an impatient breath wondering if his hunch had been wrong. He rested his hand on one of the sills and felt something wet beneath his fingers. The Inspector turned and looked down. There was a dark stain on the peeling paint. Tentatively he raised his fingers to his nose, sniffing the substance. There was no mistaking the distinctive coppery odour of blood.

He looked up and saw that the dark liquid was puddled beneath a set of double windows, one of which had been broken about half-way up, near the handle. The policeman gripped both sides of the frame and hauled himself up onto the sill, perching there for a second before pushing the two windows. They swung open invitingly and he jumped down into the building itself.

The smell of damp was almost overpowering and the Inspector blinked hard in an effort to combat the cloying darkness. There was some natural light spilling through the windows, enough to reveal to him that he was in what had once been an office. Dust swirled around him, the particles irritating his nose and throat but he fought back the urge to cough, anxious not to alert anyone who might be hiding inside.

There was more blood on the floor just ahead of him – a large splash and then droplets of the thick crimson fluid which was in the process of congealing. The trail led to the door and Randall paused before it a moment, listening. The asylum greeted him with silence and a kind of conspiratorial solitude which made him feel uneasy.

He slowly opened the door.

Corridors faced him and, after a moment's hesitation, he chose the one straight ahead.

Harold heard the noise from downstairs.

He snatched up the long kitchen knife, its blade still wet with blood, and scuttled out into the corridor his own ears now attuned to the sounds within the asylum. There was a crooked grin on his face. Someone was inside *his* home. They would not escape. His mind suddenly seemed clearer than it had done for months and he hurried through the darkened corridors as if drawn by some huge magnet, bearing down on the intruder.

It would only be a matter of time before he found the unwanted guest.

Maggie looked at her watch. The hands had crawled round to 11.49 p.m. Randall had been gone for nearly fifteen minutes. She sighed, shifting impatiently in her seat. There was a torch on the parcel shelf before her and she eyed it with a look akin to temptation. She closed her eyes for a second, trying to think about what had happened. The thought of Harold Pierce as a killer was still one she found hard to accept but it seemed clear enough. Nevertheless, if only she could speak to him, reason with him. . .

From where she sat she could see that many of the windows had been broken. It should be relatively easy to slip the catch on one and get in. She looked at the torch once again, this time picking it up. She unlocked her door and closed it behind her then she scuttled across to the nearest window, slipped her hand through a break in the pane and undid the latch. It opened and Maggie dragged herself up onto the sill. She steadied

272

herself for a moment then jumped down into the room beyond. As she switched on the torch she saw that the door ahead of her was already open. The powerful beam shone through the darkness, lighting her way. She swallowed hard and moved quietly out into the corridor.

Randall pushed open the door of a room, surprised that so many of the asylum's places had been left unlocked but then, he reasoned, no one could have foreseen anyone returning here. Why bother? He edged cautiously into what he guessed had once been the dining room. There were a number of long tables stacked at one side and, at the far end of the vast room, a long counter. It was fronted by a corrugated metal sheet which had been pulled down and padlocked. The Inspector walked across to it, his footsteps clacking on the stone floor. Large picture windows, meshed, gave him some added light but already his eyes were beginning to ache from the effort of squinting in the gloom. He stood still for long moments, listening, trying to catch even the slightest hint of movement.

Silence.

He exhaled deeply and turned towards a door nearby which was also unlocked. It was as he passed through it that the Inspector realized he had nothing to defend himself with should he come upon Pierce. He swallowed hard and moved on, finding himself in another corridor. There were rooms every fifteen yards and each one would have to be checked.

He pushed open the first door.

Harold paused at the bottom of the stairs, looking round. He could see no sign of the intruder but he knew that his quarry was here somewhere. A surge of adrenalin swept through him and he gripped the knife tighter, his breath now coming in short, excited gasps.

273

He touched the scarred side of his face, feeling the crusted flesh beneath his fingertips. He moved slowly along the corridor to his right, stopping dead when he heard movement ahead of him. His knife gripped firmly in his fist, he ducked into a nearby room.

Maggie put her hand on the bannister of the staircase and hurriedly withdrew it as she felt something sticky on her fingers.

It was blood.

There was more on the bannister, even some on the steps themselves. She shone the torch on the crimson liquid and, slowly began to climb. She wiped the blood off on her jeans her heart now beating just that little bit faster. The staircase rose precipitously until, at last, it levelled out onto a landing. Faced by two corridors, Maggie took the one on her left, tip-toeing in an effort to diminish the clicking of her heels on the stone floor.

She recoiled from a sudden, nauseating stench which seemed to drift around her like an invisible cloud. She put a hand to her mouth and stifled a cough. As she moved further down the corridor the smell became almost unbearable. Her head began to swim and she was forced to lean momentarily against the wall for support. She played the torch beam before her in an effort to discover the source of the rank odour and, as she moved on, she found that the end door in the corridor was open. Maggie pressed herself against the wall once again, listening. From inside the room she could hear soft, liquid sounds – a series of rasping gurgles. She closed her eyes for a second, at once revolted by the sounds and desperate to discover their source. A part of her was wishing she had stayed in the car.

She held the torch beam up and peered round the door.

For brief seconds, Maggie had to use all her self-control to prevent herself from vomiting. She swayed slightly, supporting herself against the door frame, then, almost drawn to the sight before her, she walked slowly into the room.

Maggie shook her head, unable to believe what she saw, convinced that, any second she was going to wake up to discover that this was a nightmare. But no nightmare could be as vile as what she now saw before her.

She shone the torch on the first foetus and the creature recoiled slightly from the piercing beam, its dark eyes glinting menacingly. It was standing, something wet and sticky gripped in its fingers. The other two were on the floor, the second one pawing at something before it.

It was a few more seconds before Maggie realized that the object was a human head.

And now, as she stepped back, her foot brushed something else. Something which rolled when she made contact. She swung the torch beam round, the gruesome discovery pinned in the beam.

The second head was partially decomposed, the skin around the neck and eyes mottled green in places. The skull had been split open with a heavy object, exposing the brain and, as Maggie turned the torch back onto the abominations before her, she realized just what the sticky grey substance was which the larger creature held. As she watched, it raised the jellied matter to its mouth and clumsily pushed some in.

Maggie closed her eyes momentarily.

The foetuses seemed unconcerned at her presence. They were more interested in the severed head they were toying with. There was blood everywhere, mingling on the floor with slicks of excrement and pieces of hair. Greyish brain matter seemed to sparkle in the light.

Suddenly, everything seemed to take on a horrendous clarity: the headless murder victims that the police had found, Harold's obsession with the incineration of foetuses and, worst of all, she now understood why only five babies instead of eight had been disinterred from the grave near Fairvale.

She stood still, frozen by the sight before her, trying to find either the will to move or the power to scream but she could do neither. She felt faint, her stomach finally beginning to churn uncontrollably and she felt the vomit begin its journey up her throat. She turned away, retching violently, the foul stench of her vomit mingling with the choking odours already filling the room. But, the action seemed to shake her out of her trance and she moved for the door.

(*STOP*)

Maggie clapped both hands to her head, the torch dropping to the ground.

(*You will not leave*)

It's my imagination, she told herself.

(*No, it is not your imagination*)

She turned back to face the creatures.

Could it be telepathy? she wondered, hurriedly dismissing the thought. Her mind was over-reacting to the situation.

(*Your thoughts are open to us*)

She gazed at them, her face twisted into an expression which combined revulsion and fascination.

"What are you?" she said.

(*Nothing. We are nothing*)

"How do you know what I'm thinking?"

A soft chuckling and Maggie felt the hairs on the back of her neck prickle.

(*There can be no secrets. We know your thoughts and your fears*)

She thought about Randall. If only she could alert him to the danger.

In the blinking of an eye he was standing before her, smiling.

"Lou," she said and stepped forward to touch him but, even as she did so, the vision faded and she was alone once more.

The soft chuckling filled her ears.

(*Thoughts. Fears. There are no secrets*)

Thought projection, Maggie wondered? Auto-suggestion? The very things which she had mentioned to Randall and now she began to realize how Judith Myers and Lynn Tyler had come to die. The foetuses were the exact size which they would needed to have been to cause the Fallopian ruptures.

"You killed two women," she said.

(*They had to die*)

"Why?"

(*THEY WOULD HAVE KILLED US*)

Despite herself, Maggie moved closer to the largest of the creatures, kneeling before it, running expert eyes over its body. It was perfectly formed, as if it had grown within the mother's womb, reaching maturity as originally intended. The most frightening thing about it was its eyes. Black pits devoid of emotion, they pinned her in an hypnotic stare.

Randall heard the sounds of movement from upstairs and he ran towards the foot of the staircase, pausing momentarily when he reached it.

Harold came hurtling out of the room behind him, the knife held high above his head.

Randall heard the vicious arc of the steel and tried to turn but Harold was too quick for him. The blade powered down, catching the policeman in the shoulder. It tore through the flesh and actually scraped the clavical as it finally burst through his pectoral muscle, the point dripping blood. Harold pressed his advantage, wrenched the knife free and drove it down again but this time Randall managed to get his hand up in time. He deflected the blow, the knife striking concrete as the two men fell to the ground. The Inspector was surprised at his assailant's strength; despite Harold's age he seemed to possess an energy which belied his years. Randall struck out with his right fist, his left arm already numb from the knife wound. The blow caught Harold squarely in the side of the head but the impact only staggered him for a minute. However, that minute was enough to allow Randall the chance to wriggle free. He hauled himself upright and, as Harold tried to follow him, he drove a foot hard into the older man's side. There was a strident snapping of bone as one brittle rib splintered under the impact.

Harold went down in a heap, the knife held in one outstretched hand. Randall dropped to his knees, grabbing for it but Harold struck out again, the wild blow slicing open the policeman's palm. He yelped in pain but closed his injured hand around Harold's wrist, banging the hand on the ground repeatedly in an effort to make him drop the knife.

The older man clawed at Randall's face, gripping him by the hair, yanking his head to one side and both of them went sprawling again. This time Harold was first on his feet and Randall saw the scarred attacker advancing on him. The Inspector waited until his opponent was mere inches away then lashed out, catching Harold in the crutch with a powerful kick. He doubled up and Randall hastily scrambled to his feet. He grabbed Harold's hair and, in one skilful movement, brought his knee up to meet Harold's down-rushing head. The older man's nose seemed to explode, splattering the policeman's trousers with blood. Randall wrenched his attacker upright, hitting him hard in the stomach, his hand still gripping Harold's hair. The knife finally fell to the ground and Randall drove another powerful kick into the other man's stomach, watching as he crashed heavily to the ground.

"Lou!" – the scream came from upstairs. It was Maggie's voice.

Randall snatched up the knife and started up the stairs.

"No," Harold shouted and staggered after him.

He caught the Inspector half way up but, the older man was weak and, as Randall spun round he drove the knife forward. It caught Harold just above the right hip, deflected off the pelvis and ripped into his intestines. The policeman tore it free, watching as Harold tottered drunkenly on the stairs, blood pouring through his fingers as he tried to hold the ragged edges of the wound together. Then, with a final despairing moan he toppled backwards, crashing head-over-heels until he lay still at the foot of the stairs.

Randall's breath was coming in gasps. His left shoulder and most of his left arm felt numb and the slashed palm of his right hand felt as if it were on fire. He turned wearily and climbed the last few steps to the landing casting a perfunctory look back at Harold when he reached the top. The older man lay still, face down in the dust which covered the floor, a dark pool spreading out around him.

The Inspector turned and walked on towards the junction of the two corridors before him, not sure which one to check out first. Then he noticed the vile stench and moved cautiously along the left hand one, the knife gripped tightly in his throbbing hand.

He reached the last door and slumped against the frame, his mind reeling from the pain of his wounds and the sight before him.

"Oh my God," he croaked, his eyes scanning the scene of horror which confronted him. The heads, the blood, the excrement and. . .

He stared at the foetuses, shaking his head slowly from side to side. Then he took a step into the room, noticing Maggie for the first time.

"Get out," he told her, gripping the knife tighter.

The foetuses turned their black eyes on him and Randall felt the first gnawings of pain at the back of his neck. He advanced slowly on them, taking in each monstrous detail.

"Lou, don't touch them," said Maggie, her voice low.

Randall seemed not to hear, he just kept moving closer. So slowly, so feebly, as if someone had attached lead weights to his limbs.

"Don't touch them," Maggie implored.

"What are they?" he croaked.

"The grave of abortions that Pierce dug up, these are the three that were missing. They've grown."

"Oh Jesus," murmured the policeman.

(*GET BACK*)

He felt as if he'd been struck with an iron bar. He reeled, almost fell and a thin trickle of blood dribbled from one nostril.

"Lou," Maggie shouted. "Stay away, they'll kill you."

Randall gritted his teeth, raised the knife in his bloodied hand. It seemed as if someone were inflating his head with a high-pressure pump. His eyes bulged in their sockets, a small crimson orb burst from one tear duct and ran down his cheek. Still he advanced on them, the pain in his head growing.

He was less than ten yards away from them.

"Lou."

His legs gave out and he dropped to his knees but still he crawled onward. The veins in his arms and neck bulged menacingly, the wounds in his hand and shoulder bleeding freely. It was like pushing open a thousand ton door, pressing against it, moving a fraction of an inch at a time. He clenched his teeth until his jaws ached, the knife clanking on the concrete as he dropped to all fours.

He almost screamed aloud as he found himself staring into the sightless eyes of Paul Harvey.

The dead man's head lay in a pool of congealing blood, inches from the policeman's face. Thick crimson streamers still dripped from the nostrils and ears. The tongue protruded over white lips. The skull had been smashed in just above the right ear and Randall could still see fragments of brain matter sticking to the hair. The cavity had been emptied, the soft tissue devoured by the monstrosities before him, torn out with their eager hands.

As Randall crawled on, he bumped the head and it rolled over to reveal the severed stump of the neck, the slashed veins and arteries hanging like dripping bloodied tendrils.

The foetuses concentrated their mind power with greater accuracy, focusing it on Randall like some kind of invisible laser beam.

Blood burst from his ears and he went deaf for precious seconds.

"Lou," Maggie shrieked. "Stop."

He was just feet away from them now, their rancid stench filling his nostrils, mingling with the coppery smell of his own blood which was flowing from his nose and dripping onto the floor. He groaned more loudly now as his efforts to reach the creatures became greater.

He raised the knife to strike.

Randall almost screamed aloud as he found himself gazing into the eyes of his daughter.

(*No*)

"Lisa," he croaked, the knife hovering above her head.

(*Don't kill me*)

He swayed, thought he was going to pass out then, slowly, he lowered the knife, eyes fixed on the vision of his daughter.

(*Put the knife down*)

He dropped it in front of him, staring at her. God,

281

she was beautiful. She lay before him, her body unblemished. He reached out his arms to touch her smooth skin but, as he felt her body, he gagged. The flesh was soft and jellied. As cold as ice. The vision faded instantly and he found himself staring once more at the foetuses.

"No," he screamed and snatched up the knife, plunging it into the one closest to him.

A huge gout of blood erupted from the wound splattering Randall who was sobbing now as he brought the knife down again, the second blow hacking off the foetus's right arm. The tiny limb fell to one side twitching spasmodically, blood gushing from the severed arteries. He struck again and again until the knife was slippery with his blood and that of the creature. The other one tried to crawl away but Randall was upon it in a flash, driving the blade down between its shoulder blades, tearing downwards to rip through its kidneys and liver. He held it by the back of the head and drove the knife into the hollow at the nape of its neck, ignoring the blood which spurted up into his face. He hacked off an ear, part of its nose, buried the blade in one of those dark pits of eyes.

The third creature didn't even move as he gutted it, ripping the small tangle of intestines free with his bare hands.

Finally, he toppled over onto his back, eyes staring blankly at the ceiling. Maggie rushed across to him, wiping some of the blood from his face with her handkerchief. There was so much of the sticky crimson gore on him it was difficult to tell which was from his wounds and which was from the creatures. She helped him to his feet, supporting him out of the room and out into the corridor.

"Got to get back to the car," he whispered, almost collapsing.

She held him, ignoring the blood which dripped from his hands and arms and stained her own clothes.

They reached the landing and began, cautiously, to descend the stairs.

"Harold?" asked Maggie.

"I killed him," said Randall.

But, as they reached the bottom of the stairs, the policeman saw only the pool of blood there. Of Harold there was no sign.

"Come on, hurry," the Inspector said, leading her back through the maze of corridors. "He can't have got far, we've got to get help."

Harold emerged from the door opposite like a vision from hell. Mouth agape, blood spread darkly around his stomach and crutch, he was on them in a second, hurling Maggie to one side. Randall tried to strike out with the knife but Harold was too fast. The older man, wounded though he was, had the element of surprise in his favour. He swung a lump of wood which looked like a chair leg and the blow caught Randall in the side of the face, felling him like a tree-trunk.

Maggie screamed and ran, looking back in time to see Harold snatch up the knife and set off in pursuit of her.

She barged through a door and found herself in the old canteen. Maggie slammed the door behind her and ran for the window, reaching it just as Harold sent the door crashing inwards. He came after her, the bloodied knife raised above his head. Maggie turned to see him gaining and, gritting her teeth, she broke the window with her hand. Crystal shards sliced open her flesh and she screamed, but she managed to push the window open and scramble out, falling heavily onto the grass below. Harold clambered after her, seeing that she was running for the car parked nearby.

Maggie reached it and tore open the door, locking it quickly behind her as Harold advanced. He struck at the windscreen with the knife and, as Maggie recoiled from the expected explosion of glass she saw that the passenger side door was still unlocked. She flung herself across in an effort to reach the lock but Harold saw her and slid off the bonnet, grabbing for the door which he managed to pull open a fraction. Maggie screamed as she tugged with all her strength on the handle but he was slowly forcing it open an inch at a time.

He snaked one hand inside, the knife driving down, missing her by inches as it buried itself in the seat.

Maggie tugged hard on the handle and smashed his arm between door and frame, almost smiling when she heard his yelp of pain. Harold withdrew his hand and she was able to lock the door. He rushed round to the front of the car again and leapt up onto the bonnet, pounding on the glass with his hands.

Maggie snatched up the two-way radio and flicked it on, babbling into the set, not waiting for an answer.

The first hair-line splinters appeared in the windscreen as Harold continued his relentless pounding.

"Help me," Maggie screamed into the two-way. "The old asylum. Inspector Randall is here too. Help."

There was a garbled answer then the set went dead.

The cracks in the glass were spreading, spider-webbing until the driver's side resembled nothing more than crushed ice. Maggie turned the key in the ignition and the engine roared into life. She stuck it in gear but her foot slipped off the clutch and the vehicle stalled.

Almost in tears, she twisted the key again.

Glass sprayed inwards as Harold's fist crashed through the windscreen, groping around blindly as he searched for her, the jagged edges cutting his wrist, trapping him. Maggie stepped on the accelerator and the car shot forward. She heard Harold's shouts of alarm for he could see the wall which Maggie couldn't.

The Chevette hit it doing about twenty-five. The impact sent Harold hurtling into the brickwork with a sickening thud. He staggered, watching helplessly as Maggie reversed. As the car ploughed into Harold, Maggie threw herself clear.

There was a blood-chilling scream of pain followed a second later by a high pitched thump as the car exploded. Pinned between car and wall, Harold could only scream in anguish as the flames licked around him eagerly devouring his flesh. He clapped both hands to his face as he burned, his false eye falling from its socket to reveal the dark mess beneath. His hair went up in wisps of smoke and the flesh peeled from his body like a snake shedding its skin. He let out one final caterwaul of agony then the roaring flames drowned everything out. The heat rolled over Maggie, bringing with it the sickly sweet stench of charred flesh.

She dragged herself upright, the pain in her hand from the cuts keeping her conscious. Mesmerized, she gazed at the burning car and, before her eyes, Harold Pierce seemed to melt away beneath the roaring inferno.

Maggie sucked in huge lungfuls of air, suddenly remembering Randall.

It was as she was heading back towards the asylum that the first of the police cars arrived.

Forty-seven

Randall had regained consciousness by the time they lifted him into the ambulance. He even managed a smile before they closed the doors on him. Maggie had kissed him softly on the lips and then watched as the ambulance sped away.

The firemen, called to the scene by Sergeant Willis, put out the blazing Chevette and then cut the remains of Harold Pierce loose. What was left of him was put into another ambulance and taken away, then Maggie led the police up into the room where the dead foetuses were. PC Fowler threw up at the sight of so much carnage and even Willis found it difficult to retain his dinner. But, nevertheless, the room was eventually cleared, each mutilated body and severed head wrapped in a separate blanket and taken away. Maggie asked for the foetuses to be taken to Fairvale for examination.

All that had happened fifteen minutes ago; now she stood alone in the corridor looking into the room, the vile stench still strong in the air. The room, for what it was worth, was to be inspected by forensic men and then hosed down. Willis himself was coming back to take Maggie home as soon as he'd dropped the specimens off at Fairvale.

She had plenty of time.

She went to the door of another room across the corridor and pushed it open.

The surviving foetus lay in the centre of the room.

No one had thought to check any of the other rooms in the building – why should they? The power of the foetuses' thought projection had been stronger than even she had imagined. So powerful in fact that Randall could not have realized that the third foetus he had killed was merely a projection of his own subconscious.

She herself had hidden the creature in this other room before the Inspector had even reached the first floor. While he had been struggling with Harold Pierce she had lifted the foetus and carried it across the corridor to its new hiding place.

Maggie crossed to it and knelt beside the body.

It *was* rather beautiful she had decided. A perfectly formed child. *Her* child. She lifted it, surprised at its weight and it looked at her, those twin black eyes glinting malevolently.

She pulled it close to her, kissing its bulbous head, allowing it to nuzzle against her. Its lips moved slowly.

The words echoed loudly, not inside her head this time but booming off the walls, all the more incongruous because of the tiny body they came from. The words filled the small room. Deep bass, thick and full of power.

"Hold me."

Other bestselling Time Warner titles available by mail: